IN THE DARKNESS, GOLDEN EYES

"I walked closer, light still shining on the animal," Phillip said. "I could see all sorts of insects buzzing about it. And then the smell . . . it was awful, something like bad vegetables. I took a swig of bourbon and as I did the light fell away from the animal. That was when I saw the eyes."

"The dead possum's eyes?" I asked.

He grinned. "I wish that were the case. No, these eyes were *alive*. As golden as the center signal on a traffic light. These eyes belonged to an Isolate."

I smiled, half incredulously, half out of discomfort. I didn't want to believe him. But something inside told me I should.

"It creeped over the far edge of the rock, just a hand at first, long fork-like fingers gripping the dead animal like a doll. Then I saw the head, and it grinned at me, bright golden eyes cutting the darkness like two beacons. It was as though it knew I was there and had waited for the right time to make its grand entrance.

"When I finally made it past the dreadful glow of its eyes, the rest of the thing's face came into focus. . . ."

Other *Leisure* books by Michael Laimo:

ATMOSPHERE

DEEP IN THE DARKNESS
MICHAEL LAIMO

LEISURE BOOKS   NEW YORK CITY

LEISURE BOOKS ®

February 2004

Published by

Dorchester Publishing Co., Inc.
200 Madison Avenue
New York, NY 10016

ISBN 0-8439-5314-4

The name "Leisure Books" and the stylized "L" with design are trademarks of Dorchester Publishing Co., Inc.

Printed in the United States of America.

Visit us on the web at www.dorchesterpub.com.

ACKNOWLEDGMENTS

In no particular order, I'd like to thank the following people for their support, inspiration, and encouragement:

Family: Sherrie Laimo, Anna Rose Laimo, Emma Grace Laimo, Mom and Dad Laimo, Bob and Larry Laimo (thanks for buying all those copies of *Atmosphere*, Bob), Samantha and John Huxtable, Mary Ann & Pat Ballaro, and the Mercury Beach-Maid gang.

Friends and Associates: Don D'Auria, Shane Staley, Gary A. Braunbeck, Tom Piccirilli, Gerard Houarner, Linda Addison, Matt Schwartz, Brian Hopkins, Gord Rollo, Gene O'Neill, Judi Rohrig, Brian Keene, Edo van Belkom, Joe Nassise, Douglas Clegg, Dallas Mayr, Gordon Linzner, Shannon Gronley & Eko Kreal of Jeans To Go, Perry Tepper, John Everson, Greg F. Gifune, Charlee Jacob, Michael Arnzen, Jack Fisher, Garrett Peck, and Clive Barker, who asked *me* to sign a book for *him*.

Research conducted at www.mayoclinic.com and www.microbeworld.com.

Written exclusively on the Long Island Rail Road, and at the Barnes & Noble Café in Melville, NY.

DEEP IN THE DARKNESS

Prologue

Dark basement.

Heavy breathing.

The grainy shuffle of feet on a cement floor. Edgy fingers tapping a table's rough surface. The reek of things moist and damp.

Somewhere upstairs a clock chimes. A useless breeze sweeps a single candle's flame.

A hand moves to a small tape recorder, sitting on the tabletop.

One hesitant finger seeks out the record button. Presses it.

Ten seconds of deep, labored breaths. Then, a voice.

"Please let me start by stating that in my opinion, the incredible story I am about to record can only be efficiently portrayed through speech. That although I have

1

recorded a series of handwritten pages discussing the events that have taken place here at 17 Harlan Road—my home if you will, though I can hardly call it *home* despite the fact I still reside here—I feel the circumstances must be recorded in my own voice, on the tapes you are listening to.

"If you, hearing these tapes, should listen to these recordings to the very end, I assume that given the complex story I have to tell, there will be more than a few hours of audio to consider. I will therefore mark each cassette with numbers indicating the order in which these tapes should be played. Of course the tape you are listening to at this moment will be marked 'Number One,' with a side-note of 'Play first.'

"It is my strong desire to spell out every detail of my experience while living here at 17 Harlan Road in an effort not only to detail it to the fullest extent, but also to demonstrate my lucidity so that you will not reject these ramblings as those of a man whose mind has been steered toward utter madness. *I am a sane man, and the story I am to tell is nothing less than the absolute truth.* I will say this only once, for I feel no reason to repeat myself in an effort to convince you, unassuming listener, of the truth of the whole seemingly implausible matter. I—Michael Cayle, M.D.—have experienced everything I am about to reveal while living in this house at 17 Harlan Road. That said, I'll defend my sanity no further.

"I must also add that I assume no involvement whatsoever in the disappearances of my wife, Christine, and my daughter, Jessica. Although *I do know* what has happened to them, I possess no knowledge at the moment as to their exact location, nor how I am able to get them back. This said, I know that my fight is far from over and there is much more I need to do, and . . . and . . .

"Maybe I'm getting ahead of myself. Again, it's my intention to reveal every moment of my story on these tapes in an effort, however vain, to not only harvest your belief, but to also help myself recall every damn torment I have been through. In doing so, I feel that I might discover something, however small a slice of experience, that might help me in the future—what little future I have left. This battle I am fighting is far from over.

"I suppose now would be as good a time as any to recount the events of the last six months, because if I meander any more, you might stop this tape before I've had anything interesting to say . . . and unquestionably, the scribblings I've left behind look like the ravings of a madman who should be spending his days and nights locked away in some faraway asylum, not a series of notes chronicling the experiences of a man simply trying to protect his family.

"So . . . I beg you, dear listener . . . suspend your disbelief and listen to these tapes . . . and give me your undivided attention. . . ."

Part One

Within the Darkness, Golden Eyes

Chapter One

If you came to me several years ago and offered me a million dollars to hand over Manhattan for a place in the country, I would have told you there was a better chance of a Subway Series taking place between the Mets and Yankees. Christ, even if you'd asked me last month, I still would've refused trading my big-city apartment for a wood-framed house in some Grandma Moses countryside, where there were more cows than people and your closest neighbor lived a half mile away with nothing but trees in between. Of course, the Mets and Yankees *did* meet in the Series, and I met my closest neighbor, Phillip Deighton, who lived a half mile away, the day I moved into the quaint township of Ashborough, New Hampshire.

The man had become the savior of our family pet, Jimmy Page, a purebred cocker spaniel who'd bounded from the minivan and disappeared into the woods alongside the four-bedroom, three-bath colonial the day we moved in. Page was really Jessica's dog, a gift from my wife for her fourth birthday last year, but we all really took to the furball quite a bit.

Fate seemed to play a role in our finding this home. It had been so easy, really, as my desire to purchase an existing practice had never grown beyond comfortable proportions; it practically fell into my lap just days after I reluctantly agreed with a very relieved Christine that for Jessica's sake we'd be much better off in the burbs. A few days earlier, I revealed to Dr. Scully that I was going to break away from his corral of internists in Manhattan. Lou Scully, who'd offered me the position upon completion of my residency at Columbia-Presbyterian Medical Center, had treated me like a little brother, and when I told him that I wanted a house in the suburbs, *for the good of Jessica*, and explained, *You know how the schools are here in the city*, he nodded and assumed I wouldn't be battling the Long Island Railroad or the Metro North every day into Manhattan. He also knew that starting from scratch would mean a harsh change in lifestyle.

Then he told me about Dr. Neil Farris, an elderly physician from New England who'd maintained a practice for thirty years in a New Hampshire town called Ashborough. A good friend of Lou's, the man was tragically killed, the victim of a dog attack. Dr. Farris had been an avid exercise enthusiast, practiced what he preached, and even at the age of seventy ran three miles nearly every morning. The week before, a mile from his home, he came across a loose mutt with a very nasty disposition. It'd been at least an hour before someone discovered Dr. Farris, and by then he'd lost quite a bit of blood. We're talking small town USA here, he was the only doctor, so he had to be taken to the nearest medical center in Ellenville twelve miles away. He died en route.

Neil Farris's wife made an immediate decision to sell the home and practice. Apparently they owned another home in Manchester. I was told her kids went to school at the university there and she wanted to be nearer to them. The sale of the house would provide for her finances and needs. *And if you ask me, Michael,* Scully said, *it's a steal. You'll never find a complete practice and such an elegant home for so low a price.*

Of course I had no intention of straying too far from the cultural offerings of Manhattan. I'd lived there for fifteen years, met Christine at the Met, had raised Jessica in a beautiful Upper East Side apartment. Putting aside the schools, which hadn't won me over, New York City did have a great deal of plusses. Long Island or Connecticut would be close enough for the weekend excursions we'd enjoyed so much and felt were important to Jessica's continuing development, and most importantly, could offer her the educational attention both Christine and I wanted her to have.

But then, this.

You really can't refuse, Lou said. *And the school is very highly rated. I had it checked out for you,* he added, handing me a folder filled with papers. I smiled and thanked him, my thoughts in a sudden whirlpool.

The next day I contacted the Widow Farris, and drove up on Saturday with Christine and Jessica in tow. We arrived just after noon. The place *was* beautiful. But Christine, who'd lived in Manhattan her entire life, broke out in tears, presumably at the thought of leaving her current life behind. And Page had a barking fit, so much so that we had to keep him in the car; I assumed Emily Farris wasn't too fond of canines these days anyway, for good reasons.

The meeting with Emily Farris wasn't as stressful as anticipated. We both felt pressured to get the sale ironed out, so there wasn't much in the way of splitting hairs when it came down to the nitty-gritty. All terms had been agreed upon in a few hours, and I drove my family back to Manhattan the next day knowing that in two weeks I'd be the next Ashborough Township physician.

Despite the stress and anxiety suddenly upon us, I tried to dwell on the positives. There'd be no worries about clientele, no competition. But there'd also be no city within ninety miles. I expected utter boredom, but put off those worries for now. The most important thing was that I'd be able to continue providing for Christine and Jessica, and that Jessica would get the educational attention we wanted her to have.

The place looked different on our arrival. *Used and abused, like a haunted house,* I thought. I shrugged off the thought and leaped from the minivan like a man with a new lease on life; this was my way of countering the fact that we were all so weary and stressed out. Jimmy Page had been barking up a storm from his cage in the back, Jessica had complained the entire trip of a stomachache, and Christine had cried a bit too much for someone who'd instigated this move from New York in the first place.

Of course my enthusiasm was feigned, and I did my best to hold back my own tears. When push came to shove, I really didn't want to live here in the middle of nowhere. Sure, I was more than willing to flee the city, but had had my sights set on a house in the burbs, a neighborhood where, if I wanted to borrow a cup of milk from my neighbor, I wouldn't have to get in the car and drive to get there. For a moment I almost suggested we nix the deal and head back to Manhattan, where the apartment we leased might still be available. I even considered leaving the yapping Page behind.

But the family followed suit, Page's enthusiasm to get out of his cage taking him like a dart into the woods alongside the house. The *house*. The place where we'd be living from now until who knows when; the place where its last owner lived unassumingly just three weeks before, sleeping and eating and working and doing the private things that no one else knew about except him and his wife and the walls around him. This man who'd left his house never intending to be mauled to death by a dog. I wondered, morbidly, if the house possessed any feelings, whether it welcomed being sold to a new, unfamiliar personality. New furniture, new people running it. If I were a house, I thought, I wouldn't be too taken with the idea. It'd be like having all your organs transplanted when there was nothing wrong with the old ones.

Nevertheless, it *was* a nice place. An old center-hall colonial with four rooms (including an eat-in kitchen) downstairs and four bedrooms upstairs. Throw in three baths—two up, one down—and you've got yourself one helluva place. And then, of course, there was the study and office attached to the house in the rear. Fit for a king! There was a separate entrance along the side of the house where my future patients would enter a small waiting room. On one side of the vestibule was an examination room, which when I'd seen it had still been filled with Dr. Farris's equipment; should still be, according to the deal I worked out with the widow. On the other side, flanking the rear, was a study, a grand room with floor-to-ceiling windows, a fireplace, and bookshelves that lined almost every inch of wall. It was a physician's dream come true, and I imagined myself getting lost in there after dinner, gazing out the windows at the dark expanse of woods in the backyard, counting the fireflies.

The backyard had a nice lay of lawn to it that even now in May possessed a healthy lavish green color. There was a large bird fountain made of cement, and further back at the foot of the woods sat a padlocked shed that I hadn't noticed before. The woods themselves went on as far as the eye could see, and from what I understood from Emily Farris, there'd never really been a line of demarcation between the property and the state's land. I figured the only thing I had to worry about was some developer coming in to build a shopping mall or a parking lot, and the odds of that happening were pretty slim. For now, I was quite willing to bet against any kind of construction in my backyard. The population didn't warrant it.

After getting out of the minivan, I gave Christine a gentle stare. She was wiping her tears away with a tissue. "Well . . . here we are." I felt a bit of anxiety, a tremble in my legs. They say that buying a house is one of the most stressful things a person can do in a lifetime, right after getting married and having a baby. I'd breezed through the latter two without a hitch, but for some reason standing in front of our new home in Nowhere, New Hampshire, felt even more intimidating than experiencing Jessica's birth. At the moment, it sure seemed that way for Christine too.

She walked over and hugged me. I felt her damp cheeks press against my shoulder. "I've never been happier," she said.

Of course she was lying, but I was damn happy to hear her say that. It meant that she was ready to accept this change in lifestyle, and that took a load off my shoulders. Being unhappy myself was a personal issue that I was perfectly capable of handling—I could *learn* to be happy again. But contending with Christine's unhappiness, that was another issue altogether. She was so damn steadfast in her emotional ways. If she decided on traveling the path to unhappiness, then I'd be screwed. For life. There'd be no changing her, no turning back. She was a rock when it came to her emotions.

She ran her eyes over the front of the house, from the front door to the empty windows to the walk that led to the driveway. I could practically hear the wheels in her mind turning, unearthing gardening ideas for the space below the bay window, perhaps charting another hundred or so decorative pursuits.

I heard Page barking in the distance, and for the first time I wondered if he'd be able to find his way back.

Jessica walked over and grabbed Christine's hand. "Mommy, I don't feel well," she said.

I'd heard that line a thousand times on the way here. As usual, Christine was more attentive to our daughter's complaints than I was.

"What is it, honey?" Christine asked, bending at the knees, rubbing a hand through Jessica's blond curls.

"I have a stomachache. I want to go home."

Christine gave me a sorrowful look. She felt badly for Jessica. Me, I figured our five-year-old might need a week or two of adjusting to her new surroundings. In a month she'd completely forget about Manhattan. Unlike me.

I walked over to Jessica and kneeled down next to her. At this level the singing birds sounded very loud. I had to admit, it was a nice change of pace from the never-ending wail of sirens filling the streets.

"Sweetheart, this is our new home." I pointed to the house.

She gave the house a quick once-over, then gently said, "Cool beans."

I gave Christine a quizzical look, then we all broke out in laughter, Jessica included. We had no idea where she picked up that neat little phrase, and figured it was better than *holy shit* or *piss my pants*, the sort of witticisms she'd undoubtedly acquire while attending kindergarten in Manhattan. That's why we moved out here. And cool beans, that was just fine with me.

I put my arms around Christine and Jessica and we all took part in a community hug.

A perfect way to start our new life together.

Chapter Two

The moment should have lasted forever, I thought, because everything really went downhill after that. I broke the family hug to fish out the house keys from my jacket pocket, and as soon as my finger hooked through the loop, Jessica threw up all over me.

Christine yelled my name, then said, "Oh, Jess honey . . ." She stood up, giving Jessica her space as she heaved again all over the front walkway. Really, though, Christine was thrilled not to have been in the line of fire, and she set herself back a good three feet to avoid getting splattered. Me, I just stood there, utterly mystified, glancing back and forth between my sick daughter and the mess dripping down the leg of my jeans.

As her heaves died down, her cries grew into wails

of dread. She sounded terrified, as if she'd just puked up a baby bird or something.

"Jessica . . ." I said, not sure what to do about the vomit on my leg. "It's all right, there's no reason to be scared. You've got a little bug in the tummy. That's all."

"But my tummy!" she cried. Her eyes were red and wet and bulging, like two cherry tomatoes.

I was at a loss for the moment. All I wanted to do was get my pants off. I still had the keys in my hand, but that did me no good because the moving van hadn't arrived with our things yet, and all I'd brought along was a gym bag with a change of clothes for that night.

"Don't just stand there, Michael," Christine said. "Do something." To Christine, being a doctor meant I had the power to bring calm to any situation, medical or not.

"What do you suggest?" My temper was rising and I thought again about hightailing it back to New York, this time alone.

"Get your pants off, Doc. Then go get your daughter some Pepto from the first-aid kit."

Jessica always became *my* daughter when things got a bit unruly. Like now. "Where should I change? I'm not gonna trail puke into the house, or the car."

"Michael . . . there's not a soul around for miles. We're in the middle of nowhere, remember? Just take them off."

I was about to argue with her, but Jessica produced a few aftershocks—three giant croaking heaves. Tears sprouted from her eyes like rain, and she cried incon-

17

solably when it was over. I staggered to the car and kicked off my sneakers and socks. The first-aid kit was in the glove compartment. I grabbed a towel from the rear seat and wiped some of the puke off my pants; it made me nauseous. I decided it might be better to take them off after all, which I did. Now, wearing nothing but boxers, I walked back to Christine and Jessica, feeling like a snake who'd just shed its skin, cold and vulnerable.

Christine had picked up Jessica. She was tapping her lightly on the back, trying to ease her hysterics.

"She's sick, Michael. Her skin is warm."

"Tell me something I don't know."

"Well . . . did you know that you're standing in the front yard of your new home with no pants on, doing absolutely nothing?" Her face was stiff, not a hint of a grin showing up. Clearly she wasn't trying to be cute or funny, as I'd hoped. She was being crass, and it made me want to scream and race into the house, to be *away* from the mess outside.

And then I did scream, but not at Christine. There was a sudden excruciating pain in the sole of my foot. It felt as though my foot had been amputated without anesthesia. I went down on one knee to investigate, throwing down the first-aid kit in a huff.

"What's wrong, Michael?" she yelled, placing Jessica down in the grass. Through the lancing pain in my sole, I could hear Jessica's cries start up again, as if someone had pushed her panic button. She clawed at Christine, then at me, looking for support, and I had no choice but to give her a gentle shove as I inspected my foot.

Of course, she fell down right in the puddle of vomit. That caused quite a furor of cries, from both daughter and wife.

I couldn't pay them any heed, though. When I twisted my foot around I beheld a gruesome sight. A rusty nail had found its way into the center of my sole. It stuck out crookedly like an old fence post. A vicious red bulge the size of a quarter had risen about the point of entry. Blood came out in a flow. I yelled again, in pain, fear, shock, whatever.

Blood and vomit! I thought crazily.

Christine had the gall to reprimand me for pushing Jessica, and amidst my own cries, I had to practically shove my foot in her face in my defense. That earned me quite a look of disgust. She cringed and turned away.

"Sure got your hands full, eh?" a deep voice from behind me said. And then I heard barking. Jimmy Page.

I turned and saw a man of about fifty standing five or six feet away. He had on a worn pair of Wranglers and a plaid shirt with gray chest hair exploding from the open collar. His skin was pale, and he chewed on the end of an unlit half-smoked cigar. He was holding Jimmy Page like a baby, stomach facing skyward. The dog's tongue lolled from its mouth like a ribbon.

"Rumor has it that you're the new doctor. Looks like you're your own first patient."

I grimaced through the pain. "Yeah, I'd say," I agreed, wondering what he *really* thought of me, considering I was in my underwear.

"Found your dog," he said, then kneeled down and

19

let go of Jimmy Page, who immediately hopped over and sniffed Jessica's vomit.

I looked up at the man, managed a smile, and said, "Thanks."

Nothing like a good first impression, I thought.

Chapter Three

Pocketing the spit-soaked cigar in his shirt pocket, the man explained how he'd been sitting on his front porch when Page came sniffing at his feet. After some petting and a slice of turkey for a treat, he'd escorted the cocker spaniel back home. "Being new in these parts, I figured he might have trouble finding his way around." Then he added, "Mighty happy fellow, he is."

While Christine changed Jessica's clothes by the minivan, I plucked the nail from my foot in a quick, calculated flick of the wrist. I bellowed just once, and even though I'd removed my share of nails and needles from patients, I'd never experienced a pain quite like it. Couldn't have imagined anything much worse, actually. Then, amazingly, it was over. At least the *bad* pain was gone. Now I was left with a dull throb, and I doused the wound with antiseptic and covered it with gauze, knowing that it'd be quite a battle just walking around the house for the next week or so. Not a good thing, considering we had a lot of unpacking to do.

"Wonder how it got on your lawn," the man said. He honored me with a witty grin, then held out his hand, which I graciously accepted. "Phillip Deighton, at your service," he said, helping me to my feet.

"Michael Cayle, and yes, I'm the new doctor."

"Mommy, who's that man?" I heard Jessica ask. Christine shushed her as they returned from the car, then smiled and introduced herself.

"Our daughter isn't feeling well today," she said. "She's had a bit of an accident." Page was doing circles around everyone, tailing back now and again to investigate Jessica's vomit.

Deighton fished his cigar back out and inserted it back into his wet lips, but didn't light it. "Pleased to meet you," he said. He kneeled down to Jessica's height. "And what is your name, young lady?" Jessica stayed mostly silent. I urged her to be polite and introduce herself. Eventually she mumbled her name beneath her breath, then buried her face in Christine's thigh.

"Welcome to Ashborough." He stood back up and offered up a most welcoming smile. Then I realized he was grinning because I was standing there in my underwear.

"Uh . . . yes, as you can tell, there's been a bit of an accident. Sorry for the messy scene." I didn't need to point it out on the walkway.

Phillip held both hands out in front of him. "No need

to apologize . . . we all have our days, and you're probably all out of sorts from the move, I'd say."

"Yes, this has been a rather inauspicious start."

Deighton smiled, then looked at Christine. He was probably getting uncomfortable with my unclothed state. "You folks are more than welcome to come by my house for the time being, at least until your things get here. You can meet my wife, she's anxious to meet you. She'll be one of your regular patients—by default, I suppose. I'm certain you'll learn all about her in Dr. Farris's files. And Michael, while you're at the house you can get that wound cleaned up. You're probably gonna want to give yourself a tetanus shot, no?"

I looked over at Christine, who gave me a half nod, half shrug. We were anxious to start exploring the house and the grounds, but without our furniture there'd be no place to rest, and the water wasn't even turned on yet. I also didn't want to refuse the hospitable offer from our new neighbor, despite the awkward timing.

"We'll fix you up some lunch. You're all probably hungry about now." He put his hands on his knees and smiled at Jessica. "Rosy has a special iced tea with honey that'll make your tummy feel all better. Would you like that?"

Jessica nodded and returned a weak, thin smile.

Well, I was hungry, Christine probably was too, and there was only a bag of chips in the car. Earlier we'd discussed heading into town to find a diner, but it seemed we had other plans now. "Sure, lunch would be just fine. Thank you." I limped to the car, got out my spare pants, and put them on. Christine gave Jess the Pepto, and the five-year-old, now beyond the trauma of throwing up, was more than thrilled to be sipping it right out of the bottle.

We all piled into the minivan—Phillip and his new friend Page in the backseat, Jessica sitting on Christine's lap in the front. As we drove off toward Phillip Deighton's house, I looked along the side of the house and saw nothing but woods.

I couldn't help but wonder how far back those woods went.

Chapter Four

The road curved quite a bit, for no good reason, I thought, as Deighton's house faced the same easterly direction as mine. The charming colonial appeared around a bend of woodland—we'd passed nothing but thick trees on the left, with open pastures on the right, each giving way to the front porches of some additional homes. Each house had its very own inviting stretch of woods in the back.

As I pulled into the long gravel driveway, I wondered why past Ashborough physicians hadn't set up an office in the center of town where the thickest flow of traffic would bring in the most patients. Perhaps it was tradition to maintain a sense of isolation, keep a safe distance from society so there'd be minimal distraction and a stream of peace and quiet. It had probably been this way since the eighteenth century, back when these houses were built by hand. Like today, there would've been only one doctor in town, with a house in the wooded outskirts that you had to travel to if you needed some fixing up. I wondered, with some dismay, I might add, if those doctors made house calls, and whether that kind of service might be expected of me. *Am I on a house call now? Could this be some kind of diversionary tactic on the part of Phillip Deighton?* I tried to convince myself that hunches like this were the side effects of a tired, anxious mind, but for some reason, I thought otherwise.

You can meet my wife, she's anxious to meet you, Mr. Cayle. She's one of your regular patients.

"Well . . . here we are. Home sweet home," Deighton said. "Been here thirty-two years. Couldn't imagine uprooting myself like you folks just went and did." He stepped from the car, Page circling his ankles, yapping happily. Jessica, in an amazing transformation from sick to cheerful, chased after the dog.

"Easy, Jess," Christine said. "We don't want to have any accidents here."

The house was much like mine, from what I could tell, a rather large New England colonial blanketed in dark wood shingles and white trim. The driveway ran like a vein alongside a generous sprawl of lawn. Like the driveway, the walk to the house was also unpaved. At the end of the walk, four wooden steps led up to a gray-painted, wraparound porch. The mild spring weather had compelled the azaleas alongside the porch to release their blooms, the scent of which hung pleasantly in the air; a few bumblebees rejoiced, buzzing in circles. Obviously, the house had more of a lived-in look to it than mine, complete with a weather vane in the grass, a cowbell on the eave, and corn husks on the front door. This was small-town New England at its finest. Phillip led us all inside, then pointed me in the direction of the stairs.

"Bathroom's to the left at the head of the steps," he said with enthusiasm.

I'd brought the first-aid kit with me, and realized with some amusement that I'd never had to use it for a tetanus shot before. I worried for a moment whether or not there would be syringes inside, as it had been so long since I'd looked through it. But my mind told me not to worry. The needles would be in there, just as surely as there was a throb of looming infection in my foot.

"Thanks," I said. I smiled absently at Christine, then looked over at Jessica, who was feeding Page a slice of bologna Phillip had gotten from the refrigerator. I started upstairs, and heard Christine begin to narrate our reasons for deciding to move out of Manhattan. I figured by the time I finished cleansing the wound and injecting myself, the whole tale would be told and we could go on our merry way back to 17 Harlan Road. Home sweet home, as Deighton had said.

The steps creaked on the way up, and at the top I made a left just as Phillip instructed. There was an open door about eight feet away at the end of a long wall-papered hallway; waist-high wainscot molding with etched floral patterns ran the entire length. A faint stale odor lingered in the air. It could have been mothballs, but might have been something else. Something *old*. Like hair that hasn't been washed in a month.

I stopped and turned for a quick moment, and saw two more doors on the opposite side of the stairs, one straight ahead, the other in the wall alongside the landing; I figured them to be bedrooms. I shrugged my shoulders, then spun back, grabbed the doorknob, and entered the room. The first thing I did was look at my watch—it was one o'clock. This might have been an instinctive diversionary tactic, a way for me to dissuade my mind from realizing that I'd made a wrong turn.

I wasn't in the bathroom. I was in the master bedroom, face-to-face with Mrs. Deighton.

She was asleep in bed, thankfully, propped up against two pillows, head tilted awkwardly and resting on her left shoulder. My palms began to sweat, but I did not drop the first-aid kit. I held it tighter as my heart began to trot in my chest. Somehow I'd either made a wrong turn at the top of the steps, or the clever Phillip Deighton had purposely misguided Ashborough's new physician into the bedroom of his first patient.

This is what you're in for, neighbor. Just a little fair warning.

Mrs. Deighton moved. It was an involuntary bob of the head, quickly followed by a knee-jerk snort that tossed her swathed arms through the mess of sheets covering her. My heart took a more forceful trot—a gallop, perhaps—and for a few tense seconds the room seemed to spin around my head. My feet were cemented to the floor, and I held my breath in what I hoped was an effort to not wake the sleeping woman—

28

but knew in my hammering heart was fear.

I probed my physician's mind for a diagnosis, and immediately came up with cancer, the malady that plagues nearly one in every nineteen Americans. The signals seemed obvious. A good portion of her lower jaw had been cut away, a crude job if you ask me, primitive-looking and carelessly jagged. But I'm not a surgeon, nor did I have any details as to the severity of the problem, so I couldn't know exactly what options for surgery existed at the time. All I could tell was that there'd evidently been a malignant tumor festering in her jawbone at one time that nobody knew about, and it had grown and grown until it was too late to save her jaw, so it was sectioned away along with a hardy portion of her cheek, and what you had left was a gaping hole that revealed a wet blackness inside that no one should ever have to look at. Let me tell you, I've seen my share of open wounds, and this baby was a doozy.

Call me foolish, but I took a step closer, my eyes probing the horrific imperfection with utter curiosity, and I couldn't help but just stare at her face. In some crazy, ridiculous way, I thought I was looking at the rind on a rotting apple discovered at the bottom of some forgotten fruit basket. The doctor in me wanted to study it. No, *ogle* it. Christ, I felt like a kid in the freak tent at the circus. What was wrong with me?

I turned and let the vision of the woman go. I focused on a photo hanging on the wall, that of a younger Phillip, an unblemished Rosy, and a younger girl perhaps fifteen years old between them. Their daughter, I assumed. There was an open door inside the bedroom, and I slipped past it into the bathroom. I found the light switch and flipped it. The room filled with a sharp yellow glow that reflected off the ceramic tiles, which climbed all the way to the white plaster ceiling. The throb in my foot began to intensify, and the feel of it against the cool air as I hurriedly removed the bandages sent gooseflesh across my skin. I pulled the shower curtain aside and let the water run in the steel-toed tub, keeping it tepid. Once the tub was a quarter of the way filled, I immersed my foot. There was an initial sting, but pain soon eased as the injury soaked.

As I stood there, I tried hard to think of the movers who were probably filling my front lawn with cardboard boxes, and how I really needed to get back to the house so I could tell them where all the furniture needed to go. But it was difficult to stay focused; the image of the woman from the next room stayed with me, *haunted* me, made me shudder. Perhaps it'd been the unanticipated sight of her that had me so unnerved; I told myself that my professionalism would take over once I was settled into my position as Ashborough's respected internist. I hoped.

After five minutes, I removed my foot from the water. Examining the puncture, I could easily make out the beginnings of infection setting in, the appearance of a warm red ring about the perimeter of the wound. In a few hours pus would start amassing—the nectar of decay. Oh, joy.

Time for an inoculation.

This is one of the perks of being a doctor. You can administer a medication or write yourself (or a family member) a prescription without having to spend a few hours seeing the doctor, dropping off an Rx, and spend God knows how much time waiting for all this to happen. In a matter of a minute I had the syringe unwrapped and fitted into the plunger, had dispensed the vaccine, and inoculated myself in the thigh. To this day I still wince at the pain brought on by the needle, no matter how briefly it lasts, and I hoped this would be the last one for a while. Two sharp pokes in one day was more than this doctor could stand.

I leaned over and closed up the first-aid case.

I saw something move.

In my peripheral vision, an elongated, lopsided shadow splayed across the tiled wall; it looked like a sea serpent's head. I jerked away, leaning into the shower curtain, then grabbing it to prevent me from falling into the tub. Three plastic rings *popped* from the shower rod and clattered on the floor; the rest held just fine, long enough for me to regain my balance. But the noise had been more than sufficient to wake Mrs. Deighton. Unless, of course, the shadow itself had belonged to the unsightly woman, now up to investigate the odd noises in her bathroom. I wondered what she would think finding a strange man in her bathroom, barefoot and clutching her shower curtain. It'd scare the bejesus out of her.

Better give her some fair warning.

I stepped toward the door, and cringed back at the same time, at first keeping my eyes on the wavering shadow, then on the open door leading into the bedroom.

"Hello?" I called, half-whispering.

No reply. Might be hard of hearing too.

I called out again, this time louder. "Hello? Mrs. Deighton? Your husband told me I could use the bathroom."

I stepped out of the room.

Mrs. Deighton was awake, all right, out of bed and standing beside the lone window in the room. Wearing only a nightgown, she was faced away, thankfully, so I wouldn't have to look at her face. Her eyes were pointed out the window, and her body swayed slowly back and forth, as though she were under the influence of some potent spirits.

She turned toward me in an ungraceful totter, eyes muddy, yet still piercing. She didn't scream, didn't make a move. It was as if my presence had been expected, or perhaps unnoticed. Her jaw still quivered, except now I could see that dark open half of her face, and the dangle of loose skin that joggled from it like a turkey's wattle. For the first time in my career I was playing with the fact that this woman might not be human after all, as ludicrous as that sounded. I felt no more civil than one of those terrified Englishmen that had chased the Elephant Man, John Joseph Merrick, down in that London subway over a century ago.

Our eyes locked, and the first thing that came to me was that hers were *different,* somehow devoid of emotion, as though they'd seen terrible horrors beyond the rigors of cancer. Then I *saw* . . . there *were* additional horrors, which seeped into my world at once and staggered my breath, sending adrenaline racing through my weakening muscles. Her right hand . . . it was gone. Somewhere between the elbow and forearm was a gnarled mass of knotty scar tissue amassed in a stump. Half the bicep on the same arm was missing, which formed a glaring U-shape. Those were the more obvious injuries. All over her exposed skin, on her arms, neck, shins, and feet, were tiny masses of white scars, some more prominent than others, but each as startling as the next.

This was no cancer. It didn't take a doctor to come to this conclusion. No, this woman had been viciously attacked by an animal. *Animals.*

I wanted to be away from her. I had no business being here in the first place. I wondered why in God's name Phillip Deighton had sent me through their bedroom when there was probably another bathroom somewhere else in the house.

Has to be another bathroom, Michael. Your new home has three of them. Hey, you said it before yourself. Good ol' Phil Deighton wanted to give you a little fair warning, wanted to give you a taste of what to expect when you open your doors to the public.

I blew out a nervous breath. I had to say something, break the alarming silence. "Mrs. Deighton? I'm Michael Cayle, the new doc—"

"You can't help me," she interrupted, but her injury made it come out like *Ooo cand elp me*. A dollop of saliva pooled out of the bottom of her mouth-hole and wavered down in a long, swaying string.

I took a step forward. The woman staggered sideways and faced back out the window, bumping her shoulder against the pane. She brought her only hand up and dragged two-inch yellow nails across the glass, producing a harsh squeaking sound.

"Mrs. Deighton . . ." I said, feeling on the defensive. "I'll try my best, I—"

"They'll come for you, just like they did for me, just like they did for Dr. Farris, like they will for everyone else in this godforsaken town!" Her voice had started quietly, but rose in volume with each staggering word, and by the time she came to the end of her bizarre statement, her voice was a virtually indecipherable bark.

My breathing had increased, was exploding from my lungs in clutches. I wanted to console her, perhaps usher her back into bed . . . but I couldn't bring myself to touch her. *I was afraid of her.* And it wasn't just the woman herself—I'd seen similar injuries, many fresher than this—it was the look in her eyes, coupled with the swilling dark void in her face. It made me crazy. It made me fearful of what had happened to her.

They'll come for you, just like they did for me, just like they did for Dr. Farris.

Suddenly I asked, "Wasn't Dr. Farris attacked by a dog?" Her injures, and then the story about Farris, had me thinking.

She remained unanswering, staring out the window, thick yellow nails *tapping-tapping-tapping* against the windowpane.

Of course he was, I thought. That's why I'm here. He was killed in a savage accident, and now I'm moving into his home and taking over his job. Christ, the whole situation, which began as a godsend, was looking more and more morbid by the minute. Perhaps he'd been the fortunate one, I thought, unlike Mrs. Deighton, who'd survived her own dog attack and was now living permanently blanketed in her injuries. I pulled my sight away from her, then paced from the room, taking long, slow, deep breaths in a struggle to soothe my dizziness. My fear-response system was working rigorously, and I needed to massage it into retreat mode.

Once in the hallway, I stopped and leaned against the wall, my thoughts waging battle. Why on earth had I been so damn afraid in there? Was it the anxiety of the move that had me all bundled up in knots? When I first heard about the jarring circumstances concerning Neil Farris's death, I'd been shaken and a bit uncomfortable having to assume his revered position in this town of daily handshakes and hellos. Now, Mrs. Deighton, my new neighbor . . . she'd suffered a similar burden, and the discomfort blooming in me seemed to fall under the lens of a microscope.

Were there wild dogs running loose in Ashborough?

I shook the unpleasant thought from my head, but made a mental note to make some checks once we were all settled in. I walked to the top of the stairs, then detoured to the first door across the hall, to the *right*.

Bathroom. Full. With a tub.

Chapter Five

Phillip had traded his cigar for a pipe, and was packing it when I arrived back downstairs. I feared that someone might've heard his wife barking at me, but apparently her shouts weren't loud enough to travel all the way downstairs. He was busy folding up the rectangular package of tobacco, and when that was done, he placed it alongside the pipe on the table; apparently this was a pleasure he'd planned to savor after we left.

"Yep," he said, taking a sip of iced tea. "Neil was a dear friend. Real crying shame what'd happened to him." Three glasses half-filled with tea sat on the red gingham-checked cloth that covered the kitchen table. On the gas stove behind them was a clear pitcher filled halfway with green tea and lemons. A jar of honey in the shape of a bear was nestled alongside it like a clinging baby. There were hero sandwiches on the table (well, heroes if you're from New Yawk; subs if you're a New Hampshire-ite); Christine had a half-eaten sandwich before her, and even Jessica nibbled on a piece of bread. My stomach immediately announced its hunger, so I sat down in the open seat and helped myself to half a turkey-and-cheese sub. Christine and Phillip discussed the local amenities Ashborough had to offer, like the shops in the town square and the sprawling grasses of Beaumont Park. I stayed mostly silent, keeping to my sandwich, and started to feel a bit better now that I had some food in me. Amazing how hunger can set irrationality into a man. Once I'd eaten, my confrontation with Mrs. Deighton didn't seem so scary after all. Still, I wasn't all that thrilled being in the same house with her—much less having to make another house call someday.

"You take care of that foot, Michael?" Deighton asked.

I nodded. "I don't think we'll need to amputate."

Deighton broke out in laughter. Christine had heard me use that one a few dozen times, so she just rolled her eyes. Jessica sipped the green tea (it was a brightly odd color for tea) and offered up a long whiny *Daaaad!* She didn't think it was funny either. The joke was meant for Phillip anyway.

Phillip kept his eyes on his glass, then looked back and forth between Jessica and Christine. I'd hoped to lock gazes with him, to see if I could catch a bit of accountability in his eyes for sending me the wrong way at the head of the stairs. But he kept purposefully stoic, then went right on talking about Neil Farris.

"The Farris family lived here long before we came to town, and this is going back now twenty-seven years. He'd been there for over forty years, and from what I understand, he replaced the last physician, who'd also lived at 17 Harlan Road, and that one had been there for a good number of years as well. So you see, there's a long history of physicians in that house, at least a hundred years' worth. I reckon that if you look even beyond that, you might even find some more doctors that used to live there, but that's just a guess. Emily Farris was a good woman, a close and dear friend to Rosy. She used to come by here every other day just to say hello and check in to see how Rosy was coming along. Needless to say, Rosy is quite upset with the sudden and rather disconcerting change of events. The moment Neil Farris checked into that old folks' home in the sky, she not only lost a neighbor in Emily, but her only friend."

"Your wife . . ." I said.

For the first time, Deighton looked me right in the eye.

"Rosy . . . that's her name?" I asked.

"Yep, named after her grandmother. Short for Rosalia."

I nodded, then said, "You mentioned earlier that she was looking forward to meeting me."

"Yep, she sure is . . . but she's sleeping now." He said this in a curt, almost insinuating tone, as if accusing me of secretly slipping into the sanctuary of their bedroom to investigate his wife's whereabouts.

There was a moment of uncomfortable silence, a rare

occurrence given the fact that both Jessica and Page were in the room. Finally I said, "Well, as her new physician, I'm looking forward to meeting her." Such a liar.

Deighton smiled, a rather forced grin, I thought. Then he said, "I do need to get her medication to her."

That was our cue. Or our green light, depending how you looked at it. "And we need to get back to the house," I added, looking over at Christine. "There's probably boxes all over the place, and we need to tell the movers where to put the furniture."

With half-eaten sandwiches and half-filled glasses before us, we stood and shuffled around the table so we could say good-bye to Phillip.

"You'll love it here," Deighton said, walking us to the front door. "Like I said, we've been here for twenty-seven years. I met my wife in Boston, married her, then moved up here a year later. Got a job at the plant on the other side of town, put in twenty-five before taking an early retirement three years ago. Rosy needed someone to take care of her." He shrugged.

"And that someone was you," I said.

"Yep. What was I gonna do?"

Jessica and Page were on the porch, and Christine was holding the door open for me when I said, "You never told me what was wrong with her." I always felt it was improper to ask someone a question regarding a family medical issue, especially outside the office, but as her doctor in waiting, I figured I had the right to ask.

"Cancer."

He was lying. I didn't need to look into his eyes to know that.

"Anyways, you folks hurry along. Get yourselves all settled. We're here all day, up late at night, and Rosy's usually her best around about dinnertime, so you all feel free to stop on by at your convenience. There's always some cold tea brewing in the fridge, and Rosy's one helluva cook." He winked playfully at Jessica, who still looked a little pale to me. "And if Page gets hungry, he's always welcome to stop by for a snack too."

"Page is always hungry," Jessica said.

"We definitely will, Phillip," I said, lying again. Lunch was good for all of us, but I had no desire to race back for second helpings. I still felt the man's foremost intention was for me to give Rosy a once-over, and that soured my taste a bit. We walked down the porch to the minivan.

"Nice meeting you, Dr. Cayle," he added. There was something sharp and glowing in his eyes that made me believe he knew exactly what I was thinking.

I smiled. "Likewise, Phillip."

We piled into the minivan, and as I pulled away I watched him walk back into his house with the sudden pain-filled stagger of a man of eighty.

Chapter Six

We spent most of the day shifting boxes around the house and directing the movers, who'd arrived while we were at Phillip's. We'd toured the house only once before, so we were still a bit uncertain as to where everything should go. In the end, however, we got it all figured out. Christine and I took the largest bedroom upstairs, Jessica picked the one right next to ours, and even Jimmy Page got his own room, down the hall next to the bathroom.

The movers pulled out around ten-thirty. By then Jessica felt better and was sleeping in her new room, Page nestled alongside her on the bare mattress, snoring quietly. Mountains of boxes surrounded them; inside were Jessica's things, countless dolls and toys and books and clothes and other childhood necessities that would become giveaways in a year or two.

Throughout the day Christine had been in charge of opening boxes and sliding tables and chairs around, as well as placing knickknacks here and there and everywhere, while I complained that her desire to decorate had kicked in a bit too early. I'd argued—we'd spent a good fifteen minutes of every hour bickering—that we needed to be more organized and settle on the locations of big things like furniture and televisions before pot holders and trivets were hung on the walls. Of course I lost this battle, so she did her thing and I did mine, with us crossing paths every now and then on the hazier matters, like where to put the beer cooler full of Page's toys.

When fatigue got the best of us, I convinced Christine that a glass of wine might be a good way to end the day. So we uncorked the bottle of Merlot we'd brought along, dug back into the crackers and cheese we'd had for dinner, and clinked our glasses in a toast, sitting across from one another at the kitchen table.

"To our new home," I said, taking a sip.

"To our new home." Christine smiled and I noticed a worn look about her, eyes red and drooping, brown hair slipping from her bun. She was tired.

"Sure looks like you could use some shut-eye."

"I look that bad?"

"I didn't say you looked bad. . . ."

"Well, you don't look so hot yourself." She smiled thinly, then added, "You should heed your own advice, Doc."

"I don't think I'm gonna be able to sleep. Too much going on."

Christine started laughing. A bit of wine spilled from her lips and she used a napkin to dab at it.

"What? What's so funny?"

"I just got a visual of you standing out on the front lawn in your underwear trying to act all pleasant and nice for the new neighbor." She laughed again.

I laughed too. It *must've* been a sight, me semi-naked and smelling puky in front of the unassuming Phillip Deighton. "His timing was less than perfect, huh?"

"I'd say so."

"And then he finds it in himself to invite us over even though Jess is puking and I'm in my underwear."

Christine said, "You know, at first I got the impression that he was aiming to have you look at his wife."

I agreed, and even though I really wasn't in the mood to discuss the matter, I told Christine what'd happened upstairs with Rosy Deighton (leaving out what she had said to me), and how I thought Phillip might have purposely misled me.

"I'm sure that if he really wanted you to see his wife, he would have come right out and asked you. He doesn't strike me as the type to play games. It was probably an accident, or maybe you just didn't hear him correctly."

"No, he definitely said to make a left at the top of the stairs."

"Maybe the bathroom off the hall was broken, or dirty. Could be any number of explainable reasons why he didn't want you to use it."

I shrugged my shoulders. Perhaps I was over-analyzing the situation. Being presumptuous, as Christine had said earlier. Then I thought of something else. "Remember that he said his wife had cancer?"

"I heard that. Terrible . . ."

"What I saw on Rosy Deighton wasn't caused by cancer. I thought so at first, but when I saw her entire body . . . without question she was mauled by some kind of vicious animal. A dog probably, and more than just one if you want my professional opinion."

"You sure?"

"Positive."

"Kind of scary, considering what happened to Farris."

"Exactly."

Christine downed the rest of her wine. There was a bit of silence that seemed to end the troubling topic of conversation. "That's it for me," she said. "I'm bed-bound. You coming?"

"No . . . I think I'm going to poke around in the office for a bit. Haven't set foot in there yet."

"Michael, it'll be there tomorrow. . . ."

"I'm too wound up, plus I'm real curious too see what kind of equipment the widow left behind. I'll only be a few."

"She said she was going to leave everything."

"Yeah . . . I'm anxious to see what *everything* is."

"Please, don't be too long. First night in the new house. I'm bound to be spooked by all the creaks and noises."

"Don't worry, you'll be asleep in no time," I said, and kissed her good night.

Chapter Seven

I felt like a cat exploring a closet for the very first time, eyes wide, searching for the light switch in the hallway leading into my new, still unexplored office. Finally I located it on the wall to the right. An exposed bulb in the center of the ceiling, weakened by a layering of dust, emitted a pallid glare across fading green walls. The hallway (that's all it was: a five-foot hallway connecting the house to the examination room and medical office like a big vein) was as bare as a prison cell with chipped plaster walls and a steel institutional door complete with the tandem security of a dead bolt and chain. I thought it strange that Farris chose to install the sort of door you would normally use to partition a garage—the impassable type that keeps the burglars out. I made a mental note to have it changed to match the rest of the paneled doors and closets in the house.

I opened the steel door. It led into the waiting room, where my patients would sign in and fidget away their time before seeing me. Two small plaid sofas hugged the walls, and were separated by another door, this one leading out to the side of the house where the patients would enter. Opposite this door was a small cut-out partition. Looking through it, I could see a small desk that was built into the short wall. Here's where my wife would do her job, greet the patients with her pleasant smile and enter all their personal information into the computer I was hoping to have set up within the next few days.

Just to the right behind the partition was another doorway, this one leading into the examining room. It was painted the same odd green color as the hallway, and I made a second note to put a fresh coat of cool sterile white over the queasy clinical decor. In the eight-by-eight room was an eye chart on the wall alongside a 3-D diagram of the human nervous system. On the opposing wall sat a stainless-steel examining table, which still had half a roll of sanitary paper beneath it. This paper always reminds me of the wrappings they use when you buy a hero, er, submarine sandwich at the deli.

I closed my eyes for a moment and fantasized about meeting my first day's worth of patients. They would be very different from the breed of people haunting Dr. Scully's practice in Manhattan. There I'd served a Medicaid population with general family health care, poor people whose green cards still had wet ink on them. Teenage pregnancies and flulike symptoms that were a result of either painkiller withdrawals or the beginnings of hepatitis. A real treat. Here in Ashborough I'd end up spending my time crawling through annual check-ups, treating the occasional flu or trifling with the sniffles and broken limbs of schoolchildren. In six months time I would end up crossing paths with most of the town's population—at last count hovering around twelve hundred—and I say most because there's always your small percentage of individuals who refuse to see a doctor for one of two reasons. Either they feel invincible to nature's harmful ways, or they're too scared to face God's music. These are the same people that come crawling to me for a miracle cure a day late and a dollar short. Sorry, Charlie, God I ain't.

There was another door two steps into the entrance of the examining room, this one also, oddly, made of steel. It led into my future sanctuary. The library. I've made myself quite clear about my hesitations regarding moving my family from the city to the country; but this room, well, let's just say that its presence made it much easier for me to look beyond my reservations. Upon walking through the door you are faced with an entire wall of floor-to-ceiling windows, and we're talking lofty, vaulted ceilings that start at twelve feet and point skyward to an apex of nearly eighteen feet high. Being in this room made me feel as though I were in a church, with cathedral ceilings and arched doorways purposely constructed to further inspire a reflection of the heavens—to induce a mysterious quiet apprehension that a divine presence is in visitation. Spooky, yet breathtaking. A room with a view, and so much more.

This room was a sanctuary. Here, I felt *protected*.

Apparently Emily Farris felt it necessary to not only leave her husband's medical supplies behind, as shown on the immediate right where two large oak armoires stood; inside were all the materials I would need to patch and mend and record and administer and perform all my doctorly duties: a fresh and wealthy inventory of medicinal furnishings and instruments. Really, I could go to work tomorrow if I had to. The widow, in an apparent struggle to vanquish all memories of her husband's career, had left the entire room untouched. And I'm not just talking filing cabinets stuffed with medical records or cases of promotional pharmaceuticals, I'm talking furniture that included the aforementioned armoires, a huge cherry desk facing out the windows, plus custom bookshelves lining two entire walls stuffed with every medical encyclopedia under the moon (*after all, it was night*). There was a coat rack by the door, original paintings on the back wall. And don't let me forget the fireplace, set with harvest-gold brick that went up the entire wall to the peaked ceiling. She even left behind a set of brass hearth tools. Magnificent.

I scanned the books, then sat in the leather chair at the desk. I pulled at the drawers, but they were all locked; someplace, I would need to locate the key. There was a small cabinet to the right of the desk, near the fireplace. I stood up, walked over to it. It was unlocked. Inside was an assortment of liquors, plus three glass tumblers. I chose the brandy, sat back down at my desk, and poured myself a drink. As I sipped the alcohol, I stared beyond the glass panes of the floor-to-ceiling windows, and for the first time relished in the flavor of my new country home, all the while thinking of my fantasy of gazing out the windows at the dark expanse of woods in the backyard, counting the fireflies on a hot summer night.

I smiled as the warm spirits softened the anxieties of the day. Perhaps I wouldn't miss the city after all.

Ten minutes passed. I downed the last drop of brandy in the glass and decided that now would be a good time to retire to bed. I placed the glass on the table, looked out into the darkness, and saw, in the distance of the woods, a brief and single flash of gold light. I walked to the window, cupped my hands around my face, and peered out. It did not come again. Perhaps one of my fireflies had paid me a visit?

When I turned around, I saw a small icebox in the farthest corner of the room. I hadn't noticed it until now, as it hugged the corner between the bookshelf and armoire. I went to it, pulled at the door, but it was locked. Rifling through the desk earlier, I'd noticed a few small keys, which I'd assumed went to the liquor cabinet. I retrieved them, then fitted the first one into the lock on the icebox. It opened with a small *click*.

Inside was an assortment of blood samples, each one labeled with a patient's name. I found it odd that Farris had presumably collected the blood of his patients, which wasn't necessarily out of the ordinary if he'd planned to send them out for testing. However, there was quite a collection here. Then I discovered something amazing.

The man had samples of disease-infected blood.

They were labeled as such: *Hantavirus, HIV +, Malaria, Bubonic Plague.* I wondered where he'd gotten them from, and what they could be used for. Was it possible that he'd had some patients who'd come down with these diseases? HIV, yes. Hantavirus, possible. But malaria? Bubonic plague? I locked the cabinet back up and made a point to research Farris's files as to why he'd had those samples on hand.

Back in the house, all was quiet. I peeked in on Jessica, who along with Page appeared not to have moved since I last checked in almost two hours ago. I felt a true, powerful sense of love for my daughter, a feeling so deep it scared me. Perhaps it was the unfamiliar surroundings, seeing her here for the very first time, sleeping so peacefully, the simple act appearing oddly precarious, as though she'd settled down in the first comfortable place she could find after a day wandering as a lost runaway.

In my new bedroom, I undressed and crawled into my half of the bed that for the time being was a stark metal frame holding up two twin boxsprings and the king-size mattress; the rest of the wood bed was disassembled on Christine's side, towering against the wall like phantom trees. I lay there for ten minutes feeling the pressures of the day waning, and all the while I listened to Christine's shallow breaths and the occasional grind of her teeth. Still, sleep seemed as far away as my life in Manhattan, and I propped myself up on my elbows and peered out the window facing the woods in the backyard. In the full moon's light, I could see the birdbath, the shed at the perimeter of the woods, and then the woods themselves, which pitched up slightly and disappeared in the distance, even at this height.

All was quiet. Too quiet.

Deep in the darkness of the woods, I saw a second brief flash of golden light. And then, like the first, it was gone.

A half hour later, while I still lay awake in bed, I thought, *Fireflies don't come out until July.*

Chapter Eight

The next three weeks were a transitional period for us, but proved to be busier than we'd ever expected. I ended up opening my practice to the public one week after moving in. It was by default. I hadn't planned on ramping things up so quickly, but as soon as the phones were hooked up they began an eternal serenade of tolls, and in twenty-four hours I had a tapeful of messages from Dr. Farris's old patients (my *new* patients) seeking checkups and appointments, all for non-life-threatening issues. Through my perusal of their records, and the general lighthearted conversations that took place during their stopovers, I realized that these people simply wanted to be the first ones to initiate some chatter with new doctor in town. It was all part of the small-town directive. She who plants the grapevine grows the most acquaintances. And while I played mayor, Christine assumed command of the household.

Jessica was having a grand old time exploring the nooks and crannies of the house, and even helped Christine choring about with an enthusiasm that'd remained previously dormant. She'd do the job that was asked of her as long as it incorporated a conversation pertaining to all the fun activities she'd soon encounter in kindergarten, plus, as Christine so duly illustrated, how she'd be the smartest kid in class because all her roots were planted in city soil. I frowned upon this type of workload bribery despite the fact that it served its purpose quite well, and hoped that Christine's ego-boosting commendation would fade from Jessica's mind before September arrived.

I'd had lunch with Phillip a couple more times, and soon enough I was formally introduced to Rosy Deighton. As it turned out, she didn't remember our encounter in the bedroom, although I still had my suspicions as to whether there might have been some ulterior motive that day on the part of her husband. Looking at her was still a little hard on the stomach (she even joined us for lunch one afternoon—I'll spare the details), but she seemed a rather pleasant lady who did her best to keep up a good attitude despite the fact that the golden years of her life had been pretty much wiped out.

Curious as to her condition and certain that cancer hadn't been the culprit, I'd spent many hours searching Neil Farris's files for Rosy Deighton's medical record, but found nothing. I'd never met Farris, and knew very little about him before I assumed his life here in Ashborough. But I'd learned that he was a very detail-oriented man. His files were immaculately kept, alphabetized by last name, and categorized by condition. There were fourteen people suffering from cancer in Ashborough (at least those who came to Farris for support), and Rosy Deighton wasn't one of them. Actually, according to the records left behind for me, Rosy hadn't even been a patient.

I never told Phillip that I couldn't locate Rosy's file—I felt this bit of information was something he didn't need to know about; the last thing I needed was the *necessity* to unearth it under his watchful eyes, wherever the hell it was. I ended up examining her (another choice by default) during my lunch breaks, and prescribed her a mild anti-anxiety medication in addition to the painkillers she was taking, something that would help her get through the mental aspect of her discomfort. That's the difference between Old World practice and New: Farris, in his seventies, mostly avoided prescribing anti-anxiety or anti-depressive meds for fear of their addictive properties, something he indicated in many of his patient files. Little did Mr. Small-town Physician know that half of America chows down Xanax and Zoloft like they're Tic-Tacs.

Although I knew the medication would help Rosy's thinking (I decided to chalk up her window-tapping outburst as a case of sleepwalking, and prescribed some Ambien to keep her bed-bound), I felt disappointed that there was nothing else I could do for her to make coping a bit easier. She'd have to live with her deformities for the rest of her life, and she'd have to deal with it, otherwise she'd end up in a padded room.

On a different occasion Christine met Rosy, and did her best to make nice with her by talking herbal teas, spice candles, and aromatherapy; as it turned out, Rosy had a bit of new age in her bones, and Christine took to that just fine, happily discussing the healing properties of jasmine and sandalwood and other essences of the mind. Rosy had mentioned how much she enjoyed children, but Christine thought it best to keep Jessica away, and I agreed. To a five-year-old, Rosy was the bogeyman. To some adults too.

Sometime during the third week I took the afternoon off so that we could tour the elementary school and get Jessica registered for kindergarten in the fall. When we first arrived there, Jessica had spotted an unruly line of older children in the hallway, third-graders, I supposed, and cast a silent wary look up at me as if to ask whether she had a choice in this matter. Suddenly, school didn't seem all the fun and games Christine made it out to be.

We met the elementary school principal, a bald and rotund fellow named Goodwin Clarke, who made a point of discussing the rheumatoid arthritis in his hands and how the anti-inflammatory meds gave him the bloodies, something both Christine and I really didn't need to visualize at the moment. Christine did her best to not look at me for fear of bursting out in laughter, and I changed the subject by promising Goodwin an appointment the following Saturday.

When we arrived home Jimmy Page was eyeing his leash. He ran to the door, then looked at me, then at the door, then at me again. I got the hint and took him for a walk in the back before he started whimpering.

Page's first and favorite spot had become the cement bird fountain, and in no time all the weeds around the pedestal were dead. They ought to market the stuff, I thought.

I spent some moments between appointments here in the backyard (not much hustle and bustle here in Ashborough, unlike New York, where you bounced back and forth between examining rooms like a volleyball), circling about the property, checking out the grass and the weeds and the sea of trees and copses that seemed to go on forever. Regardless of the amount of time, whether it was a few minutes or a half hour, each time out seemed like a small journey, and I would discover something else on the property I didn't know about, simple little things like where the water spigots were or how someone had planted a line of white rose bushes about twelve feet deep into the woods. One Sunday afternoon—soon, I promised myself—I would take a few hours to search these woods. Don't ask me what I expected to find. But since most of my life had been spent on sidewalks and concrete, I thought it'd be fun playing the role of forest explorer.

The rest of the day was spent in typical Cayle family fashion. Jessica ran about the property with Page, Christine rearranged our things while getting dinner ready, and I painted the hallway and examining room the flat-white color I thought it should be. At one point Jessica slipped into my office to proudly show off a marvelous scrape on her knee. I covered it with Bacitracin and a Band-Aid and sent her on her ungraceful way.

After dinner we spent the evening relaxing in the living room, something we really hadn't done as a family since moving in. The television was off, another rarity. Jessica was lying on her stomach on the spiral-weave rug reading Dr. Seuss, and I poked through the last of Farris's files trying to acquaint myself with the medical histories of Ashborough's families. At one point Christine glanced over at me. She was sitting on the love seat by the window that looked out across the front yard. I saw a glossy joy in her gaze, and she aimed her eyes down as if embarrassed by her tears. *Jesus,* I thought, *she wants another child. Ain't that a number you can bet on. And she wants one soon. My excuse of having no space is moot now. No more tight city living for the Cayles. We could have two or three more with the room in this house. I'd have to settle for one more.*

Then she said it. "Michael . . . I want to talk."

I stood, walked over to her, and kissed her, knowing that I'd have to give in to her appeal. Yep, she wanted another baby, and she'd start the conversation by saying, *I'm thirty-four, and I'm not getting any younger.*

Neither was I. And I wanted another child too. Kind of. "Wait until Jess is in bed, then we'll talk."

She nodded, smiling, knowing she was finally going to win this cold war.

An hour later Jessica was asleep on the floor, unaware of her mother's yearnings. Christine looked up from her *Better Homes and Gardens* with that same glazed stare. "Michael . . . I'm not getting any younger. And you know Jessica needs a sibling." She *always* started the talk that way. It was her path of least resistance, of trying not to sound too selfish. Thing was, I was starting to agree with her, more so now that we lived at 17 Harlan Road. Without any other children in the immediate area—heck, there were hardly any *people* in the immediate area—Jessica would have much to gain with a brother or sister in the house.

I said, "Let me put her to bed, and then we can discuss it." Me procrastinating again.

I scooped Jessica up and carried her upstairs, walking through the moon shadows that painted the open staircase with gray slants. I made it to the top and thought of Rosy Deighton . . . well not *Rosy*, but the woman in the room I met that day, how she rose from bed and spoke inscrutably of *them*, how *they'll* get me like they did everyone else in this godforsaken town. I'd kept this odd little tidbit of information to myself, did my best, really, to try to shove it from my mind. But it kept coming back, the image of Rosy and her gnarled face, her disfigurements, the yellow nails tapping their signal upon the windowpane as she warned me of some obscure and hidden threat.

It terrified me.

I stood on the landing for a minute, maybe more, holding Jessica, *embracing* her as though a clear and present danger positively existed in the cool unstirring darkness of my home. She fidgeted slightly in my arms; a wave of sick fear burned a hole in my stomach. Confusion beset me, strengthening the fear.

Something bad happened here, my mind told me. There was a sudden surge of anxiety torturing me. My breathing was quick and labored, matching the urgent pace of my heart; my legs felt like sodden tea bags; my feet and hands tingled, as though all the blood had rushed away from them toward my head, causing my lightheadedness. The human body responds dramatically to the perceived threat of danger, the symptoms as real as if an actual intruder emerged from the darkness with a weapon aimed in one's direction. But there was no intruder, no immediate peril. *So then why am I so damn terrified? Is my subconscious trying to tell me something? Or do I need medication like so many of the patients that leave my office with an Rx for Xanax clutched tightly in their sweaty palms?*

Something crashed in Jessica's room.

I was startled—*exaggerated response,* I told myself— then tried to soothe it away, taking long, slow, deep breaths through my nose, blowing it out across my coated tongue. My body ran with gooseflesh, and again I had to remind myself that there was nothing to be afraid of—spontaneous crashes were nothing out of the ordinary when you had a playful cocker spaniel sniffing about the house. No *what if*s here, nothing to ask the anxious mind that never offered a practical answer.

I took Jessica into her room and placed her gently on the bed. A cool breeze raced in through the screen, tossing the lace curtain toward the ceiling; the billowing fabric looked like a ghost caught in the clutches of the window frame as if it attempted to sneak its way in from the cold night. On the floor alongside the dresser lay one of Jessica's many plastic dolls, its fall obviously coming from a toss of wind, not one of Page's nosy pokes. Its head had come loose and rolled halfway across the room. I could see the glassy eyes staring up at me, unblinking, seeming to demand, *Michael, give your wife another child. I need another playmate.* I retrieved the head and tried to reattach it, but failed, the plastic eyelids blinking as it shifted in my grip. On the dresser Jessica had all her dolls lined up. There was a gap in the queue. It reminded me of a missing tooth. I walked over and fitted the doll back in its spot, alongside her teddy bear with the one button eye that dangled from loose threads, and nestled the head in its lap. I then pulled the curtain aside and peered out the open window. The woods were as dark as the ocean at night. Huge. Threatening. A monster. Psychologically, I could have been standing at the edge of the universe, or in the wake of a giant tidal wave.

That's your anxious mind speaking out again, Michael. Time to let it go.

I closed the window, swallowed a dry lump in my throat, and tucked Jessica in, snug as a bug. Gently, I ran a finger across her cool brow, moving aside a blond curl, then kissed her good night. Standing in the doorway, I couldn't help but stare at my sleeping beauty before heading back downstairs to discuss adding another child to the Cayle family household.

Chapter Nine

The fourth Sunday we were in the house, I decided it was time to strap on the work boots and take a nice long hike through the woods. Christine had brought Jessica into town for lunch, a haircut, and perhaps some shopping (as per Jessica, there was a toy store in town, a bit of information she must have gained through osmosis), and I took in the warm June sunshine with some iced tea (Rosy Deighton's recipe) while snuggled in a folding chair in the front yard. As soon as I finished the tea and stood to make my way around back, Phillip Deighton came walking across the front lawn. Page, who'd been sleeping in the shade of the chair, yipped a few times, then licked himself and went back to dreaming about filet mignon or T-bones.

"Hello, Phillip," I said. "Have a seat. Chair's a bit old, but clean. Found it in the garage."

"Looks as though you're headin' out." Phillip had on a pair of carpenter shorts, work boots, and a golf shirt. As usual, gray chest hair exploded from the collar.

"I was going to explore the woods a bit."

Phillip nodded knowingly. "Hmm . . . you know where you're going? I'm only saying this 'cause it's easy to get lost when you don't have your direction about you." Phillip painted a straightforward grin on his face: next best thing to coming right out and asking if he could come along.

"No, I haven't been back there yet. At least beyond about thirty feet."

"Well, it's a good thing I wore my boots. Gets a bit mushy back there. And there's also something back there I think you'd like to see."

Apparently I wasn't going to be spending this time alone. Not that I minded, of course. Phillip had been pretty good company since we moved to Ashborough, and when push came to shove, he was my only friend. "I could use a tour guide, I suppose."

"There's some beaten paths in and about the clearer areas," he said. "Best to find them and not stray too far. Three, four times a year the sheriff and his men end up scouring the woodland beyond the town 'cause some kids end up losing their sense of direction. And don't you think it hasn't happened to any adults either."

"As long as it isn't any trouble . . ."

"No trouble at all."

"Well, then let's go."

* * *

I grabbed two plastic bottles of water before heading out, and in five minutes we were well beyond the perimeter of the woods, to a point where I couldn't even see my house anymore. The land rose up over a hill and then down along one of Phillip's aforementioned beaten paths. I thought it interesting how the woods, quite thick in most places, cleared every now and then to give way to brambles and high grass. Still, the trees remained intimate, their branches reaching out and caressing like fingers, the leaves whispering songs down from the clutches of balmy winds. It was that special time of year when spring surrendered to summer, sending kisses of warmth across your moistening skin. It showed down my chest in a dark wet stripe. Phillip had one on his back. A product of nature's embrace. How poetic, I thought.

Phillip walked off the path, to the left. Twigs and sticks crunched under his feet. "Come this way."

"Don't stray too far. I don't want to get lost."

"I know these here woods pretty well, Michael. You just stick with me and there'll be nothing to worry about."

The path we traveled was carpeted with slick leaves and scattered pine needles, making the going a bit slow, which didn't matter much to me, as I'd intended on a leisurely stroll with Mother Nature and this was as close to pure nature as you could get (putting aside the errant soda can or beer bottle whose labels were as colorless as Phillip's chest hair). My guess was that we'd traveled about a quarter mile now, more than half of that on flat land. Eventually we stopped for a breather.

"You mentioned that you had something to show me," I said.

"Yep . . ." Phillip took a mouthful of water, smacked his lips, then changed the subject. "You've any idea where we are?"

"Forgot my compass, Phil."

"That way's north," he said, pointing. "About four miles from here is the town. If you walk in a westward direction you'll end up in someone's backyard. If you go south, well, then you'll get nothing but forest . . . probably forty miles' worth."

Something shifted in the woods about ten feet away. I felt a bit of a scare in my heart, then peered watchfully ahead. Phillip hunkered down, and I followed suit. He placed an index finger across his lips (which still had the cigar between them) and pointed. I looked back and saw it. To the right, nestled amidst a patch of ferns, a spectacular doe. Its felt was smooth and nutty, eyes wet and wide and cautious, mouth gnawing fruitfully on a sapling. This was a hunter's dream come true, I thought, and I savored every moment by admiring this tiny yet exquisite slice of God's creative pie. Man, what a rush.

And then, in a leap, it was gone.

Phillip stood up, groaned some. "Oh . . . that was a treat."

"Is that what you wanted to show me?" I asked jokingly.

He smiled, trudged forward. "Follow me."

*　　*　　*

We walked perhaps another quarter mile. My legs tightened up on a few more short inclines—the result of a lack of exercise, I thought—and I made a mental note to heed my own advice one of these days. I looked good, but I needed to start jogging again.

Neil Farris took to a daily ritual of jogging. Lot of good it did him.

The passage twisted downward, cutting in and about some very old pines, then the trees fell away in a spot home to a mass of tangly undergrowth. Roots rose up from the ground like tentacles, reaching to trip up the path. The ground here was spongy and the mud came up to my ankles at one point. But then the path rose again, and the pines reclaimed the territory, as did firmer ground. The canopy of branches here was thin and had a difficult time blocking the sun's rays, which were now lancing down from directly overhead. Sweat jeweled on my brow. My heart rate was that of a runner's.

"So where are we going?" I asked Phillip. I realized, suddenly, that he'd taken me to the proverbial "middle of nowhere."

"Almost there," he answered, wherever "there" was.

We climbed another small hill, then came back down into a rather large clearing within a circle of ivy-shouded oaks. I was filled with awe. The scene before me was unbelievable.

I described it as a *circle* of oaks because that's exactly how this area was shaped, leading me to believe that this place had been not been some casual fluke of nature; it was too perfect to have not been influenced by the hand of man. Here was a rather large area, the diameter perhaps sixty or seventy feet across the open center, the pines standing like soldiers around the perimeter. Yet, despite the oddly cut-out area, I couldn't help but find something even more incredible here, something extremely . . . ominous.

The clearing was crowded with stones, and I'm not just talking about a few random rocks and pebbles. These were great slabs of non-indigenous stone, each of them rectangular in shape and fitted into an odd configuration as though the whole had been constructed as some sort of altar or temple. I thought to myself, *This baby is old,* and I couldn't help but think of Stonehenge, or Easter Island. Some of the stones stood on end as high as ten feet, some only went a few feet in the air but were no less menacing. Others lay flat on the forest floor at seemingly complementary angles. I imagined that if one viewed the entire structure from above, some pattern would make itself present. Of course, such a feat would be impossible because, despite the large circular clearing in which these slabs of carved stone were erected, the trees here had still found a way to extend their branches out to close out the sky. This forced the surrounding shrubs and smaller trees to compete for precious sunlight, and kept this miraculous work of ancient art a secret.

Even more amazing was how nature itself appeared to have conformed to the ancient monuments. A perfect carpet of leaves and pine needles blanketed the floor around and about the stones, and yet not one leaf or needle lay *atop* them. It was as though someone had meticulously tended to the area, passing through every so often with a broom to take away any leaves or needles littering the smooth, weathered surfaces. But that wasn't the case, of course, and the more I gazed at the stones, the more I came to assume that there might be some incredible harmony at work here: the forces of nature toiling gracefully alongside some deeper metaphysical power. It sounded a bit kooky, but I just couldn't see humans being involved here, not with the *evenness* of this place. It was too isolated. Too spooky. Too perfect. Too . . . I could go on and on.

"This is amazing," I said. I walked across the center of the area, pacing from stone to stone, checking out their smooth surfaces and the crude enormity of them all. A quick count had me estimating the amount of stones to be about thirty. *Jesus*, I thought. *How did they get here?*

"I knew you'd like it," Phillip said, sitting down on one of the stones and lighting his cigar.

"This is incredible," I said, tilting my head in attempt to make out some sort of purposeful pattern in their layout. I tried not to get too crazy about it, though. Local town historians had probably studied this scene for years without finding any answers to their ancient function, design, or intent.

Although the stones exhibited no flutterings from above—at one point I saw a leaf seesawing lazily down from the canopy and magically divert its path to avoid a stone before alighting on the ground—some had had their fair share of crude carvings, and the largest stone, which lay flat and detached from its brethren in the middle of the configuration, possessed a multitude of brown Rorschach-like stains.

Blood.

I paced over and took a closer look at the stains, touched them, wanted to smell them—doctor's intuition setting in—but stopped myself from doing so. They were as dry as the rocks themselves, but didn't look as old. Common sense told me that over time they would have eroded and faded away regardless of the stones' porousness. Which meant the bloodstains—if that's indeed what they were—hadn't been there very long. That unnerved me.

Looks like an ancient altar of some sort.

I turned to face Phillip, but he'd gotten up from his spot. The trail of smoke from his cigar showed that he'd moved beyond the circle of stones. I could see him trembling, restless with deep lines of tension creasing his aging face. I thought: *He's tormented about his wife.* Given the dire circumstances, I'd be too, and again I told myself, despite Phillip's constant reminders, that Rosy Deighton had not been a victim of cancer. (I still hadn't located her file, and resigned myself to the fact that one didn't exist.) My gut told me that she'd been attacked by an animal, more than likely a dog or two. Or three. Like Neil Farris. *So what?* I thought, trying to minimize my concern. Regardless of *how* Rosy's afflictions were caused, they had been endless and traumatic and gruesome and would always be till death do them part. I offered Phillip a nod of reassurance, and he knew where I was coming from. He winked back, puffing on his cigar.

"How old are these?" I asked. One of a half-million questions rolling around in my mind.

He shrugged. "Don't know for sure. Thousand years, I guess. Let me show you something else."

We walked to the outermost edge of the circle at the opposite end of the structure. A very large stone stood perpendicular to the others, ten feet away from the edge of clearing. Crabgrass hugged the bottom in bunches, errant ivies snaking about it like lanyards. On the face of the stone were a series of heiroglyph-like carvings, illegible pictograms that decorated the upper half of the ten-by-six-foot stone. *Had anything like this ever been discovered outside Egypt?* On the bottom was a succession of straight-line markers, as though someone many years ago had kept a running total of something important. Sequenced by fives, I easily added up the notches. They totaled eighty-three.

"See those notches?" Phillip asked as I ran a finger in the indentation of one. "Four hundred years ago people used this place to make sacrifices. Each one of those markers represents an event."

"An event?"

He nodded. "Yep, a sacrifice."

"What kind of sacrifice?"

Phillip put his hands in his pockets. "Well, according to legend . . . *town* legend, that is, and I say that because nobody knows for sure how far out beyond Ashborough our little piece of history has traveled over the years. Old Lady Zellis, she'll tell you tales that'll pull your eyes out of your head, and she knows every legend that runs from Ashborough all the way to Blacksburgh and beyond, though she might be the only one. You see, each town has their own personal legend and where they originate is usually where they stay. No one cares much for the next town's folklore, and no one likes to share their stories either. I guess you can call it hometown pride.

"Anyway, there used to be a race of aboriginal people, not Indians, but a different kind of people who lived here in isolation long before the white man came and pilfered it all away. This land had been wholly unoccupied and shunned by the native folk, and for years our New England forefathers heeded their warning and steered clear."

"Their warning?"

He hesitated, looked me in the eyes, then said, "That all those who tread this land shall fall victim to the savagery of the Isolates."

"The Isolates . . ."

"This is what the Indians called them, these supposedly underdeveloped aborigines."

A silence grew between us. I took a sip of water and let the story sink in. *The savagery of the Isolates.* I moved my sights from Phillip to that large white slab in the center with the brownish stains. To me it looked like a great dead heart, the surrounding stones the fossilized remains of some long-extinct dinosaur. Again it occurred to me that the whole of all these parts seemed much too tended in appearance, very un-ruinlike for something supposedly a thousand years old, and it really bothered me.

"Yep, Old Lady Zellis, she'll tell you the story much

better than me, but she's a tough cookie to get ahold of these days, pretty much keeps to herself and her home, and if you ask anyone they'll tell you that she's a card shy of a full deck, myself included. But she sure as heck knows her lore, at least that's what all the townsfolk say. I'll never forget the day I met her. She told me all about the Isolates and of this place they used for their rituals. It was thirty-two years ago, right after Rosy and I moved to Ashborough. I was in my twenties and the old lady was even an old lady back then."

Phillip put his right foot up on one of the stones, rested a forearm on his knee. "We'd just moved into our home the week before. It'd been a real cool autumn evening and we needed some wood for the fireplace, so I took off into the woods with my ax in search of a couple of healthy branches. I suppose I could've taken what I needed right away, but the crisp air felt good in my lungs so I kept on walking, and in no time I was a few hundred feet deep into the woods. And then like magic, she appeared—Old Lady Zellis.

"I'd already heard some stories about her from the townspeople. Some folks were saying that she was all sugar and spice, and others thought she was a real bad apple—rotten to the core. Me, I didn't know her at all so I had no opinion at the time, but upon first glance I'd say there was definitely some hocus-pocus brewing up her sleeve. She's one of those kooky-odd types. Every town has their share and everyone formulates an opinion about them despite the fact that nobody really knows anything about them. She lives by her lonesome, rarely goes outside except to spend some afternoons on her porch.

"Her past, well, it's mostly a secret too, although the townsfolk say that she once lived with her mother, an old Gypsy who used to travel up north and trade for wax to make candles. Rumor has it that they used these candles to perform some kind of witchy ceremonies in their basement at night, and to this day if you check out some of the older trees in the woods in her backyard, you'll find some crude carvings in the bark just like these. It's told that her mother died when the old lady was just twelve . . . heh, I've always wondered if she was an old lady back then too! There's a grave in her backyard that's supposed to be her mother's. It's right at the edge of the woods, you can even see it from the road. Even nowadays people don't like talking about her. They say that she can see and hear everything you do despite the fact that she stays all to herself, and they'll tell you that she has a bit of darkness in her soul that can delve into your thoughts and spoil the purity of your Christian blood if she discovers you're doing something against her wishes."

Phillip went silent. I waited.

"So anyway . . . there I was in the woods. It was getting dark. Some owls had started hooting and the breeze'd picked up, making all the leaves sigh like ghosts. I'd stepped around a large tree and was face-to-face with a woman that looked older than time itself. She wore a black robe with a hood and had a walking cane in both hands, although I don't remember her using it to actually walk. I remember feeling hypnotized by her round eyes, which were brown with flecks of gold that seemed to glow slightly in the darkness. She was short, five feet tops, with a slight hunch that made her look much shorter. Her skin was white and weathered and trembled in the stirring winds. I half expected a swirl of fog to roll in, but that never happened."

"Were you scared?"

"Well, I suppose I was. I'm not really sure exactly how I felt at the time, although I don't remember feeling too pleased at the unexpected encounter. She just kept on staring at me as though she were working up some kind of harem-scarem on me, and I recall trying to back away but my legs wouldn't move. She kept her ground, then stepped to the side and in a high cackling voice said one word: follow."

"So you followed her."

"Had no choice, really. I felt as if I were under some kind of spell, although I suppose I could've broken away. Didn't matter, though, because I *wanted* to go. Fear had set in and I was too concerned with the consequences should I try to fight her. She led me to this place, talking as we went, and to this day I can still hear that gravely witchlike voice of hers. She told me all about the Isolates and about this place where they used to perform their sacrifices. She told me that the center stone was used for the killing because it was the biggest, and that it absorbed all the blood well enough so it wouldn't drip to the ground and violate the earth. They fed their people with the sacrificial meat, usually deer or moose, and had resorted to the daily rituals at sunrise after the nocturnal tribe spent a night of hunting. Soon the Isolates grew in numbers, and they eventually spread out to assume the land of the natives." He paused, then added, "And in order to feed their growing tribe, they began to hunt, capture, and sacrifice some of the natives as well."

"The Isolates . . . they ate the natives?"

"The winters were cold and hard on the Isolates, who lived with only the shelter of the earth above their heads. Food had been hard to come by, and they eventually discovered that catching a man was a lot easier than taking down a doe—one old sick Indian would be food for a night. Remember, these people were savages and would do anything to stay alive just like you and I would under similar circumstances.

"Then I'd started crying for some reason. The tears'd just sprouted, and I'd begun to have visions of these poor little outcasts scouring the earth for bugs and vermin in order to stay alive. Of course, for reasons I still can't explain, I pitied the people who resorted to cannibalism in order to live, who'd elected to be outcasts because they were too barbaric and uncultivated to commingle with the native society. Christ, it felt as though that trance she had me under had started making me feel things . . . things I wouldn't normally feel. I had sympathy for the bad guy. I wiped my tears while the lady continued talking. She'd added that the natives who apparently were no match for their shrewder counterparts had no choice but to make sacrifices of their own in order to protect their race. They hunted twice as hard, sometimes having to surrender their only kill of the day and face the night hungry rather than brave the death of one of their own. They sacrilegiously abstained from burying their dead and surrendered the bodies to the enemy, placing them right here on this rock, slicing the stomach open and exposing the innards so the scent of blood would attract the Isolates. Sometimes the natives waited in the darkness of the woods until the Isolates showed to claim their prize, their only way of paying last respects to their kin."

"Jesus," I uttered, then added uncomfortably, "This is just folklore, an ancient tale from the old lady, right?"

"Legend," Phillip replied.

"I'm sorry?"

"Legend. Not folklore. Not just a tale."

"What's the difference?"

"Difference is that legends never go away."

I felt a bit of a shiver race down my back. I drank the last of my water. "What's that supposed to mean?"

"It means that what the old lady was telling me was not only true, it was real. You see, she had a responsibility, a job, and that was to protect the people of Ashborough. I was the new kid on the block, so I needed to be educated, and protected."

"Protected from what?"

He paused, looked to the canopy, then back into my eyes. "The Isolates."

"Wait a minute," I said holding a palm up, then thought, *Why am I standing here listening to this? He's playing a nasty joke on me, the neophyte in town, just like the old lady did to him thirty years ago when he first moved here—that's if there really is an Old Lady Zellis! Deighton is either playing me for a fool or off his rocker,* "You've got to be kidding me, Phillip." I wanted to leave, but stayed and listened, as though I were . . . tranced.

Ignoring me, he continued. "So the lady just reaches down behind the large rock and pulls up a possum. The thing looked as though it'd been drugged. It was still alive, that much I can say for sure because it wriggled a bit in her arms and its eyes caught the moon in such a way that they glowed like two searchlights. She stroked it some, then placed it down on the big rock in the center. The animal crouched on its haunches and went still, as though willingly playing a role in the ungodly act about to take place. Michael, if legends were to be made, then this was one event to be handed down in history, my own personal history, just like the first conflicts between the natives and the Isolates were all those years ago."

"You didn't . . ."

Phillip nodded. "I did . . . I had no choice in the matter. The old lady's eyes started glowing this odd golden color and they had me hypnotized. I couldn't move, that is, until she came forward and handed me the knife. Don't ask me where she got it from, but it appeared right there in her hand just as sure as her eyes glowed that strange golden color, and then she ushered me to the stone and before I could even attempt to pull away from her, she began an odd chant. Seconds later I was kneeling on the stone grasping the squealing possum by its neck and plunging the knife over and over again into its body until it squealed no more."

"Jesus, Phillip . . ." I tried to speak, but a sudden lump in my throat blocked my words. My Sunday afternoon stroll through the woods hadn't turned out as relaxing as I wanted. My nerves jangled like fire alarms, and I promised myself that once I got back home I'd leave the woods to themselves for the rest of my time in Ashborough. Don't get me wrong, it wasn't Phillip's stories of Isolates, Old Lady Zellis, and cannibalism that had me all spooked out. It was Phillip himself. *His* cuckoo was in need of rewinding.

"I stayed kneeling over the dead animal," he continued, "and after a long time I finally climbed down from the rock. I still had the knife in my hand, the animal lay spread out on the rock, but the old lady, she'd upped and vanished, nowhere to be seen, as if she'd never been there in the first place. The woods fell as silent as a vacuum, as though everything out there had died along with that possum. No owls were a-hooting, no crickets chirped. I'm talking complete and utter silence, Michael. The only thing I could hear was my breathing and a sharp little hiss of gas coming from the punctured possum. After some time I looked down at my hands and saw all the blood. It was everywhere. On my hands, my shirt, my pants.

"I looked at my watch and realized that I'd been gone for over an hour. Without doubt Rosy would be at the window biting her nails, worried to death. I remembered thinking that she might've even panicked and called the sheriff. But when I finally stumbled my way into the backyard, the windows were dark. I went into the house through the kitchen and found Rosy on the couch in front of the television, fast asleep; another ingredient in Old Lady Zellis's stew, I figured. This gave me the freedom to sneak up into the bathroom, where I took a shower and bagged my bloody clothes for the garbage."

"You never told Rosy, did you?" I asked, eyeing the bloodstains.

"No, I didn't. I went to bed, and so did Rosy. No words were exchanged, she just pulled the sheets over her head and continued what she'd started on the couch. Me, I couldn't sleep. I lay in bed with my eyes closed, and a few times I felt myself nodding off, but then I would flinch awake. It was as if someone or something had wanted me to stay awake. As if there was unfinished business."

"Probably the longest night of your life."

Phillip laughed a bit. "That's an understatement. Eventually I crawled from bed and peered out the back window. There were fireflies in the backyard, and I thought that strange because it was October, and then I remembered Old Lady Zellis's eyes, how they glowed that golden color at the climax of the ritual she put me through. I looked outside again and saw the tiny lights fading back into the darkness of the woods, six or eight pairs of them.

"So with the moon shining through the windows, I got dressed and headed downstairs. I opened every drawer in the kitchen in search of a flashlight—remember, we'd just moved in a week before so I still didn't know everything's proper place yet—and finally located it in the cabinet above the sink, which of course made a creak that the hounds of hell could've heard. It made me shudder, and I listened to hear if it had stirred Rosy from her sheep-counting, but thankfully all remained calm. Oh . . . I did know where the liquor was, and I downed a couple of mouthfuls of bourbon before heading back outside; nothing like some good spirits to settle the soul. But, alas, it didn't seem to work that night. A couple of swigs and I was still scared to death, so I took the bottle with me when I went back into the woods.

"The walk seemed to take forever, perhaps half the night. I didn't really know where I was going, and I'm certain I veered off track at times. But then I saw the lights of gold again, and they seemed to say, *Follow me*, and follow them I did back into the woods."

Phillip's second mention of the gold lights in the woods reminded me that I'd seen them myself—and more than once: a few weeks ago while sitting at my desk, and then again later that night as I looked out my bedroom window. I'd written them off as fireflies. *Jesus*, I thought, my heart in my throat, not wanting to hear any more of this story that had become intimidating and significant. *Could this all really be true?*

"I drank the bourbon as I went and caught myself a healthy crock. I even fell down a couple of times along the way; those roots are hard to see even in the daytime, much less past midnight. Eventually I got to the circle of stones, and at first all was quiet. I shined the flashlight around and didn't see anything right away, but let me tell you, these woods here at night are just about the damn scariest place you'll ever want to be. Ain't nothing like the daytime with all its lovely fauna and scenic outlooks. The owls and birds call out from the trees in

79

droves—weird-sounding ones that you never hear during the day. And then there are animals moving around out there, jostling the copses and making you flinch every five or ten seconds. It doesn't matter much if the moon is full and the sky is cloudless, it gets darker than you can imagine here. And the bugs? Well, when it's dark and humid and sticky, they crawl out of their holes in a mighty playful mood—you can hear them fluttering by your head like tiny helicopters.

"So I aimed the light at the center stone where I killed the possum and sure enough, it was still there. I'd half expected to find it gone, not from the hand of an Isolate but from the claw of an owl. I walked closer, light still shining on the animal. I could see all sorts of insects buzzing about it. And then the smell . . . it was awful, something like bad vegetables. I took a swig of bourbon and as I did, the light fell away from the animal. That was when I saw the eyes."

"The dead possum's eyes?" I asked, sitting on the center stone. At this point there was no sense in trying to end this conversation. Phillip seemed determined to take this to the very end, and frankly I was intrigued by the significance of the gold lights—to find out if the ones I saw, or imagined I saw, were something more than just fireflies.

Fireflies in May, Michael?

He grinned. "I wish that were the case. No, these eyes were *alive*. As golden as the center signal on a traffic light."

"Old Lady Zellis?"

He shook his head. "Nope . . . these eyes belonged to an Isolate."

I smiled, half incredulously, half out of discomfort. I didn't want to believe him. But something inside told me I should, and I promised myself a few shots of something strong when I got back to the house. Maybe even bourbon, the liquor of occasion.

"It'd creeped over the far edge of the rock, just a hand at first, long forklike fingers gripping the dead animal like a doll. Then I saw the head, and it grinned at me, bright golden eyes cutting the darkness like two beacons. It was as though it knew I was there, and had waited for the most opportune time to make its grand entrance and scare the piss out of me, which it did, but I hadn't noticed that until later.

"When I finally made it past the dreadful glow of its eyes, the rest of the thing's face came into focus. It was no less sinister-looking. It looked like an old man's, all brown and wrinkled like a crumpled paper bag that's been smoothed out. There were some colored streaks on its cheeks and forehead, made with spoiled berries, and in its hand was a pointed spike of slate. It aimed the makeshift weapon in my direction and jabbed the air as if to say, *Come near my warm meal and I'll scalp you, you motherfucker.* Of course I stood my ground, and at that moment I felt as though I'd been scared sober, my body stiff and poised to flee at the first indication of threat. Slowly it crawled up on the rock, taloned feet gripping the smooth surface as deftly as its hands, those golden eyes not leaving me for one second as it patiently claimed its prize.

"The first thing I noticed about its body was that it had been clothed, crudely, however, with nothing more than dirty rags shrouding the groin. The torso, arms, and legs on the slight creature were emaciated, covered with patches of coarse hair. The skin beneath was thick and calloused and mottled with warts. At this proximity I could really smell the thing now, a horrid stench of bodily filth and decay. Goddamned awful. It speared the animal with the slate spike, then grinned, showing a mouth filled with thick brown teeth. And then . . . it *laughed*. Michael, the damn thing laughed at me, made this deep chortling sound that was instantaneous, and utterly deliberate."

I shuddered, envisioning the scene in my head, trying very hard not to believe him.

"It stood up on its hind legs, holding the possum above its head in a prayerful stance; from head to toe the thing couldn't have been more than four and a half feet tall. With an alarming quickness, it jumped down from the rock and darted back into the woods with the speed and accuracy of a frightened squirrel."

At that moment I wondered if there was something intrinsically wrong with Phillip. I didn't doubt for a moment that something had happened here all those years ago. After all, I *did* see the golden lights, and when I looked in Phillip's eyes I saw something sorrowful in them, telling me that he truly believed everything he saw that night. However . . . for *me* to assume this story was true would be utter madness, and I forced myself to conclude that Phillip had been the victim of a vivid dream, a sleepwalk perhaps, or maybe even some odd hallucination brought on from one of Rosy's medicinal teas.

"Somehow I found my way back, but I don't recall how. Apparently I blacked out—it might've been the alcohol, but was probably yet another flick of the old lady's spell-slinging wrist—and the next thing I remembered was waking up in bed the next morning with all my clothes on. My boots too, and for weeks I caught hell from Rosy for all the mud I'd dragged though the house."

"And you say that Rosy never found out?"

Phillip nodded. "Yep. Never told her. It was part of the deal. Old Lady Zellis told me that the sacrifice should be kept a secret from my family; otherwise they would fall victim to the savagery of the Isolates."

"Like the native legend . . ."

Phillip nodded. "Just like the legend."

Something he said then hit me like a sledgehammer. "Wait, Phil . . . a secret from your *family?* You mean Rosy? Or . . ."

Phillip nodded. At once tears filled his eyes. "You're probably wondering why I brought you here, Michael?"

"Suddenly . . . suddenly I'm getting the picture, Phil."

"Michael . . . this is extremely difficult for me to talk about. Although it's never left my mind after all these years, it also hasn't left my lips either. And if you ask anyone in town about it, they'll pretend that you're as nutty as Old Lady Zellis, but believe me, they'll know *exactly* what you're talking about. Some things are better left unsaid, and this is one of them."

"So why are you telling me?"

"For the same reason Old Lady Zellis told me all those years ago."

"For my protection?" I added an ineffectual tone of incredulousness to my voice.

"You're a resident of Ashborough now," he said. "Your new government lives right here in these woods, Michael. You best live by their laws."

"This is crazy. . . ."

He shook his head. "It's not." He pulled a fresh cigar from his pocket, unwrapped it, and stuck it between his lips. His hands were shaking a bit.

I laughed uncomfortably, then said, "Gee-whiz, Phil. For a second I thought you were gonna pull a dead possum out of your pocket."

Phillip grinned. At that moment I thought he was gonna burst out in laughter and brag about how he *really had me going,* but that didn't happen. Instead he said, "No, the animal can't be dead, Michael. It has to be *sacrificed* on the big stone."

In a sudden jerk, Phillip's cigar fell from his mouth. He brought his hands to his face as if in shock or pain. My paranoia was instantly replaced with concern, and I stepped over to him. "Phil? You all right?" He pulled his hands away from his face. There were dense tears filling his eyes.

"I didn't listen to her, Michael," he coughed. "I should have, but I didn't."

"Listened to . . . ?"

"Old Lady Zellis." His voice was a strangled mess. "This place . . . it seemed too special for me to hold inside. It'd *haunted* me for weeks, years, all day long and then in my dreams. There was no escaping it. It'd grabbed me, held on until it became a part of me . . . like a virus in my veins for which there was no cure." He sat back down on the stone and broke down in sobs. He looked like a sickly old man in wait for the reaper to come sow him into the earth.

"I'm sorry, Michael . . . I'm so sorry that I have to do this to you. But I have no choice . . . it's my duty. I know, I know, it's impossible to find it in yourself to understand me right now. But in time you will."

"I think I understand. . . ." I lied. There was no proper way to express the alarming images rolling around in my mind, nor was there a way to make this less painful to Phillip. But what I had to say wouldn't quell my sudden fear either. "You *did* tell someone else, didn't you? About that night. About the Isolates. Didn't you, Phil?"

Weakly, he nodded.

"Not once, Phillip, have you ever mentioned anything about your daughter to me. But I saw her picture on the wall in your bedroom the day I moved in, when I went upstairs to fix my wound."

He stayed unspeaking. His sobs lightened, but remained constant.

"If I'm to believe this story you're telling me, and I admit I'm having a difficult time doing it, then your daughter . . . are you trying to tell me that your daughter was killed by the Isolates?"

He nodded.

"And Rosy?"

He nodded again. "Not cancer."

"I'm a doctor . . . that much I figured out." I paused,

then said, "And it's also this doctor's opinion that you should seek some professional help. To help you deal with the trauma of losing your child. You may be suffering from post-traumatic stress disorder."

"You don't believe me, do you?"

I felt a surge of exasperation well inside my lungs, and I blew it out. This conversation, which began with intellect, had turned sharply into opinions that danced on the tips of our nerves. Phillip and Michael, we were two well-worn men more than ready to call it a day.

There was no way I could answer him truthfully; frankly, I didn't know what to believe at the moment. So on my suggestion we turned back, and kept silent while walking back home. During this time my mind raced, and it became all too obvious to me that the entire experience—seeing the circle of oaks for the first time, hearing Phillip's tale of the Isolates and Old Lady Zellis—seemed much too rehearsed, much too *convenient* to be true. I told myself that even though nature works in mysterious ways, there wasn't enough disorder here to make it all non-coincidental. I took one last look back into the woods upon crossing the backyard of my home, and it wasn't until later that night while I lay in bed that I finally answered Phillip's last question.

No Phillip, I don't believe you. Not one little bit.

Chapter Ten

The next day I pretended that none of my conversation with Phillip had ever happened. I told Christine that I'd taken a walk into the woods, spent most of my two hours there following the random paths that sprang up. But I never mentioned Phillip, nor did I say anything about the circle of stones, much less what I knew about Ashborough's shadowy legend. Withholding this information was my only way of keeping it under a shroud of secrecy, and it helped me maintain my belief that the whole tall tale was nothing more than just that: a fable strong in the hearts of the town's staunchly devoted residents.

The day was filled with patients, and that kept me mostly distracted from Sunday's events. By the end of the day seventeen people had passed through my office with minor aches and pains, both physical and mental, and my labored thoughts had been replaced with mostly work-filled specifics. That is, until Jessica came into my office.

As had quickly become a habit, I was seated at my desk itemizing the day's charts and returning the dozen or so calls that had come in while I was busy with patients. Christine still hadn't settled into her secretarial duties as of yet; the house had pretty much consumed her time. It became apparent to me that interior decorating and housekeeping were full-time jobs in themselves, especially when you had a little one vying for your attention all day long. The advent of kindergarten would alleviate much of this strain, however, and place Christine where I needed her most.

I'd heard Jessica's footsteps coming in from behind me, and turned to see her slowly approaching, looking a bit worried. Placing the folder I'd been holding down on the desk, I wondered for a moment what retirement in Florida would be like: children all grown up, far away with all-new worries of their own. The moment was silent except for the arrival of the night's first cicada, which had blared its toll from the not-too-distant woods.

"Hi, dear. Whatchya doin?"

"Uh . . . looking for Page," she said, but I could see the telltale signs of a lie in her features, the unconscious twitch of her upper lip, the quivering downcast gaze of her eyes. She leaned against the desk, wearing knit shorts and a T-shirt that said, *I may be small but I have my daddy wrapped around my finger*. She smelled of lavender, which meant she'd just taken a bath.

88

She then asked, "What are you doing?"

"I'm finishing up my work." Suddenly I wanted a shot of brandy from the liquor cabinet. Neil Farris's stock was still plentiful.

"Oh. Boring," she said.

"Yes, it is kind of boring. But it pays the bills."

Jimmy Page had sniffed the lavender trail into my office. He circled around my legs, then nestled himself under the desk for a snooze. Jessica backpedaled from the dog in a rather unusual way, as if somewhat repelled, or maybe frightened. This was odd considering the corny love she usually exhibited for him. She walked over to the bookshelf, thumbed the outside of one of the medical journals there as though she could actually read the spine, then asked, "Daddy, are there such things as ghosts?"

Once the words came out of her mouth, I knew there'd be a fair share of counseling sessions ahead of me. She'd gotten the idea from somewhere (those damn daytime talk shows; I'd have to have a word with Christine about this ASAP), and now it was sticking in her head like tar-balls on an unsuspecting wader's feet.

"Of course not, honey," I said. "And just where did you hear about such things as ghosts?"

"Scooby Doo," she revealed matter-of-factly. Thank you very much.

I laughed inside. So much for my talk-show theory. No psychics in this girl's world just yet. "Scooby Doo. The dog from the cartoons?"

She nodded. And then she blew me away. "On the cartoon Scooby can always smell the ghosts before they come. And so can Page. He smells the ghosts at night in my room."

Hearing these words coming from my little innocent daughter's mouth sent wild shivers across my skin. It wasn't so much that Jessica might've spoken of a common childhood fear of things going bump in the night . . . it was more the fact that she said her *dog* was smelling something otherworldly in her room.

"Honey, he can't possibly smell ghosts in your room because, as I said, there's no such thing as ghosts. They don't exist. Except in cartoons, of course, and in the movies. But not in little girls' bedrooms. Not anywhere."

"Well . . . I guess Page can be wrong." There was a pause, during which I smiled and admired the naiveté of my daughter. Her imagination had run amok, and I realized at that moment that the stress of moving into a new home in a whole new town had finally taken hold of her mind-strings and given them a nice healthy tug.

"Does he bark in the middle of the night? Wake you up?" I'd never heard any late-night barking before, and it occurred to me that Jessica might have simply dreamed it. Until she said: "Yes, he does bark at night. Out the window. At the lights."

"The . . . lights?" There were sounds in the room, of shuffling: Page finding a new position by my feet to lie in. His tail brushed against my exposed ankles, and it exacerbated the sudden fear racing through my blood. Her words, *at the lights,* equaled a slight form of horror, now out of the mouth of an innocent and into the open for me to experience once again.

She began to cry, not unlike Phillip Deighton had. "I'm scared of the lights! They're ghosts. Page growls at them."

I drew Jessica close to me. I felt her tears soak through my shirt. Christine must've heard the commotion, and was standing in the entrance, leaning against the door frame with eyebrows raised. I rocked Jessica gently, knowing that there'd be no battling her impenetrable fear, that for now it would remain obstinate. At this moment I realized that all people, children and adults alike, had a wonderful yet ruinous knack to turn unexplored frontiers into conclusive answers that might very well be somber and offensive. Ghosts in the woods? A fitting deduction for floating firefly lights and a dog's aggressive response to them—at least to a young child.

What about the Isolates, Michael? Those lights might be little malformed people seeking a sacrifice from the new kid in town. Certainly that would get Page all riled up.

Jessica pulled away from me, sobbing and looking awfully adorable with her big wet eyes—a timid expression thankfully shattering the black thoughts racing through my mind. *Isolates? Bullshit. The idea of their existence was ridiculous; pure folklore. Wait . . . I stand corrected. Not folklore. Legend. There's always a bit of truth in legends, right? Phillip had said that. And here, my child was feeling out the presence in its ancient golden impressions.*

"Jess," I said, "there's no ghosts out there. Those lights are fireflies. They're small glowing bugs that come out only at night. We didn't have them in the city, but there's tons of them out here in the country. Page never saw them before either, and that's why he got all excited."

I wanted to scold myself for making up this little story. After all, I really didn't know for certain that those small golden lights were indeed fireflies. I'd promised myself in the past that as a father to my child I would never make up a lie to preserve the sanctity of a situation. Yet here I was, for the sake of protecting my daughter's rationality, creating excuses for an unknown glow in the woods: the golden lights I'd seen a month ago when I first moved in. The same lights my now-distant neighbor claimed were the eyes of an ancient race of wood-dwellers called Isolates. The same lights my daughter thinks are ghosts from the Scooby Doo show.

"Fireflies?" she sobbed, sounding a bit relieved.

I nodded and hugged her once more until her tears stopped. I glanced at Christine, who, unacquainted with Phillip's clinging tale and the golden glows, smiled in a purely innocent and loving way, her beaming eyes pleading for another child that we might someday dissuade from fear.

I smiled back, then peered out the study window into the growing darkness, seeing nothing at all but feeling that something might be out there.

Watching us.

Chapter Eleven

One hour and two short stories later Jessica was asleep in bed, Page alongside her. Christine was in the kitchen brewing a pot of decaf. She forced a weak smile in my direction while digging out two mugs from the cabinet.

"Looks like our daughter inherited a bit of her father's anxiety," she said curtly, as if the entire scene tonight was all my doing. Christine was being serious again. Great.

I ignored the cutting remark. "I take it you got the gist of our conversation."

"Yeah . . . I heard most of it. You know," she said, sounding suddenly congenial, "I did hear Page growling in the middle of the night last night."

"Really?" I smiled, half amused, half unnerved.

"Yes, really. It woke me up and I thought it odd that Page would rile up like that in the middle of the night.

I heard Jess moving the sheets around a bit and thought about getting up to check in on her, but I fell right back asleep."

"Well, apparently she's all spooked out because she thinks there're ghosts in her room. When I asked her where she got such a silly idea from, she said she learned it from the Scooby Doo show. That doesn't make sense, does it? A kid frightened by cartoons?"

"She's beginning to show some signs of stress," Christine decided. "The move from the city to this small town with no other kids nearby, it's a bit testing on the mind. We've been here a month and she still has no friends. And then in September she's going to start kindergarten. That alone is a lot for a five-year-old to handle. Wouldn't you agree?"

"You don't have to tell me. I know."

"So then help your daughter."

There we go again. She's my *daughter.* "I think I did a fairly good job of cooling her spirits tonight."

She nodded but didn't look at me, which meant I did a *fair* job in her eyes. Not a great job, but passable nonetheless. Nothing she really wanted to give me credit for. "I don't want you taking her into the woods," Christine declared after pouring two cups of coffee in silence. "There're animals and bugs and poison ivy and who knows what kinds of things. It's dangerous, even unhealthy."

I shuddered for a moment, wondering if perhaps Christine might have heard Phillip's *legend* from Rosy. She peered out the kitchen window along the side of the house, into the woods.

"Chris . . . I never took her—"

"I didn't say you did. I just don't want you to, that's all. For all we know the dog that got Dr. Farris might still be out there."

My mind said, *Oh, it's out there, all right. But it ain't no mad mutt.* My common sense disagreed with my mind, however, and my words followed suit. "Not to worry. I won't."

There are moments in a marriage when you might have trouble knowing exactly which part of the ball-park your partner feels like playing in, despite how well you think you know her. Here Christine had decided to change positions, and instead of tapping soft, easy grounders in my direction, she'd elected to smack a couple of line drives at my head. Of course, this left me no margin for error lest I walk away with a fat lump of shame on my face. And there ain't no erasing *that* injury.

"I don't like those woods," she repeated. Tears started rolling down her cheeks.

"Christine . . . what's wrong?" For a moment I had a crazy impression, something like déjà vu, only with a heaping spoonful of reality thrown in. An hour before I'd had to console my weeping daughter. Now my wife was sinking into her own depression. That made two meltdowns in one night for this family man.

She shook her head, then peered up at me with wet, soulful eyes, holding out a plastic pregnancy test strip she plucked from her front pocket. "I'm pregnant."

I immediately sulked, not because I was unhappy with this revelation . . . but because I'd missed it, the weeks of obsessive-compulsive behavior that commingled with the on-again, off-again crying. It had been thrust before me like a great big vista and I, Michael Cayle, educated physician who was paid the big bucks to catch these kind of things, never saw it. I might as well have been sleepwalking all along, thumbs in my ears, pinkies up my nose. I took the pregnancy strip from her and eyed the positive result.

"Christine . . . that's wonderful news." I put my best smile on, despite the confusion of the moment.

She stared at me resentfully. "Depends on how you look at it."

Silence filled the room. "I don't understand."

She broke down crying. "We weren't even trying. I know we talked about it, but I don't remember us actually *trying*. I mean, how many times have we been together since we moved here? Three? Four times? So how did this happen?"

"You don't need a doctor to tell you that. Apparently we weren't being so overly protective."

"Apparently? This doesn't just happen *apparently!*" she shouted, banging her fist against the kitchen counter. "We tried for five months with Jessica before I got pregnant. And damn it, Michael, you were wearing a friggin' rubber."

I nodded. Indeed I had been.

"So how, Michael? How?"

"I don't know . . . any number of ways. It may have torn, or leaked at the edges. It doesn't make a difference. What difference does it make? We're going to be parents again. That's what you wanted, right?" I tried to place a reassuring hand on her shoulder, but she pulled away, quick and hard.

"Forget it, Michael," she said contemptuously, burying her face in her hands. "You'll never understand." Her sobs sounded just like Jessica's.

"I'm a doctor. I do understand. Not only what your body is going through, but what's happening in your mind as well. At least, *now* I do." I gave her my best wounded look—brow furrowed, eyes narrowed— which she didn't bother looking at.

She shook her head, clearly frustrated. "Don't placate me, Michael. Until your body goes through the same changes I'm going through . . ." She took her mug and slammed it on the counter. Coffee spilled out. She walked away and sat at the kitchen table, sobbing.

"Christine . . ."

"I don't want to discuss this anymore."

Now it was my turn to get pissed, changes or no changes. She'd dropped the bat and put on a totally different uniform. Something totally psychotic. Like Rollerball. I needed to defend myself. "This *discussion* as you call it has been totally one-sided. It's my turn to take some swings now." It was only at this moment that I realized that the pregnancy tester was still in my hand. I pointed it at her, reminding myself at that instant to put the kid gloves on. *Tread softly and carry a pregnancy stick.* "We have a smart, well-behaved, beautiful child in Jessica. And now we have another on the way. Jesus Christ, Christine, we had a talk about this a few weeks ago, about how you were getting older and that now was the time to have a baby. Consider yourself blessed." This time I was the one doing the slamming, tester on counter.

"Fuck you, Michael!" she screamed, and I cowered back. My arm struck the counter, and one of the mugs toppled off and shattered on the floor. Coffee spilled everywhere.

"Shit," I said bleakly, avoiding Christine's penetrating gaze. I kneeled down to gather the pieces, realizing that in our six years of marriage she'd never used such a tone of voice toward me. And I hadn't done anything wrong either. I think.

From upstairs, Jessica began to cry. Page soon followed with a series of frantic yips.

"Fucking wonderful," Christine said. "Wake the whole damn neighborhood, why don't you." She stood up at the table and started storming away.

I grabbed her right arm. We locked eyes, mine tearing with ire, hers ablaze with pain: mental, physical, hormonal. A triple combo. "What's gotten into you?" I asked, despite the fact she showed no intention of listening. "And what's with the foul language, Chris? You gonna start talking like that in front of Jessica now? For sure she'll need a counselor. A real one who can do the job correctly, not someone like *this* doctor who's only good at Band-Aids and boogers."

She yanked her arm away. "Don't you touch me," she spat. There was a great deal of anger in her eyes, but also a glaze of confusion that stated she had no idea why she was behaving this way toward the man she presumably loved. The man whose baby she was carrying. "I'm going to take care of my daughter." Wouldn't you know it. Jessica was *her* daughter now.

Women's emotions. They astound me.

"Christine!"

"This conversation is over, Michael," she said, running upstairs and leaving me alone in the kitchen with porcelain chips and hot coffee circling my feet, the echoes of our voices still resonating in the air. Silence resumed upstairs, and Christine never came back down. I cleaned up the mess, all the while thinking about how arguments as alien as this one grow right out of thin air; how simple differences of opinion or emotional fluxes can create a tremendous and unavoidable banging of heads. It works that way between married couples and with entire nations of people. But in the end a resolution must be made, good, bad, or ugly. All things must pass. And I was confident, as I'd been in the past, that the dust would eventually settle at 17 Harlan Road, lying quietly in wait until something unseen sent it all flying once again.

Chapter Twelve

I watched television for an hour after cleaning up the mess. It was still early, and sleep seemed as foreign to me as the woods had been the day I stepped in to explore them for the first time. In between harried thoughts of Christine's tirade (and revelation of pregnancy), Jessica's sudden fear of ghosts, and me being a father once again, I found myself getting up to peek out the kitchen window into the side woods, looking for the lights. I saw them, but these lights were greener, smaller, floating lazily alongside the house. Dangling from the rear ends of insects.

Fireflies.

Perhaps it had been denial, thinking that the golden lights had been fireflies all along. I'd only seen them twice, but I remembered them being bigger, perhaps the size of golf balls, drifting far back in the darkness of the woods for only a brief moment before blinking out.

Not fireflies.

Then what?

Isolates? No, Michael, a raccoon or opossum probably, or some other brand of nocturnal dweller whose wide, peering eyes fell into the yellow glow of the house light next to the back door.

Despite the early hour I decided to try and go to bed. I figured it was possible that Christine might still be up, although it was highly doubtful that she'd be in any kind of forgiving mood just yet, which suited me just fine; my mind was still racing like mad, and not quite into harmonizing. I peeked into Jessica's room and found her bed empty, the sheets in a bunch at the footboard. I panicked for a brief moment, but assured myself—prayed, actually—that my king-size bed would be filled to capacity. I paced down the hall and stuck my head into the bedroom. Indeed, Christine, Jessica, and Page were all sprawled out on the mattress, curled into sleeping positions. Someone was snoring lightly. Probably Page.

It was possible that Christine would wake up overcome with guilt—that come morning she would take me in her arms and plant apologetic kisses all over me. Then again, she might not. So I had no choice but to plan for the worst and hope for the best. We'd had lesser arguments in the past that'd led to two or three days of resentment and pointless brooding. Some were my fault, others hers. This time no one carried any blame; our little world seemed to have been rocked by an invisible third party plunging in from out of no-where. So who knows what lay ahead? I simply wanted to get it all over with, try to find a way to offset my sadness, my frustration, even if it meant making a first move.

I considered waking her up.

Something told me this wouldn't be a good idea.

So instead, I undressed, showered, shaved, and took two ibuprofren to help chase away a looming head-ache. I'd had enough excitement to fill two hard days, and that had set the cranial hammers into motion. By the time I crawled into Jessica's bed, my head was pounding, assuring me that sleep wouldn't come any-time soon. My mind raced in nutty circles, playing out the last two days like a bad motion picture. Phillip Deighton. Isolates. Sacrifices. Old Lady Zellis. Jessica. Ghosts. Golden lights. Fireflies. I'm pregnant. Christine. Fuck you, Michael.

And with this came images of pure anxiety-born spec-ulation: Rosy Deighton caught in the jaws of a dark monster, her hand torn free as spouts of blood punc-tuated her terror-filled screams; she trying to break free while sharp teeth rendered chunks of flesh from her body, a strong swiping claw cleaving half her face away in one monstrous swoop. Then, Neil Farris: the man whose home and livelihood I'd come to replace. I pic-tured him writhing on the ground, bleeding out on the pavement in buckets, waiting for help that would come all too late. I recalled my first conversation with Lou Scully. He'd said that a stray dog had made meat of Farris, that Ashborough's doctor had been taken to the

Ellenville Medical Center but was declared DOA. Then the Widow Farris confirmed this event. Exactly.

As if it had been rehearsed.

I shook away the thought. This was clearly my over-tired mind creating an ominous scenario, one befitting my growing paranoia. *Rosy. Neil. Isolates.* Yet, outside of Page, I couldn't remember seeing a single dog—free or leashed—in this neighborhood since we moved in.

I shuddered. What difference did it make? Neil Farris was dead, and as a direct result I owned a fantastic practice brimming with patients. On the outside it would appear that I'd been at the right place at the right time; me, I couldn't decide whether I'd been blessed or cursed. *One man's bane is another's benefit.* After an hour of mind-spinning, I got up and headed back downstairs. The clock in the living room chimed eleven. I made a peanut-butter sandwich (the kitchen still carried the aroma of coffee; I figured it would stay this way until I took a mop with ammonia to the floor), grabbed a glass of milk, and headed down through the hall into my office.

There was a small corkboard in the reception area pinned with various messages and notes to myself. Nothing was of great importance, primarily the phone numbers of patients who'd left messages on the answering machine earlier in the day. I looked down at the machine; the message light was dark. Nice.

My office was as quiet as a morgue, and I took to my desk, where I began to eat and rearrange some papers. I'd rigged the lights in here so that the switch on the wall would trigger only the desk lamp. This created a nice concentrated glow that traveled no farther than the confines of my work area, enabling me to peer out the floor-to-ceiling windows even at night. The porch light alongside the back door was lit, splaying a dull yellow glow across the expanse of grass that reached all the way to the edge of the woods. For a moment I imagined myself as some nineteenth-century muse working by candlelight on his most recent future-classic. Like Charles Dickens maybe, or Edgar Allan Poe.

I stared out the window, into the darkness, waiting for the golden lights. Instead I saw only the concrete birdbath and the old shed that I still hadn't gone into yet. It'd never intrigued me.

Until now.

I went back inside, suddenly adrenalized. I changed into a pair of jeans and a sweatshirt, then grabbed a flashlight and hammer from the toolbox under the kitchen sink. Once equipped (I'd hoped a few blows from the hammer would prove sufficient to break the rusty lock on the shed), I stepped outside via the side door in the patient waiting room. The fresh night air felt great, cool and crisp and comfortable on my lungs. Fire-flies floated by in a slothful manner, moths fluttering briskly about the house light in droves. Hordes of bee-tles clung to the screens like appliques on a Batique-style shirt. Quite a bugfest.

The woods were alive with the sounds of nature. Ci-cadas, crickets, owls, and nightbirds, all tossing their calls into a wind that embraced the sea of leaves in a soothing, static-toned sway. The trees themselves were a monstrous moving shape against the cloudless sky, front-lit from the light on the back of the house. Above, a glowing half-moon illuminated the backyard, the stars pinpoint flames burning through the great dark canopy above. A rather massive contrast to the city, this great symbiosis with nature was something I still hadn't gotten used to.

A gust of wind rippled my shirt as I paced across the lawn toward the shed. I hadn't switched the flashlight on; didn't need to. The moon and house light provided enough illumination to guide the way. The grass beneath my feet was dry and needed to be cut; the blades ran under my pants and tickled my ankles like the spiny legs of an insect.

I reached the shed, which marked the boundary of the woods. I stopped. Listened. The branches of the trees groaned restlessly in the growing wind. The ancient wood of the shed creaked and settled, making it sound alive. It scared the heck out of me, and I suddenly felt like a madman in search of a diabolical act to commit. I looked back at the house. It had a spooky charm to it, standing there in the ghostly hue of the moon's light. During the day it feigned innocence, sitting in its colonial decorum with daisy patches and painted shutters that welcomed all approachers in smiling, gleeful colors. Now at night, its true character seemed to emerge: dark, dank, full of secrets bursting at the beams. Put a jack-o'-lantern outside and it would be Halloween, just like that.

Scratch . . . scratch.

I jerked my gaze back to the shed. I heard something.

A noise, emerging from within the weather-beaten walls: like sharpened nails picking splinters away from an overly dry spot. Now I switched on the flashlight, aimed its honed beam into the quarter-inch space between the door and wall. The light disappeared beyond the slight gap, making it impossible to see inside.

Scratch . . . scratch.

There it was again. Although discreet, it gave me quite a start, as though a muted alarm went off nearby. I stepped back, the flashlight and hammer now shaking in my hands. I wanted to yell out, to see if anyone was *inside* the shed—common sense dictated this was highly doubtful because the door had been locked from the outside. Unless, of course . . . unless he, she, or it had been forcibly locked inside against their will.

This was possible. . . .

I shuddered at the thought and cursed my anxieties for allowing me to think such a thing. My jumping thoughts were no more rational than Jessica's sudden fear of Page and his ghost-smelling nose. I told myself to get a grip, be strong, to handle the situation just like any pants-wearing man of the household might: with strength, vigor, and courage.

I switched tools, the flashlight now in my left hand, the hammer in my right. The woods appeared darker, suddenly dead despite the ongoing chorus of insects. The wind picked up again and I shuddered, not from the cool gust but from a feeling of aloneness that bore down on me powerfully and aggressively.

I looked at the lock in the flashlight's beam. It dangled on the rusty hinge like a tiny piñata waiting to be pummeled. I raised the hammer a little and whacked it. It jangled against the clasp, and the subsequent clang echoed loudly despite my weak effort. The woods answered with yet another pervasive draft.

Aiming the flashlight's beam at my handiwork, I could see that the lock was still in place but the clasp appeared looser, one rusty screw gone forever in the surrounding dirt beneath my feet. I thought about whacking it again, but decided that the hammer's claw would do the job just as efficiently and much more quietly. I hooked the sharp edge of the claw behind the rusted fastener. I gave it a weak tug. It remained steadfast despite the missing nail.

Then . . . another sound. I held my breath, listening intently over the beating of my heart. Again, it had come from within the walls of the shed. But it was not the faint scratching I heard earlier. This noise was a muted pounding of sorts, something boots might make while kicking up chunks of dry soil.

"Hello," I called, my voice sounding hopeless, barely more than a whisper. Jesus, did I really expect an answer? I inhaled and knocked gently against the door with the hammer. This time I did get an answer. More grinding, shuffling, and then a knock, as though something inside had come in accidental contact with one of the four walls.

My God . . . there was definitely something inside. Something alive.

"Hello in there?" I said, a bit louder this time, but still only croaking faintly. "Can you hear me?"

No response, no sound. But there was an odor now,

a pissy-smelling waft that reminded me of the NYC subway system during August. I took another deep breath, eyes tearing from the stench, and wedged the hammer's claw behind the clasp. I tugged once, twice. On the third pull the wood splintered and the screws popped free. The fourth pull was made with less effort—as much needed to render the latch and lock from its weak foundation. They fell to the floor with a soft thud.

From inside, more scratching. Another thud. I stepped back a few feet, almost falling backward. A feeling of giddiness hit me as though the environment had been subtly shifted into an askew position. I did my best to steady myself, holding the flashlight and hammer out at equidistant positions alongside my body. Once I regained my balance, I stared back at the shed.

What the hell is inside? Person? Animal? Isolate?

No, I told myself. I knew better than to consider something horrific, something *impossible*. Here I would find a bird or squirrel that had somehow wedged its way in through a crack at the base, had starved for days until this moment when it heard its potential salvation fiddling beyond the darkened walls of its prison.

Telling myself—yet again—that there was nothing to be alarmed about, I stepped forward and gripped the rusted door handle. I opened it. First a crack. Then all the way.

I shined the flashlight inside.

At first all I could see was a bulking shape in the gloom, no real details. But as I waved the light around, everything came into view, and my legs went soft with fear and anxiety.

The smell hit me hard, as if it were something solid— like ruthless hands around my neck. A horrible blurting sound arose, and for a moment all my muscles turned to jelly as my weakened sights confirmed my first assumption. Inside the walls of the shed lay no human, no Isolate, no squirrel nor bird. Here was an animal, but one I was in no way set to contend with.

Lying on its side against the far wall of the shed was a full-grown deer, a doe. It made that half-blurt, half honking sound again (rather loud now with the door open), and when the flashlight caught the animal's face, its wet bulging eyes rolled toward me like eggs in boiling water. There was a nasty open wound on its side, a wash of glistening crimson tiding out on the earth beneath its heaving bulk. It attempted to move, four long legs frantically kicking at the ground, one coming in solid contact with the shed wall.

I began to back up, tried to grab hold of some thoughts, to figure out how this animal got in there. *You know how it got in the shed, Michael. Someone put it in there. After stabbing it in the gut. And they promptly locked the door on the way out, thank you very much.* So the question remained: who? And why?

I felt suddenly cold, as if the near-dead animal had emitted a ghostly chill. For a quick moment I thought back to the doe I saw the day Phillip escorted me through the woods, how it seemed to appear out of nowhere as if Phillip had *just known* that it would be there to add to the serenity of the environment. It had flitted away into the woods just as quickly as it had come, and I wondered with a bit of alarm if this doe in the shed was the very same one I saw that day. I shuddered at the possibility, and at that very moment the injured deer staggered to its feet. I backed away at the sudden confrontation, tottered actually, the stench of pee and shit and filth driving me back just as much as my fear did.

At that moment I remembered the hammer. It was still in my hand.

Think about this for a second, Michael . . . sure, you're a city boy totally out of his element . . . but handling this situation should be a piece of cake . . . folks round here would set some kind of hypnosis into the animal, have it feeding out of their hands like a puppy dog . . . do this: just make believe it's a mugger on Eighth Avenue and Forty-third Street, trying to snatch your pregnant wife's pocketbook. . . .

My pregnant wife.

My arm brushed into a naked bush at the edge of the woods. I flinched and the flashlight fell to the ground. I still had the hammer, though, and I readied it, just in case. Just in case . . .

It was a stare-down, the deer's eyes on mine. Its face was fouled with dirt. Blood and bile foamed at its gums, its breathing a succession of hurried bursts. It shook its head defiantly, croaked angrily, then charged me.

In a move that was purely instinctual, I leaned my weight forward and brought the hammer down on its skull, just above the left ear. The cracking sound it made, the contact of steel on bone . . . it was both horrible and amazing. It sounded like a bat on a home-run baseball. An offensive hiss shot from the animal's throat and nose, and the hammer rebounded from my hand, end-over-end, striking the face of the shed with a dull thump. It came to rest on the ground alongside the lock and clasp.

I jumped back in the opposite direction of the collapsing animal. Instinctually, the words "Oh dear Jesus" fell from my lips. I felt a warm drizzle of blood on me, my face, my arms, even through my clothes. The deer thudded to the ground, skidding a few feet toward the woods before its painful leg-kicks tapered down to mere reflexive spasms. The gush of blood from its shattered skull glistened in the moonlight, matching the wet gloss dousing its bulging eyes.

And then it stopped moving.

Moments passed in hardened silence, and it was only then that I realized that my feet had come out from under me, that I was lying on my back, head twisted in such a way that the downed animal appeared right-side-up. I pressed my hands against the ground, wet moss squelching coldly between my fingers, and sat up. Something slimy wriggled across my hand. Without looking I shook it away in disgust. The mud-covered flashlight was within reach of my right hand, and I stretched and took hold of it. I groped for the switch, fingers sliding across the plastic surface. The light came on and I shined it at the deer.

The sight of it was sickening, and if I'd thought there was enough strength in my legs, I would have forced myself to race away into the warm comfort of my home, never to come outside again. But all I could do was kneel in the damp earth, my mind and body trembling at the harsh result of my blind fury—of the instantaneous moment of do-or-die that mirrored the innate fear of the deer's just seconds before. The whole moment went *out-of-body* on me, and I felt as though I were looking down upon a madman whose nerves had raced maniacally for a fix of terror just minutes earlier, his dark deed now complete, the feral urges that drove him now utterly sated.

Of course I was just a man who'd defended himself from some perceived menace.

I took a few deep breaths, came back down to earth, then stood up and took a step toward the animal. Just one step. I looked toward my right, at the gaping entrance of the shed, and tried to peer into its fouled depths.

The flashlight showed only the blood-tainted flooring: old wooden beams withering to rot, grass and weeds sprouting everywhere, toadstools cluttering the corners in swelling clusters. When I neared the entrance the smell hit me, and I cringed, gagging. I stood my ground, and just when I thought my nausea had been tamed, my peanut-butter sandwich and glass of milk came up in a surge. I stayed motionless, hands on knees, panting until the sickness passed. When all was said and done, I clenched my teeth and forced myself to step forward into the shed, shining the light into the previously unseen section inside.

A deep revulsion that bordered on the edge of panic

fell into me, and I had to hold my breath to stop myself from puking again.

Inside the shed was another deer, this one a baby fawn. It had been dead for a long time.

Both my trembling hands grasped the flashlight, the beam bouncing up and down and back and forth like a nightclub spot, and it took a good fifteen seconds before I could steady it back over the motionless target. Slowly I moved the beam over the decaying animal's body, all three feet of it, its nutty hide long surrendered to dark patches of moss, clumps of twitching maggots, and mosquitoes that buzzed about the putrid mass in droves. Its legs were withered to bone and cartilage, the head bulging in odd directions, eyeless and nose-less with an incredible gaping wound at the neck.

The evidence was clear. This animal, like the other, had been killed too. And most likely, I thought, placed here in this shed for some unsound reason.

Although it had been obvious to me that the baby deer carcass had been here for quite some time, I still considered the fact that it had been purposely placed here, like the other, after I had moved into this home—meaning less than a month ago. The evidence was clear. Someone had trespassed on my property and committed this dirty deed *after* I had moved in. This was no leave-behind from the Widow Farris, no residue of her husband's lifestyle.

I turned and escaped the damp confines of the shed, my boots slapping against the moist soil just beyond the entrance. The moon hid behind a thin layer of cloud cover, making the yellow porch light of the house appear to shine more brightly than before. I prayed that Christine and Jessica had stayed asleep this whole time, and wondered how Page hadn't heard the clamor I'd made out here. I wiped my brow, and immediately decided to keep this event a secret from my family. Some things were better left unsaid, and this was one of them—along with my first-day conversation with Rosy Deighton.

I stood my ground outside the shed for a few minutes, and when I gathered my composure, I realized that I had to get rid of the dead animals. But how to do it?

Hey, Michael, how about running them up into the woods and placing them on the sacrificial altar of the Isolates? You know, that big ol' bloodstained slab?

I shook the crazy thought from my head, combatting it with an equally insane argument: *Phillip had said that the animal must be alive at the time of sacrifice.*

"Are you out of your mind?" I exclaimed to myself in a hoarse whisper, trudging away from the scene around the left side of the house toward the detached garage. I went inside through the side door, almost blessing the dry stale air within (and the fact that I was away from the woods), and pulled down a pair of Christine's mesh gloves from the wood-beam shelf where she kept her gardening supplies. In the corner next to the lawn mower, I gathered up the blue plastic tarp I'd used to cover the floor when I painted the hallway and office.

My stomach spun at the thought of what I planned to do. I tried to suppress it, but other gut-gouging factors were at play, like, despite my distance from the shed, the stench of decay riding the slight wind with the determination of a suckerfish on a shark's fins. I could smell it from inside the garage. This, coupled with the image of having to roll the stinking carcasses onto the tarp while their smashed bulks shifted loosely in my hands, made my insides spasm. And of course there'd be thousands of insects beneath the fawn, skittering away to find cover because their glorious homeland treasure had been recklessly shifted after days and days of immobility.

I tucked the tarp beneath my left shoulder and exited the garage, doing my best to shake away the repulsive memories that would stay with me long after this night ended. I made the trek across the back lawn slowly, passing the floor-to-ceiling windows of the library, wishing I were still seated at the desk, eating another sandwich and shuffling papers beneath the hushed gleam of the reading lamp. The walk back felt like an eternity—perhaps I tried to make it last that long—but I finally returned to the scene of the crime: the place where I'd aided in murdering a full-grown deer.

I told myself that everything was going to be all right, that I, man of the house, would muscle my way through this unanticipated chore, wrap the two animals in the tarp, and drag them a hundred yards back where they could finish decomposing into the terra firma, and then attempt to erase this night from my mind.

But it wouldn't happen that way.

I dropped the tarp, my whole face tightening as if I'd taken a hard blow in the knee. The flashlight fell from

my grasp too. But not before I saw. And knew, une-
quivocally, that from this moment on, everything *wasn't*
going to be all right.

Both carcasses were gone.

Chapter Thirteen

I stayed awake all night, but that was to be expected. Was sleep really a possibility after what had happened? The confrontation with the deer had been enough to inflict insomnia on any man, but the horrific mystery of two carcasses having vanished in a matter of minutes promised to torment me for years to come. Unless, of course, I could come up with a reasonable explanation.

It wasn't until half past two A.M. before I made it back inside. I took another very long shower, mulling all I'd just been through, my mind floating haphazardly away into territories of empty voids and giant incredulities. Soon after, I was faceup on the living room sofa, my back surging with pain, the muscles in my arms and legs twitching and jumping with exhaustion. I considered for a moment going back outside to investigate the shed again, to confirm that the baby fawn was not there despite the fact I already knew it wasn't. I'd looked in there at least five or six times, alternating between it and the deep dark woods, but I'd been able to see only a spotted trail of blood leading away from the place where the dead mother deer had lain. When the horrible truth of the matter had sunk in, I'd resigned myself to defeat and come back into the house, my mind fighting my body, and now it was clearly winning the all-night battle on the couch.

When morning came, I rose from the couch and, despite my lack of appetite, made the family breakfast: eggs, bacon, coffee, juice, toast. Christine came down and cold-shouldered me (rightly so, I'd completely forgotten about her tirade and our subsequent argument last night), but acquiesced once she saw the nice spread. Apparently the pregnancy had given her an appetite, and made her grateful for the plate of food I put down before her.

"I guess this is your way of making up," she said calmly.

I shrugged my shoulders, accepting her assumption as fact. Frankly, given the depth of our argument last night, I was a bit stunned by the ease with which she calmed her anger; in the past she'd allowed lesser quarrels to string out for days. So, as it seemed, this dispute was officially wrapped up, and for that I was very grateful. I had more pressing issues deserving my attention at the moment.

Like how those animals vanished last night. They didn't just get up and walk away. . . .

I heard Jessica's pitter-patter on the steps, and she

appeared in the kitchen with Page circling her feet. I placed a plate of food before her and she dug in with silent enthusiasm. Page skulked over to his metal bowl and munched on some Kibbles 'n Bits, a bit dejected that there were no eggs and bacon for him.

While preparing breakfast, I'd hoped to have a few words with Christine about her—our—plans for the future now that we had another one on the way. I realized now that that discussion would have to wait until later. There was a time and place for everything, and now wasn't either to tell Jessica about the pending arrival. Christine and I were in silent agreement about that.

I sat at the table and nibbled on a slice of toast, watching my wife and daughter (and dog) eat in silence. When Christine finished her food, she rolled her seat next to mine and hugged me. "I apologize for being so witchy last night. Thank you for breakfast. It was delicious."

"You're welcome." I returned the hug, feeling a bit awkward. One didn't see Christine bowing her head in defeat too often, unless it was after she got her way. Today, she demanded no prerequisites. A once-in-a-lifetime occurrence. Lucky me.

Jessica fled the scene and started digging through the foyer closet for her sneakers. "C'mon, Page!" she cried.

I looked over, perplexed. "Where are you going?"

Christine said, "Yesterday I told her I'd take her and Page to Beaumont Park. I was hoping she'd forget."

"Are you kidding? In this town of nothing-to-do, a promise like that will never be forgotten."

Jessica had her sneakers and jacket on despite the

fact that Christine was still in her sleeping gear: knit shorts, age-old T, and scrunchie. "Give me a few minutes to get changed, okay, hon?"

Jessica, leash in hand, yelled, "Okay," then hooked up Page and headed out the front door. "We'll be outside."

Christine stood up and put her dish in the sink. "I hope you won't mind if I don't help you clean up, Michael."

I didn't expect her to, really. I smiled. "No, you go and have a nice time." What I really wanted to do was ask her when she was going to start working for me. The paperwork, although manageable, was taking up more of my free time than I wanted. And besides, it'd be nice for the patients to be greeted by a happy face when they walked through the door, not a barren office. Now, with the new baby coming, I'd pretty much have to hire someone from town to fill the role before I dug myself too deep a hole. Jesus . . . all of a sudden Christine was becoming a full-time mom. So much for our little plan.

"Thanks, hon. We'll probably have lunch out too, after the park." She walked over and kissed me, and just like that all was back to normal between us. Then I wondered: *Did she call into town for an OB/GYN? That would be her next step.* I was going to say something about this, but decided against it for now. I'd gotten one reprieve, and didn't want to spoil the moment. This doctor knows a great many things, including the tempestuous pregnant-female/hormonal symmetry, and believe me, that doesn't need prodding with any size stick, especially when all biological waters are calm. So I let *that* sleeping dog lie by smiling and waving before she went back upstairs to get changed.

In five minutes she was out the door, and I was alone.

I stepped outside on the front porch and watched as Christine took the minivan to the end of the driveway. She made a left turn and disappeared down the road, the exhaust leaving a wispy trail of smoke in its wake, like the tail of Aladdin's genie. The sky was saturated with blue, the temperature reaching a stunningly dry eighty, so said the porch thermometer. Despite the fatigue in my blood, I could still easily admire this beautiful summer day in Ashborough. Sometimes the incredible contrast of Ashborough to Manhattan can be alarming to this city boy (like last night); other times it can be truly luxuriating, like now. I stood there taking deep breaths, forgetting in the span of these few moments the transient worries of my life. That is, until the clock in the living room chimed nine and whisked me away from my reverie. I had my first patient in fifteen minutes, so I forced myself back inside and drank a cup of coffee, staring at the pile of dishes in the sink that needed cleaning. I walked over, turned on the faucet, then peered out the window at the loose tarp caught at the edge of shed, the open door of the shed, and the bloody trail leading into the woods.

Chapter Fourteen

I went into my office to check out the schedule of appointments. Today's first patient was due in at nine-fifteen—about another five minutes. I'd examined her once before, a mid-thirties woman by the name of Lauren Hunter who had dyed-blond hair, expensive jewelry, and smooth skin. She'd made it quite apparent that she was more than available—cocoa eyes all deep and dreamy and pointed in my direction; low-cut blouse; a mile-wide Colgate smile—and I defended myself by making my happy marriage just as obvious, you know, talking about the kids and the family vacations we never took. Her complaints of stomach ills magically evaporated once Ashborough's new physician became virtually inaccessible (I say "virtually" because here she was again making another appointment; I wondered if she was actually sick this time).

The remainder of the schedule was light, another appointment after lunch, then two more later that afternoon. I'd noticed through Neil Farris's records that the summer months ran a bit slow—after the initial flurry of meeters and greeters, this was proving to be true. Traffic the rest of the week was going to be light as well.

I waited inside until about nine-thirty, then, assuming Lauren Hunter to be a no-show, slipped out the side door of the office. I walked to the front of the house and looked across the road to make sure she wasn't pulling in late. The coast was clear (my father used to say that to me when I was a young child, after checking my dark bedroom for the bogeyman before I went to bed). So I went into the garage and grabbed the metal lawn thatcher (best tool, I figured, for disseminating the bloody ground), then walked back to the shed, much more briskly than I had last night after retrieving the tarp. Once there, I surveyed the scene.

The brownish ghost of a bloodstain remained in a wide circle amidst the matted grass. Standing up close, I saw it possessed a fouled mocked-up look, as if someone had added another quart or so of blood later on, long after I'd gone to bed. From there a swath journeyed up into the woods, lines of blood thinning out across the soil, about ten feet away. They disappeared just beyond that, near a thicket of saplings. Hesitantly, I walked over to the shed and peered through the door. Even now, beneath the bright morning sun, darkness reigned inside. Still, there were a few gaps between the rotting slats—and the open door, of course—that allowed enough light through for me to see that there was no baby deer. Just a brownish stain, with no streaks. Whoever took it had picked it up and carried it away, nice and quickly, with no intention of being seen.

Until this moment, everything had been peaceful, nice and quiet. A typical morning, just as Ashborough liked it. The birds were serenading. The trees quietly whispered beneath a gentle breeze.

I backed out of the shed, leaned the thatcher against the door, then walked over to the birdbath, feeling suddenly giddy. This return to the scene of the crime had me unnerved a bit. I did my best to battle these bad feelings by itemizing some of the tasks that needed attending to, like filling out all those insurance forms and drug-stock purchase orders piled on my desk. But it didn't work—it seemed there was plenty of room in my mind for everything.

The birdbath was dry, and I realized now that it hadn't rained for weeks. I could remember only one instance since we moved in where it rained at all, and that was a late-afternoon thunderstorm that transformed the skies into a mean charcoal-gray color; it also had a yelping Page scurrying fearfully away under Jessica's bed. I ran my finger along the rough cherub statuette, totally engrossed in thought, thinking for a passing moment that another cup of coffee might go down just fine right now—when a scream ripped through the backyard.

I started, then bolted around as though I'd expected all along that some kind of terror was about to take place. (Stories of golden-eyed goblins? Animal bodies being dragged from my backyard? That might've had something to do with it.) I saw nothing, but a shriek as high and as sharp as a guillotine issued from around the side of the yard. This was followed by the dull thud of something sharply hitting the house.

I darted around the side of the house, and was immediately greeted with blood—at least it was the first thing I became aware of. Blood, everywhere. A lot of it: on the walkway, in the grass, on the shingles alongside the entrance to my office. Then I saw the body, and in a reflex shoved my fist in my mouth to keep from screaming.

Lauren Hunter had arrived for her appointment. But she'd run into some big trouble along the way. What exactly that trouble was I had no clue, and I could do nothing but stand frozen and stare down at her, hoping that some miracle group of paramedics would show up in their bleating ambulance, toting their black bags, IV, and stretcher while rushing to my patient's rescue. That's how it's done in New York—stand back and let the pros handle the situation. Here in this wee little township of curvy back roads and Smoky-the-Bear forests, I was the only show in town, flying solo and manning the cockpit in a plane I couldn't operate very well.

My knowledge and experience in emergency situations is limited—I'm just an internist, my specialties are sniffles and coughs, snot and phlegm. Still, the diagnosis was obvious. In a few minutes Lauren Hunter would meet her maker. Given her condition, it was amazing that any life was left in her at all. A good portion of her face had been stripped away. What remained was a bloody slab that ran from her scalp line to her trembling jaw. Her shirt had been reduced to ribbons, a dangling left arm twisted from the socket like a storm-damaged branch. Two shattered ribs swelled through the bruised skin beneath her right breast. She coughed, and blood and yellow phlegm showered out onto the grass. Then she moaned—loud enough to make me jerk back—and rolled over, both legs twitching much like the deer's had last night—as if charged with electricity. This revealed a large gouge in her waist, and when she shifted, purple-gray organs spilled out onto the cement walkway. A large pink tube wriggled out too. It looked alive, one end leading back into her body like a leash.

In my mind I heard Phillip Deighton say, *The animal can't be dead, Michael. It has to be sacrificed on the big stone.*

I became harried and distressed, and I knew for certain that if I'd been forced to say something, only gibberish would come out. It didn't matter anyway, I told myself. Nothing I could say or do would change the fact that Lauren Hunter, a patient under my care, was going to die.

She coughed again. Clotted swirls flew out with such force they spattered the shingles. Amazingly, she kept moving. In fact, she attempted to lean up. Her eyes quivered, then opened, unfocused and stirred with tiny masses of blood. Her head bobbled back and forth, and I finally kneeled down before her, my hands at once pinning her neck, mindful of the fact that the shock and trauma striking her body didn't deter it from squirting pints of blood out.

My knees slid forward and I said to myself, *The hole in her waist . . . her organs . . . Jesus Christ!* And all I could wonder was what could have possibly happened to Lauren Hunter. My crazed common sense kept saying over and over, *Same thing that happened to Rosy Deighton, same thing that happened to Neil Farris, same thing that happened to . . .* To think otherwise would be a waste of good thought. Something evil and horrible was going down in Ashborough, and damn the residents here who'd obviously accepted it as readily as a hot meal on the dinner table at supper time.

I had to shove those thoughts aside for the moment. More important right now was what to do next. I stood and thought about running inside for a blanket, but that would only ruin the blanket. Still, I couldn't just let her suffer. I needed to call for help in spite of the fact that she'd be dead long before they got here. It wouldn't ease her suffering, but it was the only option, given the dreadful circumstances.

I leaned down next to her. "Lauren?"

Her head shook. Her lips puckered like a fish's. She said, "*Ah . . . puh . . . ahg.*"

"I'm going to help you, Lauren. You just be good and try to relax. Help will be here soon." It was the grandest lie I'd ever told.

Her head turned in my direction, as though she were trying to look up at me, but there was no way to tell for sure . . . there was too much blood everywhere. I wanted to get up, get away, perhaps go inside and wait in a dark corner while she writhed to death. Instead, her one good arm jutted up like a moray from its lair and grabbed my wrist. A spurting sound came from her throat. Her tongue moved, I could see it flicking around in the swamp of blood and snot in her mouth. Some unclear sounds spilled forth, odd foreign syllables like *dar* and *uug*. I tried to make some sense of them, but I was growing more confused by the second. I tried to break free of her bloody grasp. I couldn't. She had quite a grip on me. *Reflexive bodily instinct,* they once taught us at Columbia.

They never taught anything like this during Family Practice 101, Michael.

"Isolates . . ." she barked, then choked up some lung fluid.

I gazed down at her, in total denial of what I'd just heard. It had come out fully intentional, as clear as the skies above our heads. Not as some misinterpreted hack or gurgle. And not as some stress-induced delusion on the ears. *Can't be, Michael. It can't be that she just said that word. No. It was nothing more than some ironic string of nonsensical utterances coincidentally formed into a word that's been haunting you for the better part of twenty-four hours.*

She was still looking at me. I managed to ask, my voice barely a whisper, "What?"

And then her voice changed. It was deeper, stronger, not the voice of a woman who lay buried in agony, seconds from death. "They want you . . . they're coming for you. . . ." Her eyes rolled up into their sockets, revealing bloody ruptures. The corners of her mouth drew downward, as if pulled by invisible strings.

And then my mind went back to six weeks ago, to the day we first moved in. I'd met Phillip for the first time, and he was kind enough to invite us to his home, and despite my encounter with the rusty nail on my front lawn, I'd thought everything was just going to be sweet and peachy here in Ashborough, but then I'd taken a wrong turn while looking for a bathroom and Rosy Deighton spat at me through her black hole of a mouth, *They'll come for you, just like they did for me, just like they did for Dr. Farris, like they will for everyone else in this godforsaken town!*

And now, a similar warning from a woman also in distress. Terror shot through me, changed me, made me a different man in a matter of seconds. Smaller, weaker, a man who needed to call the hospital not for the dying woman on the sidewalk, but to reserve myself a room in the mental ward ASAP. I'd been dealt a big blow this morning, and needed to check myself in fast.

Instead, I leaned close to her bloody head. At this close proximity I could see a tiny slice of white skull peeking through. It looked like an eye. I turned away, said, "Lauren . . . speak to me. What are you trying to say?"

"Christine . . ." she spat, teeth bearing down on her bottom lip. Blood poured out like a fountain.

Jesus Christ, how does she know my wife's name?

Then she let go of me and went back to her spasms. I threw myself back against the wall, looking at a kidney or a liver on the cement walkway that'd met its fate beneath my knee. Her body stiffened up one last time,

129

then released itself and went motionless. Something foul-smelling hit me like a bag of potatoes. Her eyes glossed over.

I sat there against the house for an indeterminate amount of time, knowing very well that someone, my family included, might nonchalantly stumble upon this horrific scene—items brought in loving arms would undoubtedly drop to the ground. I waited until my breathing returned to a somewhat normal rate, and shivered as the sweat on my body cooled. But then my vision faded, a gray sheet enveloping the environment around me. My head spun like mad, body swaying like a pendulum. Sickness found my gut, and for the second time in twenty-four hours I threw up. When everything found its way out of me, I laid myself down against the cement foundation of the house and allowed the gray to turn to darkness.

Chapter Fifteen

When I came to, feelings of surreality and bewilderment made me feel as if I'd woken up from a dream within a dream, although I knew that this waking nightmare would not go away. The true magnitude of how I felt then could never be described in the right words, although I imagined that this was how an addict felt after an all-night binge of needles and spoons.

I was still hopeful that an emergency team would soon stream in, but as we all know by now, my closest neighbor is a light year away and as those *Alien* movies tout, *In space, no one can hear you scream.* The whirlwind that went down in the yard on the side of my house might as well have taken place on Mars. No one had seen or heard anything. Hence, there was no help on the way. It was up to me to grab the bull by the horns with what little strength I had left.

Dizziness tried to claim me as I stood. I balanced myself with one hand against the house. The bloodprint it left on the shingles was still slickly wet, and made me realize that I'd only been out for a few minutes. I looked at the body—what was left of Lauren Hunter. In her unmoving state I could see that her injuries had been much more severe than I'd first observed, if that was humanly possible. Her legs were covered with what I could only describe as bite marks, circular-shaped punctures befitting the size and shape of a human child. The skin around the horrible gouge in her side had deep jagged impressions along the edges, indicating some crude weapon (or claw, I reminded myself). I could see four deep notchlike grooves inside the injury to her face, reinforcing my belief that she'd been swiped at by some kind of taloned fist. Once the horrific attraction wore off, and the gross realization of the situation set in, I lurched away, threw off my shirt and shoes, and stepped inside the house.

All was eerily silent inside.

I picked up the phone, noticing that there were no messages (for a change, I was thankful for the slow season), and pressed 0 for operator. A woman with no personality came on the phone.

"Operator."

I took a deep breath, tried to speak, but a dry tickle in my throat sent me into a fit of coughs. Once I had control of my voice, I said, "I need some help. It's an emergency."

"What type of emergency, sir?"

"What type?" I found it strange that the operator

would ask this. Then again, I wasn't thinking too clearly at the moment.

"I need to know where to connect you. Fire, Police, or Medical?"

Good question. Definitely not fire. Police maybe. No . . . I needed medical. Yes. *Jesus, am I losing my mind? I'm a doctor for Christsakes!* "Medical emergency," I panted, wiping my free hand across my forehead.

There was a brief silence on the other end, and in this time my mind wandered back to Lauren Hunter and the uncanny utterances that had come from her mouth. Just noisy chokes, I told myself. I must've misinterpreted these as referring to Christine and the Isolates. *I couldn't have heard her say those things*, I kept repeating in my mind, grabbing the sentences that were sticking in my head as if pinned there with thumbtacks, wrapping them up in pretty little mental boxes, and sending them off to gather dust in some room within my untapped subconscious—a room whose door had the word *denial* stamped on it in big bold letters.

I felt the phone slipping from my grasp, and I did my best to hold it against my mouth, but that only captured the mad giggles that started to swell in my throat.

"Sir . . . sir? Are you all right?"

I heard her but couldn't answer right away, and she heard me laughing, I knew. That tipped me a bit, made me dizzy. I took my hand and wrapped it across my waist to keep me here, on earth, in this plane of existence. *Yes, I'd heard only the yips and yaps of a human being drowning in the swells of death. That, and nothing more.*

"Sir, do you have an emergency to report?"

"Y-yes . . . yes I do."

"I'll connect you to the hospital in Ellenville."

Seconds passed. I tried to make myself feel better, but I couldn't help going back to those impossible moments when Lauren Hunter had spoken to me. *Damn it, she spoke to me!*

And then I was disconnected.

A dial tone met my ear. At that instant I felt like a sole survivor on some desolate planet, my only means of communication taken away by some unseen force. My heart pounded, my hands were shaking. I dialed up the operator again. This time I got a male voice on the phone.

"Operator."

"Ellenville hospital, please."

"One moment . . ." Another void met my ear; I never knew silence could be so deafening. Finally, after a minute of flexing away the tightness of drying blood on my hands, I heard a ringing. A woman answered, "Ellenville Medical." Her voice was curt. Clearly I'd interrupted something important. Tough cookies.

"This is Dr. Michael Cayle calling from Ashborough. I have a medical emergency and need an ambulance here at once."

There was silence on the other end. I could hear the woman breathing before a backdrop of rushed voices and ringing phones.

"Hello? Are you there?" Surely she heard the impatience in my voice. "I said I have a life-and-death emergency."

"You said you're a physician from Ashborough?"

"Yes . . . as far as I know I'm the only goddamned one here. What seems to be the problem?"

There was a shuffling of papers on the other end. "What is your address sir?"

"17 Harlan Road."

"There'll be an ambulance there in ten minutes."

"Thank you!" I hung up the phone, but not before I heard the other end disconnect.

I wondered at that moment if I should have simply called the coroner, but I wasn't sure whether I'd have to call into Ashborough or Ellenville—this was a poor time to realize that I'd never once looked into the names and addresses of my constituents. Regardless, wherever this coroner resided, whoever he was, he'd have to come up with a cause of death and I'd be his only material witness to a death that would clearly blow him out of the water. *Animal attack? Isolate? Close your eyes and flip to a page in the family medical journal. Here we go, she died of thanoplastic dystopia. Whatever the hell that is.* Suddenly Small-Town USA didn't seem as quaint as it once did. Beneath every charming little vista seemed to lie a cold dark enigma.

I walked to the door and peeked out the window at Lauren Hunter's sprawled body. There was blood everywhere, on me as well, and I knew that a good part of the afternoon would be spent cleaning it all up. After the body was taken away. After I gave a statement to the police.

The police.

I should've called them. I moved toward the phone.

Stopped. Something told me not to do it. Not yet.

Instead I went into my office, dug through the prescription drug sample case, and snatched a two-milligram Xanax. Zany Xanax we used to say in med class. We'd pop them after an exam, then assemble in clusters of six or eight and mellow out to some Pink Floyd before passing out on the carpet. Ecstasy for the post-grad scholar.

The phone rang. I picked it up expecting the police, or the medical team. It was Virginia Hastings canceling her three o'clock appointment. All the better.

Ten minutes had passed. No sign of an ambulance. I called Ellenville again and was put on indefinite hold.

Something didn't smell right.

Finally I hung up and dialed 911, hoping that the police might be a wee bit more prompt than the Ellenville medical team; I'd lose another two inches on my hairline before they showed up. I got a tired-sounded girl on the phone, who sounded unmotivated and bored, not spent from a hard day on the job. I reported a life-and-death situation, my voice cracking with anxiety and unsettling impatience. Another promise was made for an ambulance.

"How about the police?" I asked.

"I'll notify the Ashborough sheriff."

"Thank you," I said unappreciatively. My fear and anxiety were peaking. Couple that now with frustration and you had one shredded individual.

Another ten minutes passed. No one showed.

I went back outside. Lauren's body was starting to

pale—rigor mortis setting in. The blood had rushed to her head, which was angled off the edge of the walkway into the grass, turning it a purple color with sticky black blood pooling from her mouth and nose. There were so many questions that needed answering. I stood there realizing that I'd have to be the one, for now, to try and find out what exactly had happened. If a person in Lauren Hunter's condition popped into my Manhattan office in a similar state, we'd come to immediate assumptions: dragged by a bus (or a subway), maimed by an angry mob (or a pack of wild dogs; every now and then a trio of pit bulls goes haywire on some poodle-walking bystander in Central Park). Other than that, what else could it be? Here in Ashborough with its unexplored woodland and uninvestigated maimings and, dare I add, its ominously unpleasant lore, anything goes.

With all these thoughts running around in my mind, more time had passed, and my head had screwed itself back on to some degree. I was thinking more clearly now, and now was the time to trust my instincts.

I went into the garage and got the tarp back out. Noon was approaching and more than an hour had passed since I placed the first call for help. I'd subsequently left a message at the sheriff's office, tried Ellenville again, 911, ran the whole help-line gamut. No one had come, and that scared me even more that what'd happened to Lauren Hunter.

I laid the tarp down next to her body, keeping my eyes and ears on high alert in case someone—a patient, Phillip, whoever—decided on a visit. Christine and Jessica were probably having lunch in town by now, and an educated guess said they'd do some shopping afterward. Plus having Page with them wouldn't be a problem. She was a calm pup and small enough to be held, and I'm sure most store owners wouldn't mind a cute little canine to pet as long as she didn't lick at them too much. So, no worries about them coming home right now. Fingers crossed.

The July sun beat down on me like a hammer, and it didn't do much justice to Lauren either. The smell was like nothing I'd ever encountered before, thick and assaulting on my nose in a cesspool kind of way.

This was the first time I noticed her footprints. She'd worn tennis sneakers and their flat soles had left clear impressions on the cement path. I eyed them all the way to the right corner of the house, where the walkway angled left and wrapped around the front of the porch. But the footprints . . . they didn't lead that way. They went off in the opposite direction, on the grass.

Into the woods.

I'd never gone more than five feet into the woods on this side of the house. But I'd spent a good amount of time peering into them; the window over the kitchen sink looked out across the side yard and provided a serene view every time I washed the dishes. The addition of the bloody trail (second one in two days; things seemed to work in pairs around these parts) leading into the woods ate into the serenity like crude graffiti on a stark white wall. It began to eat into my mind as well.

I stepped into the woods, following the bloody trail,

which broke up over the choppy earth, then petered out about twenty feet in. The trail really should've gotten thicker, considering Lauren's injuries would have left quite a mess, unless . . . unless I'd veered off track by following an errant spattering.

I looked around, turned left, then right, saw an opening, then some more streaks of blood on the ground. I followed them, eventually stepping through a blood-stained thicket of shrubberies, into a small clearing.

Here I located the scene of the crime.

At this moment I knew for certain that I had to get the police here. But I also knew deep down inside that they'd be too frightened to come. Somehow it became apparent that they had full knowledge of what'd just happened here . . . just as they most likely did with Neil Farris and Rosy Deighton and God knows how many other unfortunate bastards. I had no evidence to support such an allegation, but it seemed all too obvious. All I could do was stand in place and try my damnedest to shake off the feelings of bleak dread, the indisputable realization that something very wrong had taken place here. And it was evident in the underlying chill in the air—not even the hot sun of this July afternoon could dispel it. The pinnacle of fear I'd always considered previously unimaginable, conceivable only in nightmares, had become fully concrete at the thought that a conspiracy of great proportions might very well be in play here.

Within the ten-foot clearing was a set of stones like those in the circle of oaks Phillip had shown me. A smaller representation of its larger model, they were also arranged in an equally artful manner, perhaps twenty to twenty-five white oval-shaped monuments, twelve to eighteen inches in height, erected in a circular fashion with one larger rock at the nucleus of the framework. The center stone had a douse of blood cloaking it, thick drippings slowly lining the surface and pooling at the base in small dense puddles. Stepping around to the far side of the stone revealed a hunk of tattered flesh—clearly the missing piece in Lauren's midsection—lying at the base of the rock like a huge scavenging slug. I bent down and ran a finger across one of the erect stones. A thin white film of powder coated my finger, leaving me to postulate that these stones weren't of ancient origins like the larger ones. No, these were a more recent tribute to the legendary temple, recently carved.

The dry earth crunched under my feet as I stood. Like its larger counterpart, the clearing maintained a healthy canopy of reaching branches and leaves sufficiently cloaking it from moisture. At once I felt the need to flee this place before I too fell victim to the curse of the Isolates. I staggered away haphazardly, my mind struggling to get itself into gear, struggling to explain to me that everything going on was all part of a grand scheme and that the dreadful chill in the air might be the final catalyst to some evil plot I had unwittingly become a part of.

I promised myself that as soon as Christine and Jessica returned with the car, I would immediately take them far away from Ashborough, leave the house and my business behind to the vile happenings taking place here on a regular basis.

Good idea, Michael. But tell me this . . . why doesn't everyone else leave? Do they choose not to? Aren't they affected by the local corruption? Don't they know about it?

Or are they kept here against their will?

That last thought sent horrible shivers racing throughout my body, and I made another steadfast promise to flee this godforsaken place as soon as my family arrived home. I slipped from the woods, ran up the walkway alongside the house, and realized only as I got there that Lauren Hunter's body was gone.

Chapter Sixteen

There's a time in your life when something really scares you. Not just *scares* you, but scares the *piss* out of you, and you leap and scream and your heart pounds and your skin ripples and your blood races and your breathing goes shallow, and then, in a domino-effect type of way, your head spins and your eyesight blurs. There's a tightness in your chest that simulates a heart attack, and you claw at your breastbone with sweaty palms and pray for dear Jesus to save you from the hellfire and damnation that sits at the end of your tunnel like some great black cloud blocking out the ever-saving light.

But then it goes away, and you return to the world of love and roses and all-things-sugar-and-spice-and-everything-nice with only a vague memory and perhaps

a little eye-rolling, shoulder-shrugging giggle of denial
that you were ever scared at all.

That's all good and fine.

But then there's *pure* fear. Pure fear is something different altogether. Pure fear is the type of fear that many
of us never live to tell about. It's the feeling you get
when you realize your plane is most definitely going
down and that you have only one minute left to live,
and in that minute you can do nothing but pray that
the Good Lord has decided you've lived an exemplary
life and that you deserve a red carpet to the pearly gates
despite all your forthcomings. Pure fear exists in those
precious seconds after you lose control of the car just
before it slams into the utility pole. It's in all those moments when you realize that certain death will take you
and you can do nothing but succumb to the finish and
the irrefutable fact that you can't say good-bye to your
family on your way out.

I, for the first time in my life, experienced *pure fear*.
But I lived to tell about it.

Without question, the person who survives pure fear
becomes changed. I knew it the very moment I saw the
bloodstained walkway where Lauren Hunter's slaughtered corpse had lain not five minutes earlier. Suddenly, I'd become a different man. My mind shifted into
some irreversible mode where I would now look at the
world through a starkly gray-toned filter, where my
common sense drowned in a muddied pool while my
nervous system swam in violent storm-driven swells.

Like the baby deer the night before, Lauren had been

carried away, that much I could hypothesize. There was no trail of blood beyond the puddle—even her spilled organs had been taken, perhaps scooped up and crammed back into her cavity. Now, it wasn't just the fact that I knew, with no doubt, that I was being watched, perhaps drawn into some wicked ritualistic-type game of death, that had me experiencing pure fear. It was what I discovered on the ground beside the puddle of blood that had me staring death right in the face.

Footprints. Not the staggering impressions of Lauren's tennis shoes. Not my own booted feet (I even made a point to stare at my boots alongside the house to make sure—I'd taken them off before going inside). These prints were numerous, made by what appeared to be a group of animals. They had certain reptilian characteristics, long, pointed digits with winding patterns in the soles. The only difference was that they possessed five digits in total, something purely distinctive to a biped—a human. But they were too small to carry anything more than four feet tall.

I remembered what Phillip had said during our walk into the woods:

It'd creeped over the far edge of the rock, just a hand at first, long forklike fingers gripping the dead animal like a doll.

"Jesus Christ," I whispered aloud. Was he telling the truth after all?

There were now so many questions that needed answering, none of which I knew would ever be resolved.

What did they want from me?

The animal must be alive at the time of sacrifice.

"Oh, my God . . ." I said, thinking of the deer, then of Lauren. Clear-cut clues as to what they might want. *Were they actually giving me a handicap, starting the process for me. Could it be?*

I managed to find the strength to gaze at my watch. 1:30. Time was moving along at a lightning pace. I suppose I could've left the mess there, it surely would've aided in my arguments for wanting to move out of this house so abruptly. But I also knew that this was no image I wanted in my wife's or daughter's head.

The tarp . . . oh, my God . . . it was gone too. I realized this only now. This led me to believe that whoever, *whatever* took Lauren Hunter, had used it to help with their task. I fitted my boots back on, then raced into the garage, got out the gardening hose, and attached it to the spigot in the back of the house. Twisting the nozzle to the "jet" setting, I sprayed the blood until it diluted away into the grass and soil. Fifteen minutes later, all signs of Lauren Hunter were gone, at least to the untrained eye. It looked as though she were never here.

I kicked off my wet boots, went inside, and tried calling the police again. This time I got no answer. 911 was the same story. The operator would put me on hold until I either got tired of waiting or was disconnected. The word *conspiracy* entered my mind again, but so did the word *paranoia*. I had every right to feel this way given the alarming circumstances, but I also reminded myself that this wasn't New York City and that the societal gears here weren't as well oiled as I'm used to. Perhaps help was still on the way? My hopes were still

145

alive but walking on a very tenuous rope. I figured that eventually, after fleeing this insane asylum, Lauren Hunter's disappearance would be investigated and someone would find out that she had had an appointment with the local doctor who'd just upped and left with no fair warning, and *then* the investigators would show up and find minute traces of Lauren's blood on the walkway or on the house, and I'd end up on the FBI's Most Wanted list or as a special guest on *America's Most Wanted*. Fucking great.

What to do?

I checked the time. Almost three. I paced like crazy around the property, my legs guided by a force of adrenaline I never knew I had. I told myself that this is what a caged animal must feel like, under lock and key and unable to go anywhere. I had my hands and legs tied, I might as well've been bound and gagged too. I'd have to stay put until my wife and daughter returned. And *this*, my home sweet fucking home, was the last place I wanted to be.

Chapter Seventeen

I went into the house and continued pacing back and forth between the kitchen and living room, thinking of all the blood, and those footprints. I'd tried calling for help a few more times—a force of habit at this point—even though I knew damn well that it was too late. I'd covered up the crime already: my only sensible response to the alarming absence of emergency relief here in Ashborough. The whole time inside the house my heart continued pounding like crazy, and it did not let up until Christine and Jessica got home.

Three hours later.

I'd packed up a few bags: some valuables, jewelry, clothing, and food. All essentials. It had all been done in vain, however, for when Christine and Jessica pulled into the driveway, I knew that we weren't going anywhere tonight.

Our minivan had been replaced by a ratty Dodge pickup driven by a burly bearded man wearing a Genesee Beer baseball cap. He grinned toward me in a friendly manner and tipped his hat as I stepped from the house. I was so nonplussed I almost tripped on the front steps. Christine slipped from the passenger seat, placed Jessica down (she'd been sitting on her lap), then shrugged her shoulders and burst into tears as the pickup backed out of the driveway.

Christine had actually planned on arriving home a couple of hours earlier but an accident had occurred and instead of catching me in the act of rinsing away Lauren Hunter's remains, she'd found herself staring her very own monster right in the face. She'd been driving up the road that led out of Beaumont Park toward Main Street, thinking about what to make for dinner, when an animal darted into the road (she couldn't say for certain what kind of animal it was; she mentioned that it was about the size of a dog, but lankier, sort of like a monkey) right in front of the minivan.

After she told me this, I said, "It was probably a dog."

She shrugged her shoulders, head down, face wet with tears. "There was a man jogging on the sidewalk. I didn't see him. I lost control of the car, I tried to avoid the . . . the dog," she finally admitted, "but I couldn't. I ran it over," she told me again. "I could feel the car thump, and when that happened I lost control of the car and the wheel spun from my hands and then the car shot sideways across the road over the curb . . . right . . . right into the man." She wailed, *"I killed him!"*

I knew she couldn't be mistaken, the shocking truth

was too obvious in her face, but I tried to comfort her nonetheless. "How do you know for sure, Chris?"

"I hit him and I saw him . . . I saw him fly across the front lawn of someone's house . . . it was like he'd been shot from a fucking cannon! He went forty, maybe fifty feet and hit a tree next to the house. Headfirst . . . *face* first. Michael . . . it was so fucking unreal. . . ." More tears. "His head . . . his head . . ."

Jessica was looking up at us, lost in a cloud, blue eyes buried in a welling of tears. She'd seen what'd happened too, in full living color, and I wondered what would have been worse: death number one on the road or death number two right here at home. I pulled her close to me and she snuggled against my leg, scared not only by what had happened, but also by the sudden fear-induced hostility Christine conveyed. For a moment I thought about asking her to wait for us in the house while Christine and I talked this out, but I couldn't be certain what horrors might be waiting for us next, so I kept a strong arm on her shoulder, which she graciously accepted with a comeback hug around my waist.

Christine continued, stammering through her cries, "Michael . . . he hit headfirst into the tree . . . *I saw it fucking explode!* He lay there for a minute before I could even move. I could only stand there and watch him bleed out onto the lawn. I was about to call out for help when some people came out of the house."

"Some people," I repeated, stunned at what I was hearing. "What did they do?"

"They did fucking nothing, Michael," she sobbed,

hands trembling. "These people, they looked crazy, mindless, like robots. The expressions on their faces . . . there was nothing there at all, blank, eyes all glassy, mouths hanging open. There were four of them and they never spoke a word, not to me, not to each other. One of them, a man, he had a blanket and he laid it out on the grass next to the man I'd hit. After that, they picked him up, one person holding each limb, and put him on the blanket. He was dead, I'm telling you, Michael. The body was hanging like a pendulum, dead-weight. They wrapped the blanket around him and then they picked him up and carried him inside the house. They left the door open, and I should have gone in with them, but I couldn't. I was too scared and they were too fucking spooky the way they were acting, the way they just *ignored* me, and I didn't want Jessica to see any more of . . . of . . ." She fell into my arms, wailing, at a loss for words.

"Chris . . . did the cops come?" My heart was pounding, sweat poured from my body like rain. I knew that either answer to this question would explain the lack of response I got that afternoon.

She nodded a wet "yes" against my shirt. "There were two cops. That's it. I had to give them a statement. They let me go after that, but the car was totaled, so it got impounded."

Impounded . . .

"What about emergency teams?"

She shook her head. "No."

"They give you an alcohol test? The cops?"

"No."

I thought about the car, then asked, "How could the car have been totaled if you only hit a man?" *Only a man. Jesus. Would I have made such an insensitive comment if my mind wasn't a total mess itself?*

She replied with a flurry of cries, and I found the common sense to not concern myself with the car—my means of escape—at the moment. Jessica had begun crying too. She squeezed harder on my leg, then said, "What about Page, Mommy?"

Page . . . I'd completely forgotten about our pet, justly so I told myself. "Where's the dog, Chris?"

She pulled her face away from my chest. It was painted deep red, glossy with tears. Her eyes flitted in their sockets. "He bounded from the car and ran away after I opened the door to get out . . . after I hit the jogger. We called and called for him but he never came back." Given the situation, I would've done the same thing. Run and run and never come back.

"The policeman said he'd watch out for him," Jessica added.

I looked across the expanse of front lawn, all the way to Harlan Road and then beyond to the woods across the street. I'd hoped for Page's sudden return, to see our little cocker spaniel charging gleefully out from between a couple of tree trunks—it would act, at the very least, as a comforting distraction for Jessica. But there was no dog, and I resigned myself to the possibility that we might never see him again.

Feeling closed in, I pulled away from Christine a bit. Despite the terror of her day, and the fact that we had no car, all I cared about was how I could go about convincing my wife that leaving Ashborough at once was the right thing to do. Perhaps her experience had triggered a need to flee this place, just as mine had. I prayed that it had, but somehow, knew that it hadn't.

I shoved my hands in my pockets, eyes searching the ground, mind treading waves of anxious thoughts. Death seemed to be a common occurrence here in Ashborough, and I'm not talking death amongst your bad-eating heart-disease groups or tainted drinking-water breast-cancer collectives. No, death here was of the uncommon variety—secretive slayings, shocking accidents, ritual butcherings, et cetera, et cetera—all seemingly tolerated and perhaps accepted among the local inhabitants. I thought of Phillip and his chronicles of the Isolates, of their legend and the dark lore of their sacrifices. It seemed more believable now that there might actually be some ancient curse on this town, something that couldn't be stopped. *Plus so much more,* I thought, thinking of Christine's tale of the townsfolk coming out to retrieve their dead comrade. Of the cops who let her go after a few general questions. Of the absence of a medical team at the scene of the accident.

The animal must be alive at the time of sacrifice.

Like a badly kept secret, Phillip's statement kept coming back to me. That, and then so much more. I felt strangely haunted by the insinuation *beneath* his words. I remembered how his eyes pinned me at that moment, how they seemed to say, *Remember what I'm telling you, Michael, because someday it will save your life*. The warning came from his lips with forced deliberation, as if each word had had a period following it. I recalled the deer in the shed last night, how it could have been put in there for me to find. Then, I recalled Lauren Hunter, how she'd been put to near death, then served to me on a concrete platter with all the telltale clues of what to do next. But . . . I hadn't done what was expected of me. I'd failed the test. The deer died, and Lauren Hunter died. And after death they would serve no purpose.

The animal must be alive at the time of sacrifice.

So they were taken away, two opportunities long gone to commit the deed expected of me.

What's next, Michael? Who's next?

Christine picked up Jessica. Both of them had stopped crying, and were silently staring at me as though waiting for me to perform a miracle that would make this day start over again.

I said, "The car was really messed up, huh?"

Chris nodded. "The whole front end was crushed in. Both tires on the left side were flat. That must've happened when I ran over the animal."

"Did you see it?" I asked.

"See what?"

"The animal you hit." I thought of the footprints on the walkway, and wondered.

She hesitated, then answered, "Not really . . . just a flash of a small lanky body."

"How fast were you driving, Chris?"

She looked to the ground, then placed Jessica down. "Honey, go inside, please."

I thought about stopping her, but said nothing. Jessica slowly paced away, over the walkway, then up the porch, where she remained, watching us.

I looked at Christine, and was about to explain to her my plan of fleeing Ashborough, when she ripped me a new asshole. "Michael, you listen to me and you listen real good. Your pregnant wife gets into a car accident and not once do you ask if I'm all right or if your daughter is all right. No, you just stand there and ask questions about the fucking minivan and whether or not I was doing the speed limit like you're Joe-Fucking-Deputy from the Ashborough police department. I could've been hurt or killed, or worse yet, carried away by one of those fucking zombie weirdos after they climbed out of their tomb to claim their prize cadaver. This has been one hell of a day, Michael, and I'm done with it. If you have any questions about the car, then call the Ellenville body shop. That's where it'll be for the next two weeks."

She stormed away, body stiff and bobbing. Upon reaching the porch, she took Jessica by the hand, then turned, looked at me, and proclaimed, "Jess is going to take a bath. After that I'm going to shower, then get into bed. Good night, Michael."

It wasn't even dark yet. "What about dinner?"

"I'm not hungry."

"What about the car, Chris?" I yelled as she went into the house. The screen door slammed and the cowbell on the eave tolled lifelessly. I walked up the front steps and followed her inside. Chris was already halfway up the stairs. Her shoes lay haphazardly on the living room floor like discarded hand puppets. "How are we supposed to get around with no car?"

She stopped, turned, looked at me. "Obviously, Michael, we don't."

Chapter Eighteen

Christine did as she'd promised. An hour later she was quietly nestled in bed, probably not sleeping, but unapproachable nonetheless. I'd spent the first hour while they were showering peeking out of the windows, looking for Page, looking for golden lights, looking for those responsible for claiming the dead bodies from my property. But I saw nothing. All I saw was a gradual gathering of darkness and a handful of fireflies that taunted me with their blinking lights.

Surprisingly enough, an appetite grew within me (well, I'd puked up my breakfast and was a tad too distracted for lunch, so it wasn't that much of a surprise). I ate a handful of wheat crackers and a few slices of Muenster cheese—I passed on Christine's leftover meat loaf; the image of meat didn't win over my stomach—drank a cup of tea, then treaded into the office to check for messages. Honestly, given the day's events, I really didn't give a shit about my job, and was frankly surprised that I remembered I had any appointments at all. When I got there I found that all three of my afternoon appointments, Virginia Hastings included, had called to cancel. I shuddered as I listened to their voices on the answering machine, thinking over and over again: *conspiracy . . . paranoia.* I had a very strong feeling this wouldn't be the last time these two words ruffled my mind.

Obsessively, I paraded around the house locking all the doors and windows, checking each one twice just to be sure, and of course glancing outside *just in case.* While securing Jessica's room—her bed was empty—I recalled her earlier irrational fear of ghosts, which didn't appear so irrational now after all. Had my daughter been privy to something? Should I have heeded her warning? I snuck into my bedroom via the connecting bathroom. The room was dark, the wooden blinds shuttered and closing out the hazy dusk light. I looked down at Christine, her body curled beneath the sheets. Again I thought she might've been faking sleep—also Jessica, who was lying beside her—but I let them be. Careful not to stir the blinds, I turned each window latch before tiptoeing from the room.

I went back downstairs, my plan at the moment to find some type of transportation out of Ashborough, if not for tonight, then for first thing in the morning.

If we made it through the night . . .

I tuned off all the lights in the house except for the three-bulb chandelier over the kitchen table, dimming it so that only the table lay beneath in its soft illumination. I sat down, opened the phone book and called the only cab company listed, located twelve miles away in Ellenville. The dispatcher, a young-sounding woman who identified herself as Jean, was courteous and polite throughout the conversation until I told her I needed to be picked up in Ashborough, at which she hesitated, then replied, "I'm sorry, sir, we have only two cars on call tonight and they're both to remain in Ellenville." I pleaded my case but lost. Great.

Rental car companies were non-existent, even in Ellenville. The closest airport was ninety miles south, and none of the shuttles offered a pickup service outside of the city's limits. Buses? Yeah, right.

My only potential ticket out of town was five minutes down the road.

Phillip Deighton.

The clock struck eight. The tolls, suddenly ominous, seemed to stuff the house. I waited an eternity until they finished, then picked up the phone and dialed Phillip. He answered on the third ring and I could tell that he'd been crying. In the last minute prior to calling I'd planned at least a dozen questions for Phillip, like what he knew about the "Isolates," who they really were, and if "they" might be responsible for all the mayhem in my life; like who might've put the deer in my shed. How about telling me what *really* happened to Rosy? *Oh, and Phillip, can I borrow your car so I can get the fuck out of this crazy place?*

I never got question one out.

"Phillip . . . ?"

More sobbing. Some coughs. It always pained me to hear a grown man cry—as a doctor I'd heard my share—and despite the fact that Phillip seemed to be the keeper of many dark secrets, he was still a friend— the only damn one I had.

"No, it's okay, Michael," he replied. "I'm glad you called."

"What's wrong?"

"It's Rosy. . . ."

"What about her? Is she not feeling well?" Wishful thinking. I figured out what had happened before he told me. Odds-on favorite here in Ashborough.

"She's dead." His voice was dry and mechanical, the tears suddenly cut off. A silence loomed between us . . . well, not a total silence. Phillip's raspy breathing cut through the phone like static, filtering into my head as though electrically charged.

I broke the hush with, "My God, that's terrible. How did it happen?"

More silence, and I'd hoped that some kind of revelation would overpower his lips. "Michael . . . we need to talk."

I saw this as an invitation—as well as a kind of cheap, shameful victory. It appeared I was finally going to get some answers, even though it took the death of Rosy Deighton to get them, something I for the moment didn't really care about. This doctor had become numb to adversity over the past twenty-four hours, and had subsequently fallen into survival mode. It was do or die, and now was the time to *do*.

"So . . . let's talk."

"In person . . . not on the phone."

"I'm not leaving my house, Phil." And I meant it too.

"I'll come to you."

I was about to disagree, but beggars can't be choosers, and I was teetering on the edge of damnation with my only ray of light dimming very quickly. Phillip was that last bit of hope, and as they once taught me in Bible studies many years ago, *Do as He says and you shall find salvation.* Phillip wasn't exactly *He,* but as far as I was concerned, he might just be the next best thing.

"Okay," I agreed, my voice sounding distant to me. I felt overcome with fear again. Would Phillip Deighton have some answers for me? I felt no safer letting him into my home. And to think moments earlier I'd found myself wishing for his help; now it felt as though he would be bringing more danger to me.

I hung up the phone, realizing a second later that Phil had already disconnected the line. I thrust myself away from the table, then crossed the living room and went outside onto the porch to wait for him. Darkness had swallowed up the last remnants of the day, a solid layering of gray clouds absorbing any possibility of blue moonlight. I reached back inside and switched on the porch light. By the time Phillip arrived ten minutes later, a cloud of moths was fluttering about it.

As he paced up the driveway, I immediately guessed by the pained look on his face that he'd *needed* to get away from his house; Rosy had died there and this bereaved man's first instinct was to flee the place where it happened. I also knew that this could force him to give in to the dark thoughts taunting his mind. Step one, come tell all to Michael. Step two, shake his hand good-bye. Step three, go for menage à trois with twelve inches of bathwater and a live radio. Here I come, Rosy, won't be long now.

He paced up the driveway, eyes darting between me and the gravel meeting his booted footsteps. He wore a pair of denim jeans and a jacket, and a Red Sox baseball cap that sat crookedly upon his head. When he reached the porch, he took the cap off and his dark puffy eyes met mine. His face was the color of redwood leaves. He broke down as he walked up the steps, nearly dropping to one knee at the top. I grabbed him by the forearm and led him into one of the rattan chairs, holding on even after he sat down. He shook his head back and forth, running his free hand across his damp brow. "She's suffered so much . . . and if that wasn't enough for them, they had to take her from me."

"Who, Phil? Who are you talking about?"

"You know who I'm talking about." His voice was like sandpaper. Broken by sobs. He kept his gaze away from mine.

"The Isolates . . ."

He nodded, then looked up at me. "You *do* believe me, don't you, Michael?"

I didn't answer him. "What happened to Rosy, Phil?"

He hesitated, then said, "They came in the middle of the night. As usual, I had all the windows and doors locked, but just like last time they found their way into the house. They're no different from rats or cockroaches, Michael. They have no feeling, no sense of compassion, only drive. It's all instinctual. When they want something, they just come out and get it and nothing can hold them back, locked doors included."

It was at this moment I remembered the steel doors that Neil Farris had installed in his office, two of them closing out either ends of the hallway. I'd changed them the first week I moved in. All of a sudden, I wished I hadn't.

"And last night," he continued, "they decided to take Rosy. They found a way into the house, don't ask me how, and they snatched her from our bed. Jesus, I didn't even know it'd happened until I got up in the morning and saw that Rosy was gone."

I rubbed my lips, swallowed something hard and fiery in my throat. Damn it, I believed him. I didn't want to, but I did. Still, I had to come at him with some kind of off-pitch angle, an innocent-until-proven-guilty kind of perspective. "Phil, are you sure she just didn't get up and leave? I mean, how do you know she was actually kidnapped?"

"Kidnapped? Did I say she was kidnapped, Michael? No . . . they *kidnapped* her the first time, and just look at how they brought her back to me, all *chewed up,* and there wasn't one doctor at Ellenville Hospital that'd been willing to help her. They knew what they would've been in for if they had. Oh, thank God for Neil Farris, God bless his soul, he took care of my Rosy, although now I wonder if it'd all been worth it. She suffered like a bastard for the past five years, lived in constant fear. And then Neil, he paid the price."

"So Neil wasn't killed by a dog then."

"No, no." He closed his eyes, coughed, then added,

"He was killed by *them*. And so was my Rosy."

I placed a tense fist against my chin. "You said that they took her from your bed."

"Yes . . ."

"And killed her."

"Yes."

"So where's her body, Phil?"

He looked up at me, eyes blank and looking over my shoulder as if Death itself had been standing behind me, tuning into our conversation.

"Ain't no body. They killed her . . . right in my bedroom, while I was asleep, then took her away. That's what they always do."

The deer, gone. Lauren Hunter, gone . . .

Despite everything I'd seen and heard and experienced, I was still having trouble believing him. Denial, in all its glory. "Tell me something, Phil. If there's no body, then how do you know she's really dead? Perhaps she's still alive, someplace we can find her."

He shook his head no. Then he blew me away.

Eyes pinning mine, Phillip Deighton reached into the left pocket of his denim jacket. He pulled out a small Ziploc bag. Inside were a pair of human eyes, plus a hunk of gray blood-matted hair.

I stepped back against the porch railing, shocked, utterly repulsed, not only by the contents of the bag, but also by the fact that Phillip had picked them up and was now dangling them between us like a sick show-and-tell exhibit. Instantly I hated Phillip, feared him, felt an uncommon dislike simply standing here before his frail form. I took a deep breath. A breeze swept by; the late July air felt cold and slimy. It brought something awful-smelling, like rotten fruit. Phillip put the bag back into his pocket—the eyes made a soft bloody squelching noise as he did this—my gaze following the slow rhythm of his movement as though hypnotized by it. He then put his hands in his lap and began rocking gently back and forth.

Now a familiar sense of fear prevailed, and I wondered for a fleeting moment if Christine had any inkling of the *real* danger that existed here. Probably not. I looked into the darkness of the house, the single glow of the kitchen chandelier barely making its way to the front door. The living room furniture sat like phantoms in the dark, their hulks intimidating in their motionlessness. Upstairs, my family slept, unaware of the dangers lurking. What they knew was nothing compared to the true dangers lying beneath the surface. My job was to convince them of their presence before we too fell victim to their dark intentions.

But even if you do convince Christine of the dangers here, Michael, how do you intend to leave with no means of transportation?

Phillip.

"Phillip?"

He remained silent, gaze cast down. He looked pathetic, he needed to be institutionalized. I wasn't too far behind. "I've no more reason to live, Michael. I failed them once again, and now they will haunt me until they decide it's my time. I'm fucked, royally fucked."

You've been royally fucked for a long, long time. . . .

Feeling dizzy, I leaned back against the railing, and even though I had a very strong inkling, I still asked, "What do you mean that 'you've failed them once again'?" I thought about what he told me in the woods that day, about how they'd taken his daughter, and then what they apparently did to Rosy.

How he'd "failed them" in the past.

Finally he peered up at me. He looked like he'd been through a hell of a war, cheeks hollowed, eyes dark and sunken. "I told you all about it when we went into the woods that day, when I showed you their shrine." He paused. "All the residents of Ashborough must make a sacrifice to the Isolates. And the sacrifice must be alive at the time of offering." It'd haunted me, and damn near murdered me now to hear it again from his lips.

"I'd told you all about this," he continued, "about the legend, about how Old Lady Zellis had told me the brutal truth all those years ago. It'd been her duty back then to warn folks of the law here in Ashborough. But not anymore, no, she's old and weary . . . has been for at least twenty years now. Now we do it, the townsfolk. And it was my duty as your closest neighbor to get you to make a sacrifice. I failed. You didn't do it. And because of that, they took Rosy from me."

"It was you who put the deer in the shed, wasn't it?"

He nodded, eyes downcast, looking weak and ashamed. "Both of them. I'd assumed you'd thought I was a bit nuts, and rightly so, after the whole grand tale I told you. I mean, I would've too if I were in your shoes. But I still needed to convince you that the sacrifice had to be made, and if I kept telling you to do it, then

165

you'd've thought I was totally out of my mind and you'd've very quickly separated yourself and your family from me and Rosy. You know what I'm saying? Stay away from crazy Phil, old bastard's a few cards short of a full deck. Still, I knew that if I'd just planted a seed in your head, it just might germinate and you'd start thinking seriously about the sacrifice, and maybe heed my warning. As it it turns out, it didn't work."

"So you put the deer in the shed hoping that I'd haul it up there on their stone."

"Yes . . . I had no choice but to try."

"What about the woman, Phillip? Did you send her to me as well?" My voice had a sudden shaky, distracted tone to it, one barely recognizable as my own. This was fear of my neighbor answering *yes* to this question. *That'd be the icing on the cake: My closest neighbor is a homicidal maniac too.* . . .

He looked up at me, face gone to stone with shock. "What woman?"

"One of my patients, Lauren Hunter. Lived on the east side of town. She was severely mutilated in the woods just outside my house. Spent her last breathing moments crawling to my door. Bled to death before I could get help."

"When did this happen?"

"Today."

He shook his head defiantly, burying his face in his hands. "They did it . . . they were testing you to see if you'd make the sacrifice. They're very serious about the games they play." He paused again. "Did they come for the body after she died?"

My heart started banging against my rib cage. "Yes . . . the deer too."

He nodded. "It's their way of telling you that you missed your opportunity, and that you should prepare for the next one. Dear God, Michael," he cried, raising his voice. "Make the sacrifice now, tonight, before they come for Jessica or Christine!"

A series of emotions rose up inside me: fear, anger, frustration, all rolled up into one evil brew. It made me aggressive, and I responded by grabbing Phillip by the collar. "*Damn you, Phillip! Why didn't you warn me the first day I moved in!*" He fell limp in my grasp, like a bag of oats. I let him go and he slumped in the chair. "You were so cordial and kind that day, offering us lunch, and all along you knew that my family was in grave danger, you . . . you fucking fraud!"

"I couldn't tell you!" he shouted, then took a few short breaths and continued more quietly as if realizing that he might wake up the girls. "They hear what's going on, Michael. They listen to our conversations . . . any time they want to. Don't ask me how they do it, could be super hearing, radio signals, ESP. I don't know. If I'd said anything to you that could've been interpreted as a warning, they might've killed me, or Rosy. Understand . . . I couldn't mention it at the time. That's why I sent you upstairs, into my bedroom. I knew that if you'd seen Rosy, it might've clued you in to the evil that exists here."

I cooled down, nodded, a kaleidoscope of images twisting throughout my mind. *Neil Farris, Rosy Deighton, Lauren Hunter. All dead, all dead.* "I did wonder

167

what had happened to her. I also wondered if Neil Farris's bad luck had come from the same source. I started putting the pieces together, thinking along the lines of a wild animal attack. I guess I was in the ballpark, sort of." I raised a hand to my mouth and chewed a firm nail. "You know . . . she said something to me that day."

Neil stared up at me, looking intensely interested.

"She mentioned that they were going to come for me, just like they did for Farris, and everyone else in the godforsaken town. As she put it."

"She tried to warn you. It wasn't her duty to do so. It did her no good."

"Then my patient, Lauren . . . just moments before her death she said that they were coming for me. Phil . . . she said my wife's name. I'm telling you, she must've done some checking up on me 'cause I'd never mentioned Christine to her before."

Phillip shook his head, eyes tearing. He sobbed a bit. "I'm not in the right frame of mind just now, and if I was, I'm not sure I'd know what to make of that. Could be your patient might've known something. Or . . ."

"Or what?"

"She could've heard them talking."

"What? Talking? Are you fucking kidding me?" I heard a sudden rustling in the trees alongside the house, somewhere close to the scene of Lauren's murder. I cut myself off, looked that way, squinting deep into the darkness of the woods and becoming vaguely aware of the breeze and the odd coolness and faint rotting-vegetables odor it carried. It was terribly unpleasant, poisonous perhaps. My heart slammed so hard against my chest, I thought it might soon burst. I looked back at Phil, who leaned his weight on the chair and stood. He replaced his Red Sox hat. I looked at his jacket pocket, the juicy tip of the Ziploc bag peeking out.

"I need to go back home, Michael," he said, eyes darting toward the woods. *Paranoia—here's a living breathing example of it in action.* "I'm not sure how many days I have left there," he added, at once anxious to get away.

"Phil . . ."

Here we go . . . do or die . . .

"Christine had an accident with the car today, and . . . and I tried to find some means of transportation, but I couldn't. Damn it, Phil . . . I want out of here. Now. Tonight. Let's take your car, all of us, leave this fucking hellhole." Automatically, I kept shooting glances back toward the woods.

(Paranoia.)

Are they out there now, watching? Listening?

Phillip laughed incredulously, loaded with mad volume. His tears were gone, but his body twitched as if he'd been prodded with a slight charge. He looked like a man who'd just discovered a swarm of ants beneath his clothes. He staggered down the porch steps and, in mid-stride, turned to look at me. "You ever see me drive, Michael?"

Damn . . . I hadn't. Come to think of it, I hadn't done much of anything since moving to Ashborough. Christine had done most of the shopping and escorting Jessica into town or the park. I'd left 17 Harlan Road perhaps a half-dozen times since moving here (excluding lunches with the Deightons), all of those short excursions into town with Christine and Jessica, once to the school, a few times to the hardware store, once for a haircut at the barbershop. Other than that, I'd been your typical work-out-of-the-home doctor with a grand old office to delight myself in . . . just what I'd always wanted.

Yeah, just what I always fucking wanted.

I shook my head.

"Haven't driven anywhere in four years. They won't let me. Seems as though they don't want you to either." Phillip turned and walked down the front path.

"Christine hit a dog," I said unconvincingly, taking the steps to the bottom. "We should have the car back in . . ." *Jesus, how long did she say?*

At the end of the path, Phillip turned and yelled, "Michael, I've got some very sad news for you . . . you're never gonna see your car again."

My heart leaped up into my throat, one powerful beat at a time. I wanted to cry, and might have if it hadn't been for the sudden anger swallowing up my fear. "Fuck you, Phil! I thought you were a friend. You fucking used us, now we're screwed like the rest of the poor bastards in this goddamned town!"

"I'm sorry, Michael . . . I wish I could help you, but I can't even help myself."

I started walking toward him. "I'll fucking walk out of here. Twelve miles to Ellenville? No problem. I'll get help there." I was starting to lose it. I could feel the gears slipping in my head.

Phillip, still walking away, shook his head and yelled, "Nobody there's gonna help you. Nobody here either. Besides," he said, stopping and pointing into the woods, "you won't get very far. You already know that Neil Farris wasn't out for a casual jog. Just like so many others, he'd tried to leave. And *they* got in the way."

I stopped, feeling suddenly defeated. "Fuck you," I said quietly, not sure if he heard me or not. Didn't matter.

Phillip started a slow jog down the driveway, the lamplights creating monolithic shadows of his body. "Good-bye, Michael," he called, then started crying out loud.

I stayed outside, at first watching Phillip, then staring into the woods, all the while listening to his cries until he disappeared around the curve a hundred yards away down Harlan Road.

Chapter Nineteen

Hours later, something woke me. A dog barking. Outside. I opened my eyes and realized that I'd been sleeping in Jessica's bed. Second night in a row.

My memory fell into a bit of a cloud; perhaps my subconscious was attempting to suppress the unpleasant events of the day. But the image of Lauren's death was too strong and haunted me like a ghostly illusion, as though her bloody soul had slid under the sheets with me and hugged me with the intent of chilling me to the bone.

At once I thought of Phillip, of how he'd betrayed me to protect himself and his family—all along he'd been playing his little role in this great conspiracy. Whether or not there existed an ancient race of people living in the woods, or even some sick band of cultists (suddenly the latter seemed to make more sense), I needed to protect my family from them, and that meant leaving here as soon as possible.

After Phillip had left, I came back into the house with the intention of standing guard until the morning. With all the horror and fear and anxiety racing through my body, I felt I had no choice but to stay awake while they peacefully slept, unaware of the dangers surrounding them. But then my body crashed and I found myself crawling atop Jessica's bed, putting my chin on the sill and peering out the window into the yard, seeing only the shadows of swaying trees before falling asleep.

I didn't remember dreaming, but it seemed as though the barking dog had somehow infiltrated my subconscious. Dazed, I sat up in bed. The world around me felt strangely intangible, as though I'd been put under hypnosis. I looked around. The dolls on Jessica's bureau sat like vague growths in the forest, dark and indistinct. I crawled to the window and looked outside, as I did earlier before falling asleep. Jimmy Page lay on his haunches below, out on the lawn. Gazing up at me. He barked again, then sprang across the walkway to the side of the house.

I tossed the covers aside and rolled my legs off the edge of the bed. The wood floor was cold on my feet; it sent a shiver racing across my back. On the floor next to my feet lay the head of one of Jessica's dolls—the same one that'd fallen off some nights ago. Its eyes stared up at me, two dark glossy orbs, bristly red hair splayed out behind it like anemone tentacles. The lids blinked, once at first, then again and again in a methodical fashion, producing a faint *clicking* beat; there hadn't been a breeze in the room—the window was shut—so I couldn't blame the movement on this. I looked to the shelf. One of the dolls had indeed lost its head—there was a gap in the collective shadow of dolls that wasn't there before. I closed my eyes and rubbed them. When I opened them, I saw that the head had vanished from the floor. I looked over at the bureau again. There it was, back in its place, sitting firmly atop the plastic body it belonged to.

This is a dream, Michael. You're dreaming. . . .

Page barked again. It sounded distant and echoey. Yet . . . stunningly lucid for a dream. I paced from the room, feeling as if my feet were floating inches above the floor. My body still felt cumbersome and heavy, and it took quite an effort to simply move. I turned on the landing and took the stairs one at a time, the runner itching against my feet despite the "floaty" sensation. The polished banister was thick in my grasp. I never remembered having a dream so . . . so *real*.

I crossed the living room into the kitchen, then followed the hallway (with its nice new hollow-and-rather-insecure cutout doors) into the waiting room of my office. I could hear Page barking outside just beyond the entrance, wanting to be let in. I opened the door. Indeed Page was there. But instead of clawing at the door, he bounded away ten feet, then turned around and looked at me and started barking again. I recognized this little doggy gesture; he'd done it before. It basically said, *C'mon Daddy, this way, I want to show you something*. I went outside and nearly tripped over my boots, which were still damp from my attempt to wash them that afternoon. I slid my feet in them, then walked across the back lawn to where Page stood. He barked one more time, then raced to the shed

(the shed)

where he stood and waited . . . presumably for me to follow. I stepped closer to him, and could see in the faint moonlight streaks of wet blood jeweling his furry face. It was on his paws and body too. I swallowed a very real-feeling lump in my throat, then stopped, five feet from the shed.

I looked at the slightly ajar door, twisted my head in an effort to peer into its depths. It began to move, swaying at first as if perhaps caught in the embrace of a breeze. Then, ever so slowly, it opened, the rusty hinges creaking like ghosts riding the beams of a haunted house.

From the darkness within, I heard a noise. A shuffling.

Something . . . was . . . coming . . . out.

I saw the head first. Then the body.

A deer.

Not just a deer. *The* deer.

It stood just beyond the entrance of the shed, its head crushed in, a black blotch of blood marring its neck. Its ribs jutted like white chalk lines. A wet organ dangled from its gut like a piece of peeled fruit.

I looked at my surroundings. The scene was deadly silent . . . no birds chirped, not a cricket sang. Even Page sat mute, looking up at me with soulful eyes, the moonlight reflecting glossily off the blood on his muzzle. I looked back at the deer. Somehow it had returned from the dead, its intentions dreadfully unknown. It stared at me with its one good eye (the other had vacated the socket, leaving a dark moist void behind like a rotting hole in a peach), then limped up the path into the woods. Page yipped, and followed. I stayed motionless, watching the two animals walking side by side like animated characters in a sick cartoon. They stopped momentarily, turned back to look at me. Waited. Waited for me to follow. Which I eventually did.

Surprisingly enough, I felt no fear, and understood why almost immediately. This was a dream. Dead animals do not walk, and definitely do not request my presence—even live animals don't do that. Well, maybe Page did sometimes . . . but somehow, here, he acted differently. He had an almost human quality to him, lending even more credence to the fact that at this very moment I was home in my bed, under the sheets, eyes rolling feverishly beneath my lids.

Strangely enticed, I pursued the animals into the woods. The deer bounded off at breakneck speed. Page barked at me to follow and I picked up the pace, walking briskly to the spots where he would stop so I could catch up. The path wound in and about the trees; the deer would appear out of nowhere at times, like magic, sometimes right next to me, other times in the distance. And then, just as swiftly as it would materialize, it would disappear, as if it'd been obliterated from my memory. For a brief moment I wondered why dream characters often pulled this stunt . . . perhaps there was some grand scheme going on in one's subconscious, a system or methodology that for some reason also sent you back to college butt-naked, late for an exam you didn't study for, or to the supermarket where, if you were lucky, you might find yourself playing hide-the-salami with the cute cashier in the produce aisle. Some things we simply didn't have answers for. This was one of them.

Page and the deer pressed on. I followed them, never once straying from the path. Everything felt so damn real. I could feel the brambled woodland beneath my boots: the sticks, the roots, the soil. The night wind was cool against my bare legs and arms. At one point my forehead found a low-lying pine branch; the needles pricked painfully against my skin.

Despite my lucidity and sense of control, I wasn't enjoying this dream at all. I told myself that in lucid dreams you could wake up at any time if you wanted to . . . all you had to do was try. I tried . . . but with no success. And as a result found myself suddenly riddled with apprehension. This dream held me in a very powerful grasp, one that would keep me here until I woke up—at which point I'd probably scoff cockily at all its incongruities. So I prayed for morning, wanting very badly to wake up—I felt no want nor desire to follow my little cocker spaniel and a zombie deer up into the circle of stones, the shrine of the Isolates. A place I didn't want to be. Dream or not.

The animal can't be dead . . . it has to be sacrificed on the big stone.

But like a fly caught in a web, I felt no alternative but to allow fate to run its course. I followed the animals, feeling as if *I* had been leashed and led along the path. I coursed over all the familiar rises and dips, high up into the woodland. The distance didn't appear to vary much from my real-life trek up here with Phillip. Neither did the environs: the ground got very soft in spots, my boots squelching in some awful muddied puddles. The trees towered over me like skyscrapers.

Eventually, in the same amount of time it took me and Phillip to get there, I crossed the perimeter of the circle of oaks into the shrine of ancient white stones.

Almost immediately I began to experience pure fear again. It hit me like a sandstorm in a gale, whippingly powerful and relentless. The world spun giddily. Oh, God, would I live through this?

It seemed too horrific to be true (again I had to remind myself that this was nothing more than a very vivid dream), but here she was in all her slaughtered glory: Rosy Deighton. She was slumped on the big center slab, body facing skyward, arms stretched out over her head and dangling off the edge, fingertips in the dirt. Her nightgown fell in silky tatters across her gutted torso, entrails stripped and lying prone to the canopy above. Slivers of moonlight trickled through the silent leaves, igniting her still-open eyes like two silver gems. I never felt so doomed in my life, the horror of her glistening organs exposed to the elements torturing me just as much as the age-old scars still visible on her skin.

I realized now that this was more than just a dream. It was a horrid form of trauma, one that had me hypnotized and wholly dominated. In a way it taunted me and made me realize that despite my years of schooling and professional experience, there was nothing I could do to save Rosy Deighton. Or Lauren Hunter. And perhaps, I realized with phenomenal dread, my family.

A silent breeze picked up, pushing the branches of the canopy aside, bathing the center stone with horrid radiance. The Stonehenge-like stones, in all their towering brilliance, cast dark chiseled shadows across the entire area.

Page and the deer stopped alongside the center slab. My playful little cocker spaniel leaped up into the stone and settled down between Rosy's legs, duly burying his tongue in her open cavity. The deer barked once, and Page looked up at me, bloody maw shriveled back from his teeth. His once-golden coat lay matted against his body in a ghostly phosphorescent hue, gray and spotted with blackened smudges.

The dog jumped down from the rock.

Rosy Deighton began to move.

First one arm, which had been horribly dislocated from the shoulder like a section of loose rope, twitched a few times, then swung forward in a quick-jerk maneuver across her chest. Then her eyes, which had already been open, grew even wider and rolled in their bloodied sockets; crimson teardrops trickled down her cheeks. Her mouth—that ghastly black maw—moved in its only one possible quiver, spewing forth an alarming blend of coagulated fluids and gurgling moans. She sat up horridly fast as if controlled by strings, then looked at me, eyes still rolling, mouth still chomping.

Pure fear felt like a fairy tale at this moment . . . the

horror, the terror I felt was unfathomable. It rose in me and filled me up so much that I simply couldn't take it anymore. I felt as if I might very well implode . . . but at this point realized with dismay that I'd have to begin the horror anew, because in dreams one never really dies. You wake up on impact.

I'd woken up, all right . . . right back into the dream. The *real* waking world wouldn't come until this script had run its course to the very bitter end.

As if pulled by ghosts, Rosy rolled off the surface of the stone onto the forest floor. A small cloud of dust rose around her fallen body, which lay utterly motionless while her head twisted and jerked on its own accord, the maw spitting inhuman growls.

Michael . . .

I heard my name being called, a woman's voice, sweetly nice and tender. Yet . . . it rode a haunted echo, proof of otherworldly origins. *It's nothing but a dream voice, nothing but a dream voice.* . . . I peered in the direction of the voice—to my right—and shoved my fist in my mouth to keep from screaming, realizing from the moisture on my cheeks that I'd been weeping uncontrollably. A new horror stood before me . . . one too vast, too extensive to accept.

Lauren Hunter was here too, walking out from behind one of the stones. She leaned crookedly against the white slab, half her skinned face covered in dried blood, her hair a nappy padded mess. She smiled maniacally—a taunting rictus grin of death rife with chattering teeth—then creeped across to the front of the stone, dragging her intestinal leash along with her, which snaked away from her body around the back of the stone, dried out and peppered with flakings of twigs, leaves, and soil. She staggered toward me, arms outstretched, smile wide and frozen, head bobbing in a blackly comical way. So goes the cliche: She looked like a fucking rag doll.

The last remnants of my lucid mind tried desperately to wish it all away. I even closed my eyes and thought maybe, just maybe, I'd find myself naked in the classroom porking the supermarket cashier.

I opened my eyes.

She was still there.

Closer. Still smiling. Reaching for me. Tendrils of green smoke seeped from the open wound in her torso.

I tried to scream. Nothing came.

She stopped, as if surprised by my failed attempt to wake up. Her smile disappeared. "The animal must be alive at the time of sacrifice." Her body jerked and twitched. Her eyes turned up their sockets, exposing pus-blood whites.

I looked back at the center stone. Page was there, on all fours, tongue lolling from his bloody mouth. He panted, in a respite so it seemed. I staggered over to the center stone and fell to my knees before the dog; the earth felt soft and moist on my knees. Lauren Hunter walked over too, fell on the ground beside the sprawled body of Rosy Deighton. The deer had pulled another vanishing act. Both of them stared at me, Lauren in a direct line of vision despite lying on the ground, Rosy in a sidelong glance, unable to twist her inverted head in my direction. Each of them seemed to exhibit a bit of empathy—or so my imagination told me—but these looks were more likely consents: go-aheads to commence a very tragic resolution.

I wanted to scream, but didn't. I knew it wouldn't come.

"Do it," Lauren said. Rosy said something too, but the words were unintelligible. Still, the meaning was there. It was time to make the sacrifice to the Isolates. No avoiding it now.

This is just a dream, just a dream, just a dream . . .

"The animal must be alive at the time of sacrifice, or you and the ones you love will fall prey to ruination." A breeze picked up and carried Lauren's threat into my lungs—I could taste the rot of her words on my tongue.

I looked at my dog. Jessica's dog. My mind struggled with the thought.

Do it, Michael, do it like they say, and then the game will be over, and so will the dream, and you will wake up in bed with the morning at your disposal, plus the entire day to flee Ashborough.

I reached over, petted the dog's fur. Sticky blood filled my hand.

I took my other hand, placed it around the dog's neck. Page didn't resist.

I squeezed.

Hard.

Harder.

I pressed his skull against the stone.

I felt bones moving. Snapping somewhere in his head. Something warm seeped from his mouth.

I looked toward the woods, unable to witness my own crime.

Oh, my God . . .

What the hell . . . ?

The woods . . . they were filled with golden lights. Hundreds of them at varying distances, floating indiscernibly in and about the trees and copses.

Staring at the lights, I slammed Page's skull against the center stone, over and over again, until the world and those ghostly golden lights whisked away from me in a dark swirl of ugly gray tones.

Chapter Twenty

"Mommy!"

I heard Jessica's voice, as crystal clear as any reality that had come my way over the years. Yet I immediately thought it was another dream—another dreadful nightmare. I heard some noises, pots and pans banging, the scrape of something plastic.

"Come here, honey . . . don't go outside."

Christine's voice, keeping a leash on our daughter. I opened my eyes, still assuming that this was all a dream: my tempered breathing, the sun-specked walls, the dolls in Jessica's room meeting my tired gaze. I felt no less alert than I had last night when I began my journey.

I stretched out under the sheets, feeling like a swimmer coming up from the bottom of a deep pool, reality's light growing clearer and brighter as I waded toward the stirring surface.

"Mommy! I want to go look for Page!"

Jessica's voice came through loud and clear, her call to Christine from somewhere near the bottom of the steps a "real world" shove through my dream-water's surface: I'd woken up. This was no illusion. To be sure, I remained silent and still for at least five minutes, listening to their conversation as it filtered into my blooming consciousness.

And thinking of Page.

It was all a dream, nothing more than a crazy, nutty dream. And that was simply good and fine, a nice little positive in a world suddenly exploding with negatives. But there were still all those negatives to contend with. No small potatoes.

Speaking of which, the smell of something cooking wafted upstairs. Eggs, home fries, bacon. My stomach growled. Despite my torment (and a bastard of a headache), I smiled. This was perhaps Christine's way of making up—I'd done the same exact thing yesterday in an effort to mend a hole in our relationship. A nice warm meal would feel plenty good right now, and might be in order before breaking the news to the family that we'd be leaving Ashborough immediately, once and for all. Car or no car.

Neil Farris . . . dead.

Lauren Hunter . . . dead.

Rosy Deighton . . . dead.

Jimmy Page . . . dead?

Jessica's voice came from downstairs: "Can I wake up Daddy? He'll help me look for Page."

Christine: "We have no car right now, honey. It's in

185

the shop. Don't worry, Page'll come back. We'll go out and call for him when Daddy gets up."

I looked toward the window. Jessica's dolls were there, all of them, heads included. Sunlight poked through creases in the blind, slashing the walls and floor. The clock said it was nearly nine o'clock; apparently Christine had decided to let me sleep in today. She and Jessica had turned in rather early last night, and probably got up at the crack of dawn to do this, that, and the other thing. I wondered with no care at all as to whether I had an appointment due to arrive at any moment. Apparently Christine didn't give a hoot either. If this were any other day, I'd've been pissed off, and would have let Christine know all about it too.

But today . . . it was different now, wasn't it? The world had taken on a new perspective. There'd be no time nor energy to be angry. It all had to be aimed toward my new directive: the safety of my family.

I heard Christine make a *hum* sound and clang more pots and pans. There were some footsteps, then a call from the bottom of the steps. "Michael, I think there's someone knocking on the office door."

Shit. I'd had an appointment after all. They'll have to wait. "Christine, could you lean out the kitchen window, tell them to wait about ten—"

At this very moment I glanced down at my hands, and my words hit a roadblock.

My hands were covered with blood.

My breathing immediately went shallow, came in painful bursts. My heart jostled in my chest like a punching bag. In a panic, jaw locked, skin crawling, I ripped the covers aside. *Jesus*. Messy streaks of blood, everywhere, staining the cool beige sateen. I looked at my hands again.

There were coarse hairs all over them, stuck in the blood like insects on flypaper. They were wedged under my nails.

Dog hairs.

Jesus Christ . . . I feel as if I'm going to die. I think I'm having a heart attack.

A cannonball of terror blasted up from inside me, suffocating me as it lodged itself in my throat. The real world had taken on another identity, one that consisted solely of fragments that'd seeped their way in from my dreams. I plucked a single hair from my hand, held it up, and peered at it curiously. Brown, caked with blood.

Jimmy Page's hair.

Now was the time to pack it all in, to pull the tainted covers over my head and allow the madness to assume control of my mind. It'd be so much easier to live the rest of my life via straitjacket and padded room.

"Michael, did you hear me? There's an elderly woman outside. She must have an appointment with you."

I stayed unanswering, my words still held captive.

"Michael?"

I thought I heard her coming upstairs, a bang or two near the bottom of the steps. I scrambled in a panic, pulling the sheets back over my body, keeping my hands way down below, near my hips. There was no viable excuse for my appearance, except perhaps that

I'd killed someone or something in the middle of the night. Which, boys and girls, I apparently had.

"I'll be down in a few minutes," I answered as loudly and as optimistically as possible. "I . . . I have a stomachache. Tell her to give me about ten minutes." My mind screamed with confusion, and nothing I could say would make any sense to me. It all seemed a blur.

There was another bang near the bottom of the steps. Christine, placing some objects on the lower steps to be carried up later. Not coming up, thank God.

"I need to go to the bathroom," I called. "I'll be down in a few." The words felt like rubber balls on my tongue, bouncing away with no meaningful destination.

"I made you breakfast. It'll be in the microwave when you get down. I'll offer the woman some tea and let her into the office."

"Okay."

I heard her walk away, back into the kitchen. I ran a hand over my eyes, unaware until now that I was probably smearing Page's blood all over on my face. In another wave of panic, I jerked my eyes open for fear of falling back into a dream and seeing myself face-to-face again with Lauren, Rosy, or even Page; I couldn't let that happen again, not now. I got up in a hurry, yanked the sheets off, and shoved them under the bed. Then I went into the bathroom and ran the water until it began to steam, keeping my gaze away from the mirror for fear of what I might find. *Blood, blood, everywhere!*

The hot water felt like a godsend. I soaped my hands and face, scrubbed them clean, feeling as though I might even be washing away the very real events of my dream.

I toweled down, then got dressed in a rush. During this time, the tears came and I cried my eyes out, so strongly that my chest burned as I gasped for air. I was terribly afraid, not only of everything that'd happened, but also of what might happen. Eventually my cries tapered away and I dried my face with the damp towel. Feeling a bit more in control, I retrieved a set of clean sheets from the linen closet in the hall. I left the blood-stained ones under Jessica's bed, where I hoped they would remain forever, at least until after we were gone. I put the clean ones on, telling myself that simply sleeping in them for two nights in a row would serve as an acceptable reason for changing them.

I went downstairs into the kitchen. Christine had a purse draped over her shoulder. Jessica held Page's leash and was tapping the floor in a forward motion as if tethering an invisible puppy. The scene had been cleared of all breakfast-making evidence, with the exception of a pitcher of dark green tea—Rosy Deighton's recipe.

Rosy Deighton . . .

Christine offered up a forced smile. Clearly she noticed my face, eyes red and puffy. "You okay, Michael? Heard you crying upstairs." She said this so matter-of-factly, without an ounce of concern. Apparently she was still sore at me; last thing she'd want to do now was leave town.

"I . . ." I was at a loss for words. My family was hustling and bustling about the house as if there was nothing wrong. *As if there was nothing wrong! Michael, the only thing they've experienced is a bad traffic accident and some very creepy people. Well, those very creepy people are reason enough to get the hell out of here! Hauling dead bodies away? See you later, folks!*

"Christine," I said, grabbing her arm as she cold-shouldered by me. "We need to get out of here. Out of Ashborough. Now."

She turned to Jessica, who was standing by the front door. "Honey, could you please wait outside on the porch?" Jessica nodded, then left the house in silence; I saw her plop down in one of the rattan chairs on the porch. Christine looked back at me, eyebrows triangled with anger. "Michael, what in God's name are you talking about?" She pulled away from my grasp, as if I were some wild-eyed stranger accosting her in the street.

"Things . . . things just aren't right here. You'd said so yourself. Those people yesterday, the ones that dragged the body into the house after your accident—that's not normal, Christine. It's fucking freaky."

"Well, maybe I overreacted, Michael. They probably just wanted to get him into some shelter."

"Shelter from what? You said you killed him, that his head exploded when it hit a tree!"

"Well, it looked that way . . . but I was in a bit of a panic at the time and, well, I just didn't have my wits about me. It looked that way, but I couldn't tell for sure. He may have just hurt himself."

"Just hurt himself? How could you not tell? Jesus, Christine, you said they covered him in a blanket before carrying him inside!"

"Well, yes, I did see that."

"So?"

190

"So it's certainly no reason to leave here. What's gotten into you, Michael?"

"What's gotten into me?" Now I was yelling. Actually screaming. My faculties had just hurdled the first drop on the emotional roller coaster and were now plunging down at top speed. "This town is fucking cursed! We need to get out of here, now!" I was repeating myself, and not getting my point across.

She shook her head. "You're out of your mind. . . ." Then: "Are you taking something?"

I didn't want to say it, but I had to. I had to mention the existence of the Isolates. To Christine it would appear utterly irrational—I had no plausible evidence nor proof to back me up. It was my word against the world's, one David against a million Goliaths. My revelation would appear as the ravings of a madman. But Jesus, did I have any other option at the moment?

"Christine—"

But then she said, "I'm taking Jessica out to look for Page. Your daughter is very upset, and frankly, I am too—"

I grabbed her arm again. She tried to wrest away, but I held on tight. Our eyes locked. "Listen to me Christine . . . there's something evil living here, in the woods. A race of people called the Isolates. They're keeping the entire town hostage. I know this sounds insane but I beg you to believe me. Please, we need to leave here now. We'll walk . . . or take the bikes. Please."

I loosened my grasp and she gently pulled away, keeping fearful eyes on me. I thought for a moment that she might've believed me. Then she said, "Where'd you get this crazy idea?"

I swallowed something cottonlike in my throat. "Phillip told me all about them. He said—"

"You're kidding me, right?"

"No, he told me not to say anything to you . . . but I felt it was the only way I could convince you that we had to leave here. Christine, please, I implore you. Let's get out of here right this minute. Once we get out of here I'll explain everything to you."

She moved toward the stairs, grabbed her house keys, which had been tossed amongst some other things on the third step. "Did you mention anything about this to Jessica?"

"Of course not." I felt suddenly winded and crashed down on the sofa, wondering just where I'd find the energy to either walk or run out of here. Then Phillip Deighton's words entered my mind: *Neil Farris wasn't out for a casual jog, you know. Just like so many others, he'd tried to leave. And they got in the way.* I shuddered.

"I doubt very much that Jessica got frightened yesterday just from the ghosts on some idiot cartoon."

"Jesus, Christine, are you implying that I had something to do with that?"

She walked to the door. Jessica rose from the chair outside and stood on the porch, looking in at us with wide concerned eyes. Christine shook her head, clearly dismayed. "I suggest you go to your office and see your patient. It might do you some good. We're gonna go out and look for Page. Take a few moments to think about what you're saying, Michael. Hopefully, by the time we get back you'll have some better explanation for this behavior of yours. See you later." She walked out, the screen door hitting the jamb in an unintentional slam.

Utterly frustrated, I began to giggle. Then I broke out in laughter. I couldn't stop. It occurred to me that fear might make a person do something irrational, totally absurd even. Here I was doing just that: laughing up a storm. But in a minute the laughter subsided, and I paced to the window. My wife and daughter were walking hand-in-hand down the driveway, calling out for a dog that would never be coming home again.

This made me laugh again. Even harder.

Chapter Twenty-one

When the laughter evaporated, I went into the kitchen and heated up the breakfast Christine had left for me. I ate it and washed it all down with some tepid coffee, which at once made me feel better. I realized then that from Christine's point of view I must've appeared crazy. She hadn't the slightest clue about my encounter with Lauren Hunter or about my dream, which apparently wasn't a dream after all. Plus she'd had an experience of her own yesterday, and although she'd broken down a bit, she also appeared to have rebounded nicely after a good night's sleep. To the unknowing and stable frame of mind, I looked like the lunatic I clearly imagined myself to be.

I suddenly remembered the bloody sheets under Jessica's bed. Before I forgot again, I raced upstairs, retrieved them, then came back down and put them in the washer, thereby eliminating the evidence. After I did this, a sense of the commonplace filtered in, and despite the cloudy sensation ushering me about, I decided to shove everything aside and move on with the day as though the war had been waged and won. *After all, Michael, the sacrifice has now been made. You've been freed. You may now live your life like any common man, woman, or child. You've paid your dues, now it's time to move on.*

Strangely enough, this idea brought on a small wave of relief, as macabre as it seemed. Perhaps things would be different now. Maybe I could go on and live the rest of my life in peace and quiet. I put my dish in the sink, then peered outside and thought about Christine. Ever since revealing her pregnancy, she'd grown irritable, impatient, yet adversely independent and distant. If I'd have come to her with a problem in the past, she would have sat down and listened intently, offering up some well-thought-out advice on how to tackle it. But lately, it appeared as if she wanted nothing to do with me, mostly seeking arguments as a way to avoid conversation. Like this morning. My overt fear and outright irrational concerns would've alarmed even a perfect stranger, much less a caring family member. Christine had brushed off my behavior as common silliness, as though I'd been joking, and gone on her merry independent way.

Suddenly, something hit me.

Lauren Hunter.

In the throes of death, she had uttered: *Christine* . . .

I shook away the alarming thought, trying to convince myself that everything would be okay now, that Christine was simply going through a hormonal-induced phase, and that her ship would settle down to earth in due time. I focused out the window into the side yard. Damn hard to believe that a death had occurred there yesterday. The sun was beaming high and proud. The blooms alongside the house tossed their balmy scent in through the windows, making everything smell fresh and clean. Summer was in full gear, and I decided that I should be happy with it. No sense in worrying about the past. If I did, then I'd definitely break down and there'd be no more Cayle family outings, no more tucking Jessica in at night, no more making love to my beautiful wife.

I looked to the right and peered down the walkway where just yesterday a woman died—where I'd washed away the bloody evidence. For a quick moment I considered trying the police again, then decided against it. Heck, I was fine with the way things were at the moment—it was all okay with me. No sense in tossing another fly in the ointment. *It's called denial!* my conscience screamed, but I shrugged that probability off defiantly. Perhaps when Christine returned later I'd feel differently, but for now maintaining my sanity was my number-one priority, and I didn't care how I went about doing it.

Yes, everything was just okay at the moment.

But that would last only a minute.

A single minute. That was how long it took me to

walk the length of the hallway into the waiting room, and then into my office, where I greeted my first patient of the day.

And fell again into terror.

Chapter Twenty-two

My mind began to whirl. I pushed it aside and walked into the patient waiting room.

For a brief moment I wondered what I must've looked like, whether the stress was showing on my face. But at this point in the game, who cared? Did it matter what my patients really thought of me? No, probably not, considering the possibility that they too were all in on the conspiracy, and that I was just a little pawn in their wicked game.

The waiting room was empty. I turned around, but curiously saw no one. The only evidence of anyone having been there was a half-filled glass of Rosy's dark green tea on the small end table alongside the couch. Absently, I walked behind the cutout and thumbed through the day-planner, locating the page for today's date.

I had no appointments scheduled for today.

Or for tomorrow. Or the next day. Or . . .

My heart rate sped up. What had started out as a busy practice had gone completely dead on me—cut off as if the patients had gone on strike. The very odd thing was that up until Lauren Hunter's death, I'd been moderately busy. But then the appointments . . . they'd stopped—the empty day-planner was the true evidence in black and white. As was the lack of messages on the answering machine. And that frightened me, not for the fact that there'd been some obvious boycott of the town physician, but because I hadn't realized up until now that I'd have absolutely no work to do from this moment forward. No source of income. *Did it really matter? Didn't you plan on leaving here anyway?*

So . . . who came by today?

And were they still here?

Christine had mentioned an elderly woman. I scanned the waiting room one more time, then peeked around the bend into the examining room. It too was empty.

That left my office.

I walked into the office, looked right and then left at the bookcases that ran the entire length of the room; the only sound was the ticking of the pendulum clock on the fireplace mantle. The tightly shuttered blinds covering the floor-to-ceiling windows closed out most of the day's light; the room swam in a gloom of dusky shadows. A gentle wind rattled the panes. Somewhere in the distance a dog barked. I thought of Page.

I strolled to the desk, looked at the papers piled there,

hands searching in my pockets. For a moment I'd for-gotten that I'd been looking for someone, and that was when the rug seemed to waver under my feet. I leaned forward, combatting the dizziness, hands now on the desk for support. I slumped into the chair and breathed heavily for a minute, trying desperately to stop the stress from taking over.

Out of the corner of my eye, I saw Page's bloody collar sitting on the far right corner of the desk.

I blinked, rubbed my eyes, wished it all away, but it came into clearer focus as my eyes adjusted to the gloom. Bits of hair jutted from the metal rivets embed-ded in the tan leather. Heart racing, I pressed my feet against the carpet to see if they still touched solid ground; I hadn't passed out yet. I surveyed the office once again, running a very quick replay of the events of the night before, and had a very solid image of the circle of stones in my head when someone spoke to me.

An old woman's voice, coming from behind me.

"Don't turn around, Michael."

A shudder of fear ran through me, so powerful it could have been charged. My lips went to speak, but only choppy air came.

"We need to talk," the voice said. The sound of it was slow and staggering. An ancient fortune-teller's words on forty years of Marlboros.

I tried to turn, but a terribly numbing discomfort struck my legs and arms. "Why can't I see you?" I asked feebly.

"You need to only listen, and nothing more. But . . .

listen good, Michael, I shall not repeat myself."

I hesitated, swallowed, eyed the liquor cabinet, and wished for some brandy. "Okay," I answered by default, nodding slightly.

"It took you time, but you did what was expected of you. Those around you are now safe . . . for the time being. But . . . they will come with more demands, and when the time comes, and it *will* come, you must be here for them, ready, willing, and able. Do not deny them. Do not resist them. Do not attempt to leave. And most importantly, do not tell a soul of this. You must isolate yourself, then adhere to my words, and to their demands."

"Who are you talking about?" I asked, feigning ignorance. I already knew she was referring to the Isolates.

"Those that govern the land. Their way is the law, and it must not be broken. He who denies their command shall suffer through the torture, pain, and mortality of their loved ones."

"God, are you saying—?"

"Do as I say, Michael . . . live your life as if nothing at all has occurred, and do nothing out of the ordinary. Separate yourself from your family, from your daughter, Jessica, and your pregnant wife, Christine. And then, when the time comes, heed their call and do as *they* say, and no harm will come to your family. Much will be expected of you. I suggest you prepare yourself. Your role is one of great importance."

"My role?" I asked, horrified.

"In time, you will find out. Remember, repeat nothing of this to anyone, most of all your family. Their lives will be taken should you not heed this warning. I promise you that."

Silence followed. I could hear the air leaving my lungs in hurried bursts. I fought the numbness in my legs and spun the chair. I used my toes against the rug to stop it, catching only a glimpse of the woman as she fled the room. It was enough to unnerve me for a lifetime.

She'd looked over her shoulder at me the moment I laid eyes on her: the magnetism of the moment carried great strength, her gaze locking not only my eyes but my entire body into full numbing inaction. It was at this moment that I realized she must've used some kind of unearthly ability to paralyze me. I could see the proof of it in her eyes.

Her golden eyes.

They lay framed in a brown-colored face chiseled with deep wrinkles; her face was craggy, with the dark grimy complexion of a woman who lived a life bathing in soil and sunlight. Gray hair fell to her shoulders in matted scraggs, dirty clothes shrouding her body like oily service-station rags. Her approximate height of four and a half feet didn't detract from her supernaturally menacing presence.

I raised a hand, tried to speak to her; a wispy "Wait" fell from my lips. Her eyes glowed gold, lighting up the corner of the room as she slipped away into the waiting room.

I forced myself to stand. My legs wobbled precariously, then gave out, and I crashed down to the floor. "Wait!" I called out again, this time louder and with a bit of newfound strength; apparently the woman's spell had left along with her. I scrambled to my knees and staggered out of the office into the waiting room. As I passed between rooms, I caught a rather unusual scent, something spicy, earthy. Like sodden leaves on a forest floor.

All that was left of her.

Old Lady Zellis.

Part Two

A Matter of When

Chapter Twenty-three

Summer segued into fall. The trees shamelessly shed their leaves after boasting a month's worth of bold colors. Jessica had started kindergarten and was in the full swing of modern education, dressing up as a bumblebee for an in-class Halloween celebration of cupcakes and candy corn, compliments of Ashborough's proud and gleaming parents. The fridge was adorned with harvest decorations, including a cock-eyed turkey with four movable tail feathers that Jessica made in school (little did Mr. Tom Turkey know, apparently, that we humans would eagerly carve up his kind after basting his sorry little ass for five hours at a blistering 450 degrees). Jessica was proud of her artistic creation and of a newfound knowledge of the peace-and-friendship Thanksgiving dinner that took place between the Pilgrims and the Indians four hundred years ago. Little did *she* know that the white man would pretty much pluck and torch those poor Indians after the celebration was over. They didn't teach land-pillaging in kindergarten.

My patients slowly but surely came back to me, and I planted myself into a comfortable routine of appointments in the morning and clerical work during the afternoon, doing chores like filling out insurance reimbursement forms and restocking medicinal supplies. Place-order applications were sent out daily along with pharmaceutical-sample requests. And then, when that was done, I'd spend the rest of the day returning phone calls and making certain that all patient records were accurately updated.

Afterwards, I'd spend some quality time with Jessica, talk to her about her day and find out what other worldly wisdom had been conveyed to her by the now famous and well-regarded Mrs. Ehlers. We'd spend dinner together as a family, eating mostly in silence, and then at eight o'clock when Jessica went to bed, I'd quietly retire into my office, pour a shot of brandy, and stare out the window into the darkness of the woods.

And wait.

Eventually I'd turn in around midnight—long after Christine went to sleep. We still slept in the same bed together, but never held each other anymore.

We also didn't speak much. This was mostly my doing. I'd gone virtually mute on her.

At first my silence angered her, then it concerned her. Then it downright frustrated her. She'd grown distant from me after getting pregnant, and I'd assumed that my silence would be mostly accepted. But soon she discovered that living with someone who refused to engage in conversation wasn't exactly what she'd wanted, and she began an ineffective struggle to get to the root of the problem—my repression, she assumed—by trying to talk to me, or yell at me, or cry out loud. Sometimes things would get really bad and she'd insist on a reason for my silence by grabbing my collar and getting right in my face like a drill sergeant, releasing tears of indignation and sometimes a sidelong fist or two. I'd squeeze my eyes shut and scream and push away from her, then flee the house and walk on down the road to Phillip Deighton's place, where we'd drink bourbon and talk about how hopelessly damned we were.

I'd talk about Christine and how she'd changed and how it nearly killed me to have cut off almost all forms of communication with her; about how our marriage was treading a very rocky surface. I'd explain that I'd gone silent on her because I was concerned I might slip up or say the wrong thing and inadvertently refer to the existence of the Isolates, who were still waiting in the wings for me, watching, listening to every word I'd said. And I knew that if I *did* say something wrong, they would punish me by hurting Christine or Jessica or even the unborn baby, just like they did to Rosy and Phillip's daughter. Just like they'd probably done to so many others too. Silence . . . it was the only protector in this instance, and I pleaded my case to Phillip time and time again, and he would nod in agreement and tell me that I was doing the right thing. He'd ask if I'd done any talking to her at all, and I'd reveal that unless it was over something completely necessary, like her pregnancy (Christine is showing quite a bit for someone only four months pregnant—they say that this always happens the second time around), or when Jessica isn't feeling well, I'd pretty much clam up and keep to myself.

And when that conversation was over, we'd begin to talk about how the time hadn't yet come for me to assume my role in the grand scheme of things. Here Phillip would turn the page and go mostly silent on me, leading me to believe that he had some knowledge as to what the Isolates had planned for me; it only stands to reason that Neil Farris may have once had this role before I came along, and now that I'm in his place . . . well, Phillip's been around long enough to know the comings and goings in these parts.

Phillip would offer up replies such as, *When the time comes, you'll know,* or, *Honestly, Michael, I've no clue as to what they might have in store for you.* I never pressed the issue. He'd been through a lot more pain and suffering than me, and it wasn't my place to dig. After all, I was doing the same thing to Christine: withholding information. And I was doing it to protect her. Perhaps Phillip was trying to protect me as well. Maybe. Then again, he might still be protecting himself. After all, his family was now gone. I've still never forgiven the man for setting me up, but he was the only damn soul I could talk to about *it*. Somehow I felt that there was a safety net around him, as if he were the only exception to the whole damned unprincipled rule. That with him, I could say anything I wanted. Apparently, it appeared this might very well have been the case, as there hadn't been a single incident at 17 Harlan Road since the night I sacrificed Page upon the center stone. And for that, I was very thankful. Without Phillip to talk to, I would have gone crazy a long time ago.

Time had passed slowly since the sacrifice, and the images of Lauren Hunter and Page (oddly, Jessica had completely forgotten about her dog; she hadn't mentioned him since the days following his "disappearance"; I considered this dismissal as yet another tiny gear in the great scheming machine) had faded from my memory. Oftentimes I wondered if Lauren Hunter had had a family, and whether or not they grieved over her disappearance. The *Ashborough Observer* never made a mention of her, or of Rosy for that matter. The only obits were for those who'd lived long and prosperous lives only to have succumbed to the God-given gift of old age. As one can well imagine, I was very thankful that the upsetting episode with Lauren had pretty much dimmed from existence: I would have had a difficult time explaining it to her family, the jury, and the judge. Now, after three months, I was able to set it aside and concentrate on the more personally pressing issues at hand, even though the images of her death still haunted me at night. Like many of my patients back in New York, she endured like a distant dream, a television show, or a resonating echo.

Isolates . . .

They want you . . . they're coming for you . . .

Christine . . .

On Thanksgiving, Christine had informed me that she

and Jessica would be having dinner with the Cleggs, a family whose son was in Jessica's kindergarten class. I'd met Mrs. Clegg only once. She'd come by the house one time to take Christine and Jessica food shopping when our car was in the shop. Seemed like a nice enough woman, but as you can probably guess, I didn't trust anyone a lick in those days.

Oh . . . the car. Another mystery in the whole Ashborough scheme. It remained in Ellenville for about a month, and during that time I stayed holed up and unspeaking in my office, catering to the few patients who slowly filtered back into my life. Christine got around by catching rides with some folks she met through Jessica's school, until the car was eventually delivered back to us in pristine shape. I wasn't able to go near it at all for fear they might come after me . . . like they did the day Christine hit the jogger (another event that had simply gone away; we never heard another single thing about that). It was my assumption that the animal she'd run over had not been a dog, but a brave, conniving little Isolate. Who knows.

Since then she'd been driving Jessica to school daily—they'd leave before I got out of bed. Then she'd run around the town, shop for groceries, perform numerous errands until school let out. Eventually she'd return home and make dinner (all she'd drink was that green herbal tea, Rosy's famous recipe; I wondered whether this was healthy for the baby, but suppressed this concern as well), at which time I'd finish up my day and sit down in silence so that I could see my family for the very first time. Very few words were exchanged between us during these tense minutes, and when all was eaten I'd shuffle Jessica off into her room to talk about her day. I felt no threat speaking to my daughter. I'm not sure why I felt this way. Perhaps her age and naiveté had something to do with it. Maybe it was because I knew the subject wouldn't ever come up.

Are you sure about that, Michael? She did mention something about ghosts one time. . . .

And then came my nights. As mentioned, I spent these hours in solitude, in my office, seated at my desk. I stared out the windows into the darkness, waiting for my beckoning from the Isolates so that I could discover my role in the grand scheme of things. Sometimes I wondered whether they'd ever come, but then I reminded myself that it was not a matter of *if*, but a matter of *when*.

One can only imagine how my mind raced during the hours of eight to twelve—four total hours of pure unadulterated hell on the brain. I thought of the past. I thought of the future. I second-guessed every move I'd made and every one I planned to make. I always thought back to that day three months before when I met Old Lady Zellis.

I knew I couldn't live like that forever. I guess I was simply waiting for them to call on me so that I could pay my dues, so to speak, and move on with my life, with my family. I still hadn't written off the possibility of getting out of there . . . I'd no definitive plan as of yet, but the boilers were roiling in the back of my mind. I'd be prepared to flee any time if the opportunity presented itself.

The very first day we moved in, I remembered an intense feeling of wanting out. It was just after Jessica had thrown up and I stepped on the nail. A feeling that I wanted to flee, on my own, back to Manhattan to start my life anew. Without my family. It'd scared me to death. I realized now that perhaps it was an omen of sorts, because two months ago I'd had the same feeling once again, and I'd considered it seriously, going so far as getting dressed in the middle of the night, fishing out Christine's keys, and walking outside to the car. I'd wondered if I was essentially murdering my family by doing this . . . if I'd left would the Isolates fulfill Old Lady Zellis's warning to me? The proof of that lay a quarter mile down the road at Phillip Deighton's house. His family had been taken away because he didn't play by the rules. But then again, Neil Farris's family had been spared (although he had not). It was a gamble . . . me or my family? The risk seemed too great.

But there I was ignoring the warning signs, standing outside at three in the morning jingling the keys to the minivan and struggling with the most insane decision I'd ever have to make. As I stood there thinking, I peered into the woods at the side of the house, and saw, as bright as beacons in the ocean, two glowing golden lights. Eyes. They were watching me. I stared at them for as long as it took me to decide that leaving might not be a good idea after all, and when I turned to go back into the house, they disappeared. I went back inside, shed my clothes, and slid back in bed. I spent the entire night gripping the sheets in my fists, dreading the fact that I'd have to start the whole damned routine all over again in the morning.

And wondering whether those eyes would ever shine through the floor-to-ceiling windows in my office, beckoning me to fulfill their demands.

My days of wondering came to an end on Thanksgiving Day.

Chapter Twenty-four

"We're leaving."

It was the first thing she'd said to me all day. Nothing out of the ordinary, I suppose. I looked at Christine. She'd gained quite a bit of weight, her stomach nearly twice the size it should've been at this stage of pregnancy. She wore a light blue sheeting maternity blouse, something left over from her pregnancy with Jessica, and a pair of jeans with a knit-stretch pouch in the front. She looked like a kangaroo, I thought crazily. Her dark puffy eyes told a miserable story, one of depression, anxiety, and sleeplessness; her mussed-up hair indicated that she hadn't the strength nor desire to disguise her unhappiness. I'd seen similar looks on some patients' faces in the past, and had treated them with heavy doses of Alprazolam or Valium. I considered offering her some medication, then realized it probably wasn't right, given her pregnancy.

I nodded in understanding. Her disgusted eyes pinned me with all the vigor they could muster, then pulled away to the floor. Jessica, also drawing back into a reclusive shell and looking a bit depressed, sidled up next to Christine and reached out for her mother's hand. Although Jessica and I still talked, the tone and length of our conversations had dropped rapidly. Pretty soon, I'd imagine, we'd end up strangers, just as Christine and I had become. God . . . as much as I hated living like this, I was not sure there was anything I could do about it unless I chose to put their lives at risk. *God forbid I utter one single word, one wrong word.*

Shouldering her bag, Christine marched to the front door, then stopped and about-faced and looked back at me. I didn't move from the safe distance of the kitchen. Tears sprouted from my eyes, and in that moment I realized for the very first time that the holidays this year were going to be intensely depressing. I'd always considered myself one of the fortunate ones, a man with a wife and daughter who cared and loved me to no end—the proud patriarch of a family whom I could love in return. Now I knew firsthand why some people threw themselves under moving trains this time of year.

"Michael . . ." I could tell she wanted to run forward, toss her arms around me, and cry it all away. But she didn't. She held her ground, steadfast. She tried to say

217

something, but all that came was a miserable choke. Soon, she was sobbing into her hands.

This was a definitive moment. I wanted to walk over and comfort my wife, tell her that everything would be all right. But doing so would make me a despicable liar. I tried to convince myself that it'd be no different from the time I'd explained to Jessica that those ghosts Page had barked at outside were fireflies. I wondered for a moment if lying in this situation might actually be the right thing to do. It would certainly ease the burden of the moment. But then it would make the eventual outcome seem all the more terrifying.

That moment between us seemed to last an eternity, and for its entire duration I felt extremely confused. I nearly took a step forward, but the old lady's words came back to me in a terrible reminder: *Separate yourself from your family. . . .*

That stopped me from taking any action. Jesus, I *couldn't* step forward. I wanted to, but I couldn't. I again told myself that by maintaining my silence I was protecting my family from the greatest menace to ever threaten them. From the outside looking in, the situation had no rhyme or reason. But neither had anything else that'd taken place since we moved in.

I felt ashamed. I had no choice in the matter. I bowed my head and walked away.

There'd been no cries in reply. No hurled insults. No words at all. Only the slam of the screen door as Christine left to have Thanksgiving dinner with people who were complete strangers not two months before.

Chapter Twenty-five

I spent Thanksgiving alone for the first time in my life, slouched gracelessly at the kitchen table with a bowl of bran cereal and my racing thoughts. Christine had left around five. Since then I wondered if she would even consider bringing home a plate of food to me. God knows I could have used it; I'd lost at least fifteen pounds since moving here. But I also didn't deserve such thoughtfulness, and wouldn't hold one ounce of resentment toward her if she decided against doing it.

I looked at my fingers. The way they trembled made me break up again. I couldn't help it, I could only sit at the kitchen table staring at my hands, laughing and crying and crying and laughing for as long as it took the clock to chime eight.

At this point I did my best to gather my composure, then stood up and left the harsh environment of the kitchen for the darkened security of my office, where I once again sat at my desk to wait for the golden eyes to appear.

During that time I placed my hands out in front of me, seeking out the stability of the desk in an effort to rid my mind of the day's sad events. My sight roamed casually around my office with its hardwood floors and crowded bookshelves, to the locked liquor cabinet and then to the towering brick hearth. The room lay in pure silence, the mere creak of a settling beam amplified as if a bone had snapped. I peered through the floor-to-ceiling windows overlooking the moonlit garden (Christine, in her solitude, had taken up a hobby of herb gardening; now there was a twelve-foot patch back there that looked like witchgrass and weeds. She enthusiastically used these "weeds" to spice our dinners and brew pitchers of that green-colored tea) and the fountain birdbath. That was the only activity that helped stabilize my mind, looking out into the distant woods, even if the scenery suggested only fringes of itself in the pale moonlight. That night was no exception.

The lamps were out in the office. Earlier I'd made a fire, and now only a few glowing embers remained, leaving the moonlight shining through the bay. I thought about starting a fresh fire, but decided against it.

I set my eyes back outside, noticed a few drops of water cascading down the sides the bird fountain.

And saw them. Two golden eyes.

They were as round as crystal balls, glowing as if

charged with electricity. They floated a foot above the ground alongside the base of the fountain, remained there for at least a minute, then climbed the night air to a height of perhaps four feet. They blinked, and in a smooth and unhurried pace, advanced through the herb garden toward the window; the body they had been attached to seemed not to take steps forward, but moved in some other way I really couldn't indicate, as though drifting.

My body started doing things it had never done before, my insides *churned,* and I immediately wished that I'd taken a Valium or at least a shot of bourbon before sitting down tonight. I shut my eyes in an effort to calm my slamming heart, but the image of the fiery eyes stayed with me much like the lingering impressions of a dream immediately after waking. When I finally opened my eyes again, the nightmare had preserved itself, *enhanced* itself, and I could only stare, frozen with an icy fear as something grotesque pressed itself against the glass, *staring* in at me.

Although common sense told me otherwise, it looked like a street person from the city, the kind that huddles in a cardboard box in some foul alleyway. Its clothing was dark with sweat and hanging upon its body; long lank hair fell in damp strings; scars—one a red twisting streak—ran across its scrawny cheek. But the appearance of the bulbous eyes quickly proclaimed it not born of human genes, but of something other-worldly.

Isolates . . .

Like a wizard in mid-charm, it methodically raised its

221

angular arms and scraped ten lengthy yellow claws against the glass of the window. I shuddered as the terrifying screech passed through my body like a powerful drug, paralyzing my senses.

I stayed unmoving for what seemed forever, helplessly charting a territory in my mind previously unexplored. I wondered (in vain) if it were an aberration, whether more like him were hiding nearby, waiting for some cue to commit their filthy deed.

An immense pain darted through me. I wanted to move but couldn't; fear owned me now, settling into my body like an extreme paralysis, making me feel like I had upon my first and only encounter with Old Lady Zellis.

Still staring, still scratching the glass, the thing pulled its dirty cracked lips far apart and flaunted a mouth rife with gnarled brown teeth.

At once I had the sense of hearing words from those gaping jaws, as if they'd somehow loomed from its silent mouth directly into my mind. But I heard and recognized the words in my *own* voice and not the distorted growls most apt to escape its throat. Nonetheless, it didn't matter, for the meaning was all the same, and I finally found the will to shudder again as it reaffirmed something I'd known all along. What I'd been warned of.

Of why it came.

It *needed* me.

I tried to move. Fear still held every muscle in my body immobile.

Then, something horrible happened.

Beneath my pants leg, between the calf and knee, I felt a stroke, gentle yet determined.

Sickly confusion struck me. I looked down and beheld a smallish figure like the being in the window stooping under the desk, its clawed hand no longer caressing me, but now gripping my shin painfully hard, its mutilated stare meeting my terrified one, its golden eyes glowing beneath a black mask of soot.

I tore my sight away, so strongly wanting to believe that somehow my bleakest, most terrifying nightmare had escaped from my subconscious and entered my home to terrorize me.

But my poor fortune would have it otherwise.

Somehow I tried to hobble from the chair, to no good purpose as the demon beneath the desk held me firmly, and I stumbled to the floor. I managed to look up, saw another golden-eyed demon only feet from me, coated in ashes like the one still gripping my leg, facedown on the floor but pushing itself up on all fours. Behind it another wriggled in from the tight sweep of the chimney, arms dangling, reaching for the brick hearth. Rustling sounds emanated: more were pushing their way down the chimney!

Coming for me.

An unnameable, gristly odor invaded my nostrils, and my eyes automatically released sour tears. A gray cloud veiled my sight, and simultaneously a multitude of tiny scraping footsteps pattered about the hardwood floor all around me.

And all I could see were their eyes, flying about my

head like fireflies *(like fireflies!)*, eight, ten, then more than a dozen golden lights, dizzying me.

Many hands groped me, tore at my clothing, dragged me helplessly across the floor.

Sweat, hot and odorous, formed upon my skin. Transient whispers brushed my ears.

I prayed for death to take me, and thought it had. Until I woke and found myself in Hell.

Chapter Twenty-six

I woke in the same position I had passed out in. On my back.

I heard murmuring throats, grinding teeth, then the soft sounds of movement, of tentative feet shifting stealthily about me. Breath—hot primitive sighs—danced across the surface of my skin. I suspected more movement, but could not see quite yet. I felt a dark shadow looming over me, a misshapen silhouette, eyes shining through the curtain of haze obscuring my vision. A rough, hard object touched my face. A claw. I shivered.

The gray haze cleared and in the flickering midst of an unseen flame, I saw a horrible manlike creature hovering over me. It was emaciated, a living skeleton coated with tendons and filth, arms and legs as thin as whittled broomsticks. It crawled on all fours, then bowed its head and sniffed my leg from ankle to thigh. I could see its face and it terrified me, a mutated demonlike visage, two holes for a nose, mouth and eyes much too large for its tiny head. The eyes rolled up and looked at me across a loose wisp of weblike hair, then glowed a gold-colored light that ignited its horrid filth-covered features.

Somewhere nearby a noise erupted, and the creature next to me scurried away on two legs, pushing up clouds of dust before disappearing into a hole in the dirt wall about twenty feet away. A chorus of growls and grunts spewed out from the mouths of many. Not three or four or even a dozen. *Many.*

I forced myself up on my elbows, peered out into the distance, and saw at least a *hundred* glowing lights crowding the gloom of a smallish dirt cave.

Eyes. All of them pointed in my direction. I'd quit praying years before, traded religion for scientific beliefs. But now I had no choice but to quickly return to my faith. It was my only hope.

Quickly I looked around. Indeed I was in a cave of some sort, the walls constructed of dirt, roots sprouting from them, dangling from a ceiling not six feet above my head. It smelled awful, of sewage and of things gone to rot. Breathless, I dared to look at the creatures staring at me with their golden eyes, but the collective glow of them hid their faces, leaving only jerking fragments of their bodies visible.

A single beast approached from the crowd, stood before me for a minute, then kneeled down to eye level and stared into my face. It had an almost humanlike

quality to it, brow arched downward as if in deep con-
centration, as though *I* were a curiosity. Perhaps I was.
It possessed a grand collection of awful features on its
face, deep wrinkles, warts, and moles the size of beans,
bristles of coarse hair sprouting everywhere. It peered
at me for another fifteen seconds, golden eyes unblinking the entire time.

Then it smiled. It fucking *smiled*. The expression was
long and broad and intentional upon its deformed
face—a face with a gash racing along its cheek, and by
this horrid feature I recognized it as the creature that
had first appeared at my window.

It stood up. Still staring at me, it raised its sinewy arms
in the air, and yelled *"Kahtah!"* The crowd, a multitude
of voices, repeated the foreign gesture: *"Kahtah!"*

I remained silent, stunned. *They can speak,* I thought,
terrified. *Jesus Christ, I am so fucked*.

It drew a claw into its body. *"Fenal,"* it proclaimed,
head tilted, voice deep and gravelly. There was a damn
frightening silence. Then it said . . . no, demanded,
"You . . . help."

Then something amazing and totally unexpected
happened. A second Isolate appeared. It too stared at
me with a lengthy expression that could only be described as awe. When it appeared to have had its fill of
me, it reached around, grabbed something from behind, and placed it at my feet.

My medical bag. I'd packed it the day after we moved
in, and kept it in my office in case of emergencies. Inside were the bare necessities like gauze and antibiotics, fresh needles and syringes—the usual house call

requirements. After I'd stepped on the nail I'd realized that anything could've happened at any given moment and that it was always prudent to be prepared. As it turned out, I'd ended up using the bag on my visits to the Deightons when seeing Rosy. That seemed so long ago now.

The creature—Fenal—grabbed me by the wrist and forced me to my feet. Two more came, seized my arms, and hurried me into a cavelike corridor lined with red soil and dark slimy moss. Many more of them were ahead and behind, running along the path and crawling on the walls and ceiling like giant insects, forcibly ushering me forward, their eyes igniting the way. I felt horribly nauseous from the brutal odor here; it reminded me of the summer stench that rides the wind over from the neighboring farmlands, only more intense. High hoots and hollers whipped about the tunnel in an echoing frenzy. Brisk, meandering activity surrounded me as the twisting passage widened, some sections breaking off into branched corridors. Bodies scampered by, shrieking. My head spun crazily. Eventually I choked and gagged, then vomited. But I didn't stop moving. They kept pushing me, and I could do nothing but continue on, the blind being led by an untrustworthy source, my feet sinking deep in the muddy ground, my stomach churning in twisted knots. My muscles screamed. I groaned in pain. I cradled my medical bag close to my body as if it were my only means for survival.

Soon, they stopped moving. The sea of filth parted, many of them scampering away like cockroaches in sudden lamplight. I stood my ground, heaving for breath. Eventually a single Isolate appeared alongside me, grabbed my thigh, and urged me forward. I moved in that direction, turned a corner, and at once found myself before a wholly intimidating sight.

I stood at the forefront of an immense room. It appeared at first glance to have been either constructed within a mountain of dirt, or built entirely underground. Hundreds of hovels had been dug out in the muddy walls of the hub, multitudes of glowing eyes peering out from within their faraway depths. Hundreds of torches burned, igniting the chamber to a ghostly yellow luminescence. I saw a large group of Isolates gathered at one of the gouged-out areas at the opposite end of the room, maybe two hundred feet away. A cool breeze struck me.

Fenal appeared at my side and gently ushered me forward. Every damn creature in the place had their golden eyes pinned on me; I thought crazily, *This is what a human astronaut might feel like as an exhibit in an alien zoo.* There was virtual silence except for the errant squeal, which was subsequently answered by a silencing bark. I stopped, suddenly sick again, then leaned over and puked once more, all the while trying desperately to ignore the reek of sweat, urine, blood, feces, and God knows whatever else might be festering in the air. I gagged and coughed again, then eased back up and followed Fenal's lead through a sea of groping limbs all the way to the opposite end of the dirt chamber, near the gathering at the far wall. Upon my arrival, the crowd there dispersed, some on two legs, many dashing away on all fours. A few were fighting over the last scraps of meat on what looked like a human leg bone. Fenal pulled aside a burlap bag used as a curtain, and allowed me access to a smaller chamber scooped out in the wall.

The interior of the room was damp and miserable, cramped. I could barely stand up. A couple of small torches carved the dark interior with their flames.

"Help . . . Cerpdas," Fenal stated, pointing.

I followed its bony finger to a being—Cerpdas apparently its name—lying bare-chested and trembling beside the slime-ridden wall. A spread of rags acted as a mattress beneath it. She—and I say this as the appearance of breasts, however flattened and mottled, were evident upon the exposed torso—had been covered up to the waist with a burlap bag.

I gazed at Fenal. It peered back at me, the same desperate emotion I saw through my bay window again pasted upon its deformed face. Suddenly, for reasons I could not explain, I no longer felt fear. I felt only pressure, for I realized now that I'd been brought here to perform what might very well be an impossible task; the endowment of my medical bag was evidence of this. Fenal squatted next to the injured Cerpdas and stroked her shoulder. Her eyes rolled up, the golden glow diminished to a dull luster. Sick.

I placed my bag down, took a deep breath of rotten air, then hunkered down next to the creature and slowly peeled down the burlap bag a few inches at a time, until I saw the first splash of crimson washed across its distended abdomen. A powerful stench of

230

waste and rot assaulted me, hinting to me that it had been lying in this spot for quite some time.

Wanting to get this over with, I tugged the cover away . . .

. . . and stared in horror at the freakish sight before me. It was beyond belief. Yet here it was, much too real to renounce.

The female creature's legs were spread-eagled. A pool of blood and substance tided from the vaginal canal.

A gnarled claw protruded crookedly, wriggling like a worm out of earth.

"*Help Cerpdas,*" Fenal begged, gently stroking the rotting strands of hair on her pear-shaped head. "*Help.*"

So I set to work, trying not to think about what I was actually going to do because now was not the time for me to doubt my abilities or ask myself questions. All I could do was remain strong—and sane—and convince myself that this was just another patient, a woman in need of an emergency C-section (something I've never done, mind you), and not whatever else she might be.

I retrieved a scalpel from the bag, placed it on the burlap bag. I doused the creature's abdomen with alcohol, then with a topical painkiller. Taking a deep breath, I wished the whole scene away, wondering if perhaps this might be a dream, but knew wholeheartedly that this time I wouldn't be waking up in my bed with just blood on my hands.

I took the scalpel and slowly cut her open. Brown blood spilled from the wound, running down the sides of her gaunt torso. A tiny hand poked free from the split, tossing a spray of blood into my face. I used my forearm to wipe it free of my eyes, only to see a second hand emerge, five bony fingers replete with yellow claws flexing in the free world for the very first time. I hesitated in touching the thing, but Fenal barked *help . . . help . . .* over and over again, so I closed my eyes and reached into the open cavity, grabbed the bawling creature—I felt the tug of the protruding leg slipping back inside—and plucked it free of the womb.

Arms outstretched, I held it out before me. I opened my eyes and beheld the hairy demonlike beast, all swollen like any human baby might be, eyes open and peering about with stunning alertness. Its toothless mouth choked out a garbled mess of fluids, which I sucked free with a plunger. I turned and handed the bawling infant to a waiting Isolate, which in turn hurried it away into a darkened corner of the room.

I faced the mother. Her eyes glowed weakly, as if mustering the strength to thank me for what I'd just done. I cleansed her wounds and crudely stitched them back up, then buried all her injuries under a thick layer of bandages. I fed her a dose of penicillin and resigned myself to the fact that this was all I could do.

I staggered up and backed away against the dirt wall in the shelter, the back of my head pressed against a pulpy patch of fungi. In the soft glow of the flames I observed the others in the room with me: perhaps a dozen Isolates, all silently scrutinizing me, their glowing eyes now full of questions. One being, horribly deformed, separated itself from the horde and writhed across the room, its leg dangling helplessly behind it. It confronted me, tracing a finger through a damaged gnarl of skin on its thigh.

Another leaped from the group, pushed aside the fiend in front of me, and grasped my arm, tears flowing from one golden eye. The other hung shriveled and lifeless from the socket like a pendulum, the miraculous gold converted to a stone cold gray.

Fenal leaped forward, intercepted. *"Pentaff! Blah-tah!"* The Isolates scrambled away. He then gazed at me, his golden eyes glowing with admiration. "Savior," he said.

Savior?

Oh, my God . . .

Dizzied, I stumbled from the room back out into the large antechamber. The creatures immediately rushed forward, groped me with broken bones and mangled limbs, mouths dripping fetid with disease, their wails echoing in helpless pain, desperate for my aid. Jesus, it was all too clear now, my purpose. My role in the grand scheme of the Isolates. I could see it on their suffering faces, the clear desperation that I would be the one to nurse them all back to health, give them a chance to thrive as they once did, just as Neil Farris had for thirty years. Just as the doctor that lived at 17 Harlan Road before him had.

Savior . . .

Calloused hands grabbed me. Monstrous cries filled my head. My breath escaped me.

Overwhelmed, I felt a wave of darkness consume me, and I collapsed, gratefully succumbing.

Chapter Twenty-seven

I woke up.

It had taken me some time to realize that I'd actually survived the night. When I tried to move, a crippling numbness seized my body, forcing me to speculate that I'd been lying facedown for a long period of time. I was also blind, and all I could really do was lie there and try to catch my breath, which kept a sufficient distance from me despite my best efforts. Soon my senses returned to me. A breeze tickled my skin, the earth soft and grassy beneath my palms and face. The distant calls of songbirds stirred me even further. Eventually, I found the will to open my eyes and found myself surrounded by an early morning darkness, fading starlight and the soft shuck of the moon tossing slight shadows across my surroundings. Here was enough evidence to make me believe that perhaps I'd survived—been spared—the night after all.

When I regained full control of my breathing, I tried to stand, anticipating a swimming head. Oh, it did swim, and it sent me careening across the short sprawl of lawn in the backyard. The presence of my office windows brought reality back to me in a very hard thrust, and made me realize what I needed to do with them as soon as humanly possible. The image of the steel doors Neil Farris had installed, which I hastily took down, came to me; my next step would be an even more drastic yet necessary move. I slid crookedly along the side of the house, then entered the waiting room through the unlocked door. I wondered if any of the Isolates had come here to help themselves to my belongings while I'd visited their home. I didn't see any mud tracked on the carpet, leading me to assume that they hadn't, but I wouldn't put it past them.

I felt my way across the lightless waiting room, through the hallway, and then into the kitchen, where I blindly shuffled to the table. I fumbled for the cord to the chandelier, grasped the air a number of times before finally locating it. I yanked it. The room fell into rude light. It attacked my eyes like lasers. When my sight finally cleared, I found a cellophane-covered dish filled with Thanksgiving dinner leftovers sitting on the table.

I should've been happy about it. But I wasn't. A shudder ran through me instead, and a million paranoid thoughts assaulted my mind. Like, *What if the food is poisoned?* Or, *Is this some kind of trick?* I told myself that no act of kindness could be trusted, even a seemingly generous gesture on the part of my wife, who'd apparently made this last-ditch attempt to save our marriage. I sat down at the table, thought about eating the food, but just stared at it. Believe me, I wanted to eat it, but I was scared to . . . plus it didn't look good to me. Not at all. Along with my soul, my appetite had also stayed behind in the domain of the Isolates. I stood up and took a drink of water from the sink, then closed the light and staggered to the living room couch, where I curled up into a fetal ball and waited out the rest of the night.

I must've fallen asleep at some point. Sometime later, something came out of the darkness and touched my dangling hand. I heard a dreamlike voice call out to me. I screamed in panic, eyes and mouth fully opened. Jessica was there, surrounded by the morning light, eyelids fluttering in sudden fear. She screamed and fell back in a defensive twist, then landed on her back. In a flash she righted herself like a cat and raced from the room, crying hysterically.

Christine hurtled in, dropping her pocketbook, which had been draped around her shoulder. She looked sick. Eyes dark and puffy, skin sallow, no makeup. A thicket of her hair escaped the bun on her head, obscuring her angry face. "Are you fucking crazy?" she yelled.

Her words burned through me like acid. She screamed something else, but her voice was like mud in my mind. Gibberish. *Jesus,* I thought, *if she only knew.* I stood up on achy legs and limped away, shoulders hunched as if expecting her next move. By the time I reached the steps, she had gone back into the kitchen and returned with the plate of food she'd brought home for me. She ran forward and threw it at me. Her aim was bad. The plate shattered against the front door. Most of the food ended up strewn about the living room in a storm of cold chunks, although some pieces hit me in the chest. Fearing another attack, I turned and raced up the stairs to the landing, stopped, turned, and looked downstairs.

The sounds of Christine sobbing and Jessica crying could be heard, and it damn near killed me to hear my daughter in such distress. I covered my ears with my palms, then spun away from the top of the steps and ran down the hall. The bathroom door was open, and I banged my knee against the jamb at about the same time I heard the front door slam shut. Pain barked up into me from the point of contact. I bit my tongue and grabbed my knee, then moved inside and looked into the mirror and nearly leaped at what I saw. Mud. On my face, in my hair. On my clothes. Jesus, I looked like a fucking monster. Quickly I peeled off my filthy clothes and slid into the shower, where I sat for an hour or more, washing away the disease of the night and trying hard to rinse my mind of its memories. I realized it wasn't going to work, that the events of the night would stay with me for an eternity.

Eventually I crawled out of the shower—the water had turned cold by now—barely able to lift my tender legs over the tub. A towel wet from Christine's earlier shower hung limply on the bath-hook. I used it to dry off, smelling the soft feminine aroma she'd left behind in the cottony fabric. Gooseflesh hurdled across my skin, and at one point I put the towel in my mouth, trying to taste the pleasures of my past.

Dear God, how I wanted that past back again.

So badly.

The beautiful, glorious past.

Half an hour later I was dressed in fresh clothes, my mind brimming with the determination to retrieve everything I'd lost.

There was only one way to do it, I knew.

I'd have to fight this damn thing to the very bitter end.

Chapter Twenty-eight

The living room had retained a bit of an odor. Kind of like, well, Thanksgiving dinner. I did my best to clean away the mess of hurled food. It'd been nearly impossible to get everything up (I'd made up my mind not to tackle the wall beneath the steps, which had a surreal-artlike spattering of mashed potatoes and cranberries on it). But the bigger pieces of turkey, stuffing, and yams all ended up in the trash.

Eventually my body called out for food. My stomach loudly protested its emptiness with lionlike growls, so I quenched it with a bagel, banana, and instant coffee—the most food I'd consumed in one sitting for at least a week. As I sat at the kitchen table, I planned out my first task, which wouldn't be an easy one. I decided to secure the house from any possible intrusion. Every window, every door, would have to be completely shuttered, now that I knew what was *really* out there. I didn't want one single night to pass without being sure my family would be fully protected. Then, once this was completed, which would take me most of the day, I'd consider making some plans for a means of escape from Ashborough.

I'd have to be smart about it. No rushed exits.

Fuck the "law" and its battalion.

I peeked out the window.

A man walked by.

Shit. I hadn't considered at all whether I'd had any appointments.

Apparently, I did. And here he was, Mr. Punctuality, showing up at exactly nine-thirty on the dot.

I stood from the kitchen table, peeked into the small mirrored backsplash set above the stove, and saw a wretched beast of a man peer back at me (what did I expect?), then moved through the connecting hall into the waiting room. Here on the love seat sat a rather slight, ordinary-looking man of perhaps forty. His legs were crossed, hands on his knees, near-bald head resting back against the upholstery. As I approached him he gazed up at me, smiling congenially beneath a few days worth of beard. He stood to shake my hand. His grip was weak and cold.

"Hello Dr. Cayle, nice to finally meet you. I've heard so much about you."

"And you are?"

He hesitated for a moment, and ran a nervous hand through his thinning hair, eyes narrowed and head cocked, giving off a sense of sudden perplexity. "Sam.

Sam Huxtable. I didn't have an appointment."

Given another minute I might have simply gone through all the motions Sam Huxtable expected. The smile, the trading of pleasantries, the silent stroll into my office to proceed with the examination. But I acted with the arrogance of a man in the throes of paranoia—a man riddled with ultra-high levels of anxiety along with the will and sudden strength to survive the elements. I couldn't help it. I instantly had to take my frustrations out on somebody. And that somebody had become Sam Huxtable.

Using both hands, I grabbed fistfuls of his shirt, twisted him around, and slammed him up against the wall. The Monet print there toppled off the hook and landed with a bang on the floor. I brought a knee up into his groin. He doubled over, giving me the opportunity to assume full control of the situation. I threw him to the floor, flipped him on his back, and straddled him, one hand still gripping his shirt, the other successfully seeking out the few strands of hair left on his head.

Tears sprouted from his tightly squeezed eyes. His mouth was wet and twisted with fear. "You're hurting me. . . ." he cried.

"It's my intention to," I said.

"Please stop."

"I will . . . when you answer my questions."

His eyes darted open. They were wet and red and glossy. I let go of his hair and fisted his collar to make sure he didn't go anywhere, then slammed him a couple more times against the floor just to reaffirm how serious I was.

241

"Questions? I . . . I don't know if I can. . . ." His words were interrupted by a fit of coughs.

"You can, and you will. Ready?"

He remained silent, unmoving.

"Ready?"

"I'll t-try. Jesus, don't hurt me."

I kept my grip tight. Clearly he didn't want to talk. Probably knew he couldn't because common sense told him that the new doctor in town had finally come in contact with Ashborough's strange governing body and wasn't all that ready and willing to give in to their decrees yet. But Sam also knew he had to keep everything he knew under lock and key so the little fuckers in the woods wouldn't drag his wife or son or daughter into the woods and send them back with a limb or two missing.

The thought of all this made me want to kill the man. I really wanted to fucking *kill* him.

I took a deep breath, tried to get a grip on myself. "No . . . you'll do more than try," I said. "You'll tell me everything you know, 'cause if you don't, God help me, I'll break your arms and legs and drag your sorry ass up there into the woods and plant it on that big bloody stone and feed you to those motherfuckers. Would you like that? Huh?" God help me, I meant it too.

"Let go of me."

"What? I don't think so."

"You let go of me and I promise I'll tell you what I know."

I pressed down harder. Cramps shot through my hands. Sam grunted in pain, then coughed. Dapples of

242

saliva hit me in the face. His already pale skin went whiter when he realized what he'd done.

"I'm sorry . . ." He coughed again. More spit. "Sorry . . . just please let go of me."

"How do I know I can trust you?"

"You have my word . . . I'll tell you everything I know."

I loosened my grip. "Everything . . ."

"Everything I *know*," he stressed. Meaning don't expect much. He again added, "Please don't hurt me."

I loosened my hold, then stood up, pulling him up with me. We staggered a bit, but I gained a foothold and dragged him into my office. I shoved him deep into the room, then closed the door. He caught his footing against my desk and stayed there, unmoving with the exception of his heaving chest; evidently he hadn't been used to this level of activity. *Start exercising and cut out the high-fat foods. More fruits and more fiber. Doctor's orders.* We both took a moment to catch our breath. I then swept an arm toward the chair in front of my desk and told him to have a seat.

Sam's eyes avoided me like the plague; he'd been defeated. Never had a chance really, and he knew it. He nodded, then paced like a wounded soldier to the chair and sat down, keeping his eyes pinned to some nondescript spot on my desk. His shirt was torn at the collar. A juicy red spot appeared on one of his cheeks. Tears streamed down his face. He looked pathetic, though probably not as much as I did.

As I stared at Sam Huxtable, a gale of sudden remorse whacked me, and I felt ashamed of my actions. My frustrations and determination had driven me to this point, and now that I was here, guilt riddled me like a virus. I'd just committed an irreversible act, and had chipped away a bit of my soul in the process. What little soul, that is, I had left. I told myself that all my actions had been utterly necessary, all for the well-being of my family. I'd had no choice in the matter. Do or die.

Sam gazed up at me. "You look like shit," he said rather brazenly. Given his predicament, he should've kept his mouth shut, but he probably saw through my weak facade. I was no murderer. Far from it. And he knew it too.

Yes, but would a man murder to protect his family?

I shoved my hands in my pockets, seeking false comfort and finding nothing. "So do you . . . at least now you do."

"I was feeling like shit before I came here."

I nodded. "What's wrong?"

"You said you wanted to talk," he remarked angrily, ignoring me. His priorities had taken a bit of a shift; I'd taken the ball away from him and placed it in my court, putting him on the defensive. Now I could press forward and slam-dunk some info out of him.

"I have some questions, Sam, and I think you know where I'm going. I'm the type of person that doesn't like to be kept in the dark about certain things, especially when they affect me and my family. And let me tell you, I've never been more affected in my life, as you can well imagine."

Sam stared at me, but said nothing.

I continued. "Basically I've been fucked up the ass

just like you and everybody else who lives here in Ash-borough, if you want to call it living . . . it's more like a modern Inquisition if you ask me, wouldn't you say? The only difference is that I'm not gonna stand for it, and I don't give a shit if everyone here, and in all the surrounding towns for that matter, are in on their dia-bolical plot. I've paid my dues, and now I'm gonna take my family and get out of here."

Sam grinned incredulously. Suddenly he had a voice. "What a genius . . . don't you think I've tried it, that hun-dreds of others over the years have tried leaving here? You don't understand, Doctor. They're everywhere, like goddamned cockroaches. They hear all and see all. And just when you think it's safe to pack up your things and slink out of here, they'll come at you twice as hard and make life miserable for you and your family. They have no qualms about killing, I'm sure you've seen some of their handiwork by now, right? But that's why you're questioning me now, isn't it? Because you've seen what they can do and you simply don't want to take a chance. Paid your dues? I don't think so. You haven't even scratched the surface."

"Yeah? Well . . . then how can they possibly stop me in my car?" Somehow I knew they could, but I wanted to hear it from a man with experience, someone who had more answers than me.

"Why don't you try it and see what happens? They'll fuck with the engine or even toss themselves under your wheels if they have to. Anything to stop you. And you want to know what's really fucked up? Afterwards they'll come and get you, dear Doctor, to fix up their

245

injured martyrs after they've committed their nasty deed. Yeah, go ahead. Go and get your family and make like the wind in your minivan. You'll be mending broken arms and crushed ribs for a week."

I thought about Christine and the mysterious "animal" that had darted out in front of the car. Then, about my visit last night to their dwelling. How one of them had crawled over to me after I'd completed the cesarean, *how it dragged its leg behind it as if it had been run over by a car.*

"Jesus," I said, suddenly sobered.

"I tried to leave once," Sam said. "It was in the middle of the night. I had my wife and son in the car, and at the time I didn't think they knew anything about the Isolates. But I was wrong. I ran inside to get the keys, which I'd forgotten on the kitchen table, and when I got back outside the car was teeming with them. I couldn't even see the wheels. It looked like a piece of candy swarming with ants. My family was trapped inside for hours, and I couldn't do anything but stand there and watch helplessly until morning came. The Isolates eventually skittered away—all at once, mind you, a real frightening scene—and at that moment I still had the mind to get in the car and start driving, but my son had hyperventilated himself into a coma and nearly died. Thankfully, Dr. Farris took care of him, although I'm not sure if it was the right thing to do. Now every day I have the pleasure of waking up and seeing Josh lying in bed all curled up and twisted, full of bedsores."

"You . . . you never brought him to the hospital?"

Sam rubbed his tired eyes. "You're not listening to

me, Doctor. The hospital is in Ellenville. I couldn't even get my car out of the fucking driveway."

I was going to ask him why he hadn't tried calling another town, even the city. But I'd had the frustrating experience of trying just that, and it'd gotten me nowhere.

"Jesus, this doesn't make sense to me . . . I mean, how is it that the whole outside world is conspiring against Ashborough? What about the fucking government? Jesus, let's call the goddamned National Guard and have the fuckers smoked out of here."

Sam folded his hands on his lap. "You have a drink?" he asked.

I nodded, went to the cabinet, retrieved two shot glasses, and poured us both some brandy.

He sipped it gingerly, then continued. "It's a buffer effect. There are five towns within fifty miles surrounding Ashborough. Ellenville, Claybrooke, Townshend, Beverly, and Beauchamp. Between here and all those towns lie thousands of acres of woodland. Within those woods live the Isolates. I'm assuming you've been to their den by now."

I nodded. "Yeah, I've had the pleasure."

"The den . . . the one you've been to, here in Ashborough, is the largest. But there're dozens of smaller ones all over between here and those towns. It's a great labyrinth, they're all interconnected, and they can travel between them with amazing ease. The Isolates keep eyes on the people living on the outskirts of the towns. These are the town 'officials,' who make sure that all order is kept and that no information about the

Isolates leaves Ashborough. They keep track of who goes in, and make sure that no one comes out."

"Are you saying that the Isolates have spies? Human spies?"

Sam nodded. "Like you and me, they're under strict watch and constant threat by the Isolates. They have no choice but to adhere to their demands, otherwise they and their loved ones will fall victim to them."

"I've heard that before."

"And undoubtedly, you've seen it. These aren't animals we're dealing with. They're a cunning, intelligent race of, dare I say, people who for hundreds of years have had things done their way. They live by a strict set of mores and practice them with utter determination. There's no escaping them, Doctor. I suggest that if you wish to live as normal a life as possible, simply go about your duties as you normally would, and do as they demand, when they demand it. And most importantly, remember that their laws do not allow any discussion of their existence."

"So . . . why are you talking about them now?" I asked.

"You threatened to kill me."

I nodded, again feeling remorseful. "I'm sorry. . . . "

"Don't apologize, Doctor, I know where you're coming from. I've been here for five years now. I do the best I can, given the situation with my son, but frankly I'm tired of seeing him the way he his. I'm wondering whether he might be better off as . . . as . . ."

"Don't say it," I said. Sam Huxtable was talking because he wanted the Isolates to come take his son. But who's to say, I thought, whether they might come and torture the poor kid even further? Or perhaps lay claim to his wife?

His wife . . .

"You mentioned to me that when you tried to leave you didn't think at the time that your wife and son knew anything about the Isolates. What did you mean by that?"

He took another sip, then downed the rest and grimaced. I refilled his glass. "Just as I'd been keeping my knowledge of the Isolates a secret from my family, terrorized by their threats, my wife Janice had also come in contact with them. She too had been threatened by Old Lady Zellis, and had been keeping it all pent up inside, doing only what had been demanded of her. For three years the Isolates had separately manipulated myself and my wife, neither of us having any knowledge of the other's torment, keeping the existence of the Isolates a secret out of fear of them hurting Josh. Eventually Janice broke down, tried to overdose on the anxiety medication Farris had given her, which simply made her vomit for twenty-four hours. At this point we found out that each of us had had a run-in with Old Lady Zellis and were being tormented by the Isolates, had been for quite some time."

Lauren Hunter's attempted warning shot back to me like a missile, now, suddenly, making sense: *Christine . . .*

"So what you're saying," I said, the horrible truth of the matter setting dread deep into me, "is that I may not be the only one being tormented by the Isolates?"

Sam nodded, then stood up. "I believe it's time for me to go."

I was too stunned to speak. I gazed up at Sam, a sudden underdog in this conflict. "Why did you come here?"

He looked at me, dark eyes pinning me. "The Old Lady told me to."

And then he walked out.

Chapter Twenty-nine

The trees were a great shifting shape against the cloud-filled sky, backlit by a sun whose rays found it difficult to warm the air. A threat of rain loomed, cool wind rippling at my shirt as I went outside.

I stood at the entrance to my office, wondering which way Sam Huxtable had gone: either home to the left or right into the woods to report his confrontation with Ashborough's good doctor. He'd left about a half hour earlier, and I'd spent that time glued to the chair behind my desk, seeking the strength to accomplish what I'd originally set out to do.

Eventually, reality had taken over and I'd risen from my desk and gone outside. I paced across the yard with all the energy and enthusiasm of a man who'd just broken the finish line of a marathon. For the millionth time I mustered some hidden strength to stave off insanity, then made my way into the garage, where I planned to spend the next hour or so wrenching down the slats of wood piled up in the loft. The garage proved a vital breeding ground for mice and insects seeking warmth from the cold air, and they all let me know how pissed they were to have their dwelling unsettled. I also let them know that I was in town to do business, and took out my aggressions on as many of the skittering devils as I could with a healthy chunk of two-by-four.

The store of wood here led me to believe that Neil Farris must've planned to shutter up his house at some point, but had never gotten around to doing it. In addition to the collection in the loft, a stack of four-by-eight planks leaned neatly against the rear wall alongside a stack of new and used beams. I also found a few sets of nails still in their clear packages, plus a fairly new claw hammer with the price still attached.

Hastily I began shifting the wood planks around, finding it easy enough to move them until I tripped on an errant slab and took a splinter of wood the size of a shish-kebab skewer deep into my palm. The pain at once reminded me of the nail that had lanced my foot the day we moved in; now that episode seemed a long-lost warning of the shapes of things to come. Plucking the wood from my hand proved no less painful or gory.

Instead of treating it, I set right back to work, wincing through the pain that exploded beneath the work gloves I put on. I started the formidable task of replacing the two steel security doors at either ends of the hallway, both of which I was now thankful to have not thrown out. The two panel doors that came down ended up across the left half of the front window. A couple of closet doors from the bedrooms fitted perfectly over the other half.

I wore out a path between the house and the garage, carrying all the wood planks and beams outside and spreading them out the on the grass like a collection, examining the sizes and shapes of each piece and carefully considering which windows they would adequately barricade.

As I worked, the day grew cooler and a gray mist formed at the foot of the woods, like a great white capsule. I'd stopped many times during the course of the day to gaze into the woods, feeling as if they had become a sentient force, conspiring with the Isolates.

Plus, there were *sounds* in the woods. Errant bustlings, twigs cracking, leaves swishing. I went about my work, ignoring the sounds despite the fact I shivered uncontrollably every time I turned away, as though invisible eyes bulleted icy gazes into my back. I worked for hours under these circumstances, wondering if they might leap out from their hiding places to rip away my efforts.

Many hours, and many minor injuries, later, every possible entrance to the house had been barricaded except my office windows, the office entrance, and the solid oak front door, on which I added four bolt locks. The steel doors now back in place would keep the beasts from entering the remainder of the house—the Isolates had already proven themselves quite capable of entering the office through the chimney, which I also left clear. *I* was the one they wanted, and as long as I kept myself available to them, my family would be safe.

In an odd instant, Sam Huxtable's words flitted back to me, like a snapping dream-bubble bursting with insight: *I suggest that if you wish to live as normal a life as possible, simply go about your duties as you customarily would, and do as they demand, when they demand it.*

Then I was reminded of our conversation about his wife, how unbeknownst to him she'd been under a similar threat by the Isolates, how all along she too had been forced to commit ghastly deeds in order to assure the safety of her family, just as they'd done to him. All this had gone on for years without the other's knowledge. Examining the possibility of this occurring with Christine brought some issues out into the clear. It very well explained her sudden anger and resentment toward me, as well as the ongoing frustration riddling her arguments and how she'd treated the pregnancy as an ill-fated event.

Jesus, Michael, she'd said, *you were wearing a goddamned condom!*

I was. And we hadn't done it much prior to that, perhaps three or four times, if that. I shuddered at the sudden dark mystery that my wife had become, and wondered if she too had played some role in the *Grand Scheme*. She'd shunned me (not unlike I had her, but I had a reason; was her reason the same?). Then her pregnancy, how she seemed to treat it as a curse. Jesus, when we had Jessica (thinking of the past, the happy past, really fucks with my head) she acted like the Cinderella she presumed herself to be, a woman reveling on cloud nine and taking every precaution to ensure the safe delivery of her baby. Now? Nothing. No pre-natal vitamins. No motherhood literature. Nothing to convince me that she had done anything for her un-born child. Damn, she never even tried to talk about it.

Why should she? You closed yourself off from her months ago.

Suddenly, and perhaps irrationally, I considered con-fronting her again. This time, instead of confessing my knowledge of the Isolates as I had done rather futilely many months ago, I would insist on her confession, as to whether *she* was withholding any secrets, whether she too lived under their constant threat.

The sun began to set behind the cloak of clouds, dimming everything to a stark gray. I paced about the backyard, gazing at the upstairs windows that used to look through into my bedroom and master bath. Now sloppy wooden barricades faced me, like blinded sock-ets. I took a deep breath and turned to face the woods.

All of a sudden, there came a sound, and I remem-bered it clearly from my journey into the den of the Isolates: a laugh. A shrill cackle that could have been a cry. It was cut short, then returned to rise maniacally and freeze my blood. The wind picked up and lifted the fog to the branches of the trees, swirling it about in ghostly eddies. The laugh descended into a wheeze, then faded away . . . but its resonance continued on, penetrating me, tearing my senses to pieces.

"Fuck you," I said, my voice barely a crack. "I'll beat you."

I hesitated for a moment, then walked around to the side of the house, this time keeping my sights on the woods, and seeing for the briefest instant two glowing golden eyes fifty feet back beyond the perimeter of the woods.

Fuck you.

I kept on walking around to the front of the house, where I saw Christine pulling the minivan into the driveway.

She stared at me from the driver's-side window.

I stared back for a second, then turned away, suddenly *afraid* of her. And completely unsure of what to do next.

Chapter Thirty

That day I rediscovered fear. Again. It came at me from a completely different angle, one I'd known existed all along but had been ill-prepared on a mental level to confront. The enduring threat of the Isolates had been directed against my family since the day we'd moved in, but *I* had been the only one to my knowledge who'd witnessed any of their horrors firsthand. Now, the possibility of Christine having also experienced them had become conceivable, but to this point remained unconfirmed.

And then there was Jessica. Would my five-year-old be capable of recovering from experiencing even a fraction of what truly existed out there?

Daddy, are there such things as ghosts?

I wondered—quite seriously this time—if Jessica had ever witnessed the Isolates, had perhaps seen the golden eyes hovering in the woods. If Christine had indeed been taken by them as I now surmised, when had she confronted them without Jessica present? Was she too spending her nights in the woods as I had? Had she been forced to secretly perform a sacrifice as well? So many questions, and no answers.

Despite the threats, I decided to confront Christine.

She got out of the minivan and walked along the walkway to where I was standing, Jessica followed the path a few feet behind, empty eyes staring soullessly to the ground. Christine attempted to walk around me, but I blocked her. She kept her eyes away from mine, shifting back to her right.

I grabbed her arm and pulled her toward me, our faces inches apart.

"Let me go," she snarled. She was immediately angry, yes, but it was overshadowed by the pain and trepidation in her eyes. I could read her mind: *I don't want to talk about it, Michael. I can't talk about it, and you know why.* "Please let me go," she said again, this time quieter, more desperate.

"We need to talk," I demanded. These were the first words I'd spoken to her in more than a month. It felt incredibly strange, as if I'd just committed a crime.

She remained defiantly silent and tried to tear away from me, but I held on to her arm. We wrestled back and forth like this for ten or fifteen seconds, and then she began to scream. *"Let go of me! You bastard!"*

That's when Jessica ran away, around the side of the house.

I called after her, and so did Christine, but she didn't answer.

Finally, by default, I suppose, I let go of Christine. She pushed me away roughly, crying hard. I ignored her and hurried quickly around the side of the house, calling Jessica's name. When I didn't see her I raced into the backyard, my feet seeming to move by themselves.

I saw her running. Far back into the gathering darkness of the woods, and disappearing fast.

I screamed her name, then ran after her like a madman. But she kept on running, blond curls bobbing about, before dipping behind a crest in the land a hundred feet ahead. Brutal horror grasped me in the moment she slipped from my sight, far beyond even that of my trip into the den of the Isolates. I ran after her as quickly as humanly possible, calling out her name as thoughts of her coming face-to-face with one of the demons tortured my mind. I could hear the faint echoes of her distant footsteps crunching leaves and snapping twigs, and they helped guide me along her chosen path, where the canopy above blanketed me in shadows as I continued yelling, *Jessica! Jessica!* looking for any sign of her.

I heard her scream.

I sped forward, sidestepping reaching roots and scattered brush, wondering how in God's name her little legs had taken her so far, so fast. I climbed hills, skidded down peaks, again calling *Jessica! Jessica!* over and over again. Twigs poked my skin. Wet leaves made the going treacherous and I slipped full-length on the ground. A stab of intense pain lanced my lower back, and for a moment I didn't think I'd be able to get up, but then I heard Jessica yell *Daddy!* and that was enough to help me climb back up and move on.

I pressed on. Pine needles jabbed the skin beneath my clothes. I kept on yelling Jessica's name, again and again, but my voice was weakening, and here in the darkening woods the critters were bustling to welcome the night, serenading in the millions and making it virtually impossible to hear. The land sloped further upward.

Even in the darkness, the environment I approached took on an alarming familiarity.

Jesus . . .

I climbed over a hill, crossed a flat of land thick with trees, and saw it.

The circle of stones.

I finally found her. She was standing motionless within the arena of ten-foot stones, knee-deep in a blanket of dead leaves alongside the bloodstained altar. A disemboweled raccoon lay on the stone. She stared at it, eyes bulging, jaw hanging.

How did she come this far? I ran as fast as I could, yet she made it here way before me. . . .

I took a step forward. Then it hit me, like a great rush of hot air. *The smell*, the familiar foulness of decaying leaves and excrement and rot, rising up from an unseen source.

Why I hadn't smelled it when Phillip had taken me here, I can't explain. But it was here. I had found it. Somewhere beneath her gentle footsteps was the dwelling place of the Isolates.

"Jessica," I said, my voice cracking. "Come here." I tried to step forward, but my legs immediately froze, taking me no further than beyond the outer perimeter of the stones.

Fear had me in its grasp again, not because I was afraid for myself, but because I was terrified for my daughter.

Right behind my daughter was an Isolate.

Jesus, it seemed so nightmarishly surreal, so weird, as if I were looking at some image from a book of nineteenth-century ghost photographs. But it was real, mere feet from her. A face, staring at me, its golden eyes dulled to a drab shade, like dirty lamplights. The gnarled, knobby head shifted ever so slightly. It looked like an anglerfish nestled in the sand awaiting its prey at sea bottom.

As my eyes adjusted to the surroundings, more came into view. Jesus, there were perhaps a dozen demons here, all masterfully camouflaged within the brown earth-toned environs. Hideous, gnarled faces with downcast brows, staring at me, stirring ever so slightly as if to alert me to their presence, but not so much as to make themselves apparent to Jessica.

She looked up from the dead raccoon, waved at me, unaware of the threat only feet behind her.

Then, from the corner of my pained eye, I saw something. A burrowing-like ripple below the leaves, approaching her from behind. It stopped at her heels and I froze, paralyzed, heart pounding, breath short and stagnant.

Like a worm unearthing itself, a brownish face appeared, a hideous mask squirming out from the layer of brush and tangle. A single clawed limb rooted out alongside it, reaching for her ankle.

It had to have been sheer will (it certainly wasn't my bravery), but Jessica ran to me at that moment, as if my mental pleas had somehow coerced her. She leapt into my arms, crying, and I quickly embraced her.

I ran back to the house, holding her tightly the entire way.

Christine waited there, racing forward, face swollen and damp with tears. She grabbed Jessica from me and hugged her against her pregnant belly and repeated through her sobs, *"Oh, my baby, my sweet baby. Thank God you're okay,"* rubbing her head and kissing her.

She walked away toward the house, and I wondered if she even noticed that all the windows had been barricaded. She brought Jessica inside, going in through the office entrance. I'd left the steel doors unlocked (would she notice them too?) so she'd had no problem getting back into the house. I wanted to go inside, speak to her, but it became clear that Christine wanted no part of me . . . not now anyway.

I took a deep breath, a million thoughts racing through my head, none of them making sense.

Except one.

They had Christine.

Chapter Thirty-one

The day's veil of clouds had dissipated into fine air, allowing the near-full moon to wash its pale blue beams across the backyard. In this light my house looked haunted with its boarded-up windows and chipped shingles. It had been all along, I suppose—and reflected that with its dreadful appearance. Slowly I gazed around the dark yard, at the matted lawn, the poisonous woods, and Christine's herb garden (it had overgrown rather quickly, making it look like something out of a Lovecraft tale, particularly with the cement birdbath casting shadows over it).

I paced awkwardly across the yard, checking the windows repeatedly to make certain no Isolate could make its way in. A few nails had come loose, but the barriers remained secure. Eventually I went back into the house via the office door, then into the kitchen, where I sat at the table, staring at the clock, which read eight-thirty. I made myself a cheese-on-rye sandwich and chased it with some milk. My appetite was virtually nil and it took me some time to force it all down—the food felt like Styrofoam against my dry scratchy throat. When I finished, I went upstairs, quickly showered, and changed into a clean pair of jeans and a sweater. Christine had sequestered herself behind the bedroom door, and I figured that Jessica might be in there with her. I peeked into Jessica's room anyway, just in case, and surprisingly enough found her asleep in her bed.

My princess was motionless beneath the quilted covers. Her tattered teddy bear lay curled in her grasp, its one button eye peeking out from the edge of the comforter, dangling from withered threads. I ran a hand through Jessica's curly hair—one of the simple pleasures, I realized now, still left in my life—then gazed through the upstairs window alongside her bed into the dark of night. The wind picked up and whined sharply against the glass, startling me a bit.

Staring into the woods—sometimes hours at a time— had become an outright obsession with me, for I needed to be ready to act the instant the golden eyes appeared; it was the only option I had to protect my family. Christine had suffered great pain, I knew that now, although not for the reasons I'd originally assumed. At first it seemed clear that her anguish had come about because of my sudden paranoia, my drastic change in personality. All along I'd carried a great burden with me, knowing that my actions had gravely hurt her.

But if what Sam Huxtable had said was true, it seems I'd been horribly wrong. The cause of her suffering had not been my cold, dreadful behavior. It had been the same torment afflicting me all along. That Christine had had her very own experiences with the Isolates, and had been tortured by her inability to communicate with *me*.

Sam Huxtable was right.

Lauren Hunter was right.

They had her.

But to what degree? What sort of threats had they made to Christine?

I had to find out.

Chapter Thirty-two

With my hand still tenderly caressing my daughter's hair, I backed away from her bed with every intention to go into Christine's bedroom—*our bedroom*—and open up the lines of communication again, when, by force of habit, I looked out the window.

I saw them immediately, escaping from the woods and slowly approaching the house. Golden eyes, perhaps a dozen of them, floating like fairies from a child's fable.

The sight jolted me. My hand slipped from Jessica's head and accidentally tore the teddy bear from her grasp. It fell to the hardwood floor with a quiet, graceful thump, slightly stirring the five-year-old from her dreams, but thankfully not waking her.

Leaving the teddy bear on the floor, I quickly escaped her room, went downstairs, and scampered through the kitchen into the hallway leading to the office.

Once in my study, I seized hold of my medical bag, which I'd restocked earlier with all the appropriate tools necessary for curing their ills: bandages, antibiotics, a variety of clamps and scalpels (the latter having performed the C-section), and went back out the office door, into the night.

At once the golden orbs in the backyard signaled me, and I followed their lead into the dark woods.

Once in the woods, the beasts aggressively clutched at my clothes, hissing alarms, probably indicating that I had arrived. They led me through the woods along a familiar path, their claws poking and scratching me when my tired pace lagged too much. I stumbled repeatedly along the way, and at one point fell down and considered staying there and feigning death; somehow, I didn't think they'd fall for it, and it was this thought that got me up and moving again. I ran a hand across my mouth and came away with blood; I'd cut my lip in the fall. "Fuck," I muttered, grasping my bag and continuing on. Five minutes later, I reached the circle of stones, where the Isolates were darting all over the place like dogs chasing a ball. In the starlight I could see two hidden doorways slowly rising up from beneath the brush on the forest floor, each constructed of mud and thatch, leaves and twigs intricately woven on and around them to permanently disguise their existence.

Two Isolates abruptly forced me through one of the entranceways, which fell into a steep narrow passage. Nearly falling forward, I stretched my arms out in front of me, carefully feeling my way through as my shoulders scraped along the dark soil walls, my head against the low ceiling. The passage twisted and turned as it wound down into the darkness; in some places it widened, other times it thinned out. Sections broke off every so often into branched corridors where more Isolates appeared for a glimpse of their "Savior." I felt bodies scampering by as I stumbled further into the earth, harsh voices hooting louder and louder, limbs groping me, guiding me, only their bulbous golden irises visible in the utter blackness.

A flickering of lights appeared ahead. Once there, I beheld a familiar sight: the immense subterranean dwelling. Hundreds of burning torches lined the soil walls, igniting the chamber to a ghostly golden hue.

A single Isolate jumped out, mere inches before me. I was startled, and dropped my medical bag, which I'd completely forgotten I was holding.

Fenal. He silenced the advancing crowd, positioning his wiry body now three feet in front of me. His limbs swayed in a purposeful dance. His grin was brown and rancid, brimming, the scar on his face wriggling like a snake. "Savior." A spectrum of whispers came from the crowd.

I remained silent. I could taste blood and sweat in my mouth.

"Heal us," he said.

A mob running three deep surrounded me, each creature suffering from some kind of sickening ailment. Two creatures dangled broken limbs before me as if bestowing gifts; many picked at open festering sores so that I could clearly see them; another had experienced a failed childbirth, and miraculously crawled over trailing its uterus behind like a piece of luggage. Fenal broke through the pleading crowd and guided me into a separate antechamber to the left where, one by sickening one, I was forced to treat them.

Hours passed. I spent them under the firelight, binding the Isolates' broken parts, sealing their wounds and administering antibiotics, delivering their babies. It was a terribly fatiguing process that seemed to never end. Before I was done, I treated a total of twenty-one Isolates. Four of them were dead before they got to me; two died under my "care."

They were a race weakened by injury and disease, that much I could ascertain. I realized now that it was my job, as their so-called "Savior," to heal them and help them flourish, to multiply further, to help them gain strength and vigor and reestablish themselves as a breed. Just as Neil Farris presumably had.

Oh, they eat their dead.

Coming here tonight, I had dreaded the possibility of an untreatable demon lying before me. The third Isolate presented to me had not been bitten nor scratched by a forest animal; wasn't broken-limbed nor the ill-fated recipient of a newborn infant.

No. This demon had been suffering from disease.

It had lain in a separate hovel, shivering atop a burlap bag, its gnarled teeth clenching and grinding in agony. Blood and feces surrounded it like a foul moat. Its golden eyes had lost all their luster, now dulled to naked gray hues. Upon close inspection, I observed that it had been bitten in a multitude of places, on the legs, stomach, and groin, probably by a rat. I administered penicillin, but knew it would do no good.

An hour later, the Isolate was dead.

The panic I felt could never be described by words alone. Would they kill me for not living up to their expectations?

I found myself suddenly alone in the tiny alcove. Behind me they had all emerged from their resting places into the core of the den, crawling slowly and quietly, the grinding of their teeth and claws sending wicked shudders throughout my body, and I nearly collapsed at the sight of them. There were more of them than I'd ever imagined. Their clan was so huge that I couldn't imagine them not needing to branch out soon into newly settled territories, perhaps beyond Ashborough.

I could only kneel at the edge of the dirt chamber, staring out at the hundreds of golden eyes, which all stared back at me. Carefully, I stepped down from my platform and edged slowly away, keeping my eyes at my feet and feeling their bodies brushing by me.

A loud scuffling ensued. I cringed, expecting them to leap on me. When they didn't, I turned to see what it was that had had them so suddenly excited.

I beheld a gruesome sight.

A few of the demons had ripped the dead body from its resting place in the alcove and began tearing its limbs away. In mere seconds many more had feverishly pounced it, and I was horribly reminded of a documentary film I'd seen where a pride of lions competed for a share of a downed wildebeest. Rancid jaws locked onto muscle, tendon, and bone, pulling away as much sustenance as possible. Wild screeches and howls followed, and before I could grasp my sanity, the dead creature had been reduced to mere gristle lodged between the spaces of their twisted teeth.

I shouldn't have been surprised. After all, I'd seen the damage they did to Lauren Hunter and Rosy Deighton. But . . . to finally see them in action . . . it threw me for a loop. When this feeding ritual was complete, Fenal led me back into the first hovel and sent in additional Isolates to be treated.

Finally, when I felt I could handle it no more, they stopped coming in. I felt afraid to move, so I sat in the cave and at one point even drifted off into a light sleep, my head resting against the muddy wall. I dreamed of better times, of living in Manhattan in our cramped apartment; how foreign the bump and grind of city life seemed now.

I startled awake to find two Isolates forcing me to my feet. Bewildered, I stumbled from the small cave into the den. The entire mass of Isolates had gathered, their golden eyes aglow and pointed in my direction.

Fenal stood before them, staring at me. I stared back at him, wondering if my time had come, and to some odd extent, hoping it had.

Fenal raised his arms high. I saw a black beetle nesting in his armpit. It circled there for a few seconds, then skittered down the side of his mangy torso. *"Katah!"* he screamed. The hundreds of golden-eyed night dwellers squealed and screeched in a roaring frenzy, waving their broomstick arms in all directions.

Something seemed wrong, and I felt that my life might be coming to an end right there—that my last breathing moments would take place in this den of hell. I prayed to God for mercy, asking him to protect Jessica and Christine.

A flurry of activity arose behind Fenal, a jostling of bodies. Then, a scream.

A human scream.

Deep, guttural, exhausted, pained, it was most surely that of a man. I craned my neck to peer past Fenal and those Isolates crouching menacingly alongside him, but a number of the breed were holding me firmly by the arms and legs, keeping me in place, and I couldn't make out the cause of the commotion, or the source of the scream.

Fenal gazed at me, his eyes glowing as bright as the torches providing light to this hellish pit. Those hunkering near him suddenly darted away like frightened cats, their squeals echoing about the chamber.

I stared back, waiting, never imagining for even the slightest moment that any worse nightmare could exist beyond all I'd endured for the past six months. I was wrong. It did.

I saw something move and I did my best to focus on the continuing activity just behind Fenal. The head-Isolate stepped aside and in his place I saw a figure loom, that of a man, hunched and obviously wearied. I could not see his face at first, but I recognized the dark denim jeans and flannel jacket he wore.

In an instant two Isolates pounced on the man, digging their claws into his clothes and skin. He screamed and they grasped him by the hair, mocking his screams with wild howls of their own. They pulled him to his knees, and a shroud of flickering torchlight washed across his trembling face, badly beaten, bloodied, bruised.

Phillip.

Fenal approached me, cracked bulbous lips inches away from my face. He whispered, "Savior." His dirty breath stank of decay. *"Maltor . . ."*

The entire clan repeated the foreign gesture, hushed, yet deep and caustic. Hundreds of golden lights glowed in the distance. Confusion beset my tortured mind.

Maltor?

Phillip's eyes, what little life remained in them, pleaded with me. His bloodied lips trembled, the voice coming from them cracking with fatigue and fear. "I shouldn't have told you anything, Michael."

Jesus. The Isolates were punishing him for breaking their law. That night on the porch to my house, when we spoke, Phillip had told me about their ability to spy on people, to listen in on others' conversations. He'd also shown me what they'd done to Rosy, and that was much more than they could ever allow above and beyond his attempts to get me to make the sacrifice.

They'd been in the woods listening to our entire conversation. And they didn't like what they'd heard.

Now Phillip would pay.

And so would I.

Fenal slithered over. He came within inches of my face. He forcibly handed me a club of wood that looked as though it had been crudely carved from a

273

woodland tree. I grasped it, suddenly aware of their dreadful intentions for myself and for Phil.

Maltor. Kill. They wanted me to kill Phillip Deighton.

I held the wood club in both hands, sweat pouring from my palms, my mind circling in a vain attempt to find the logic behind their perverse request. But I could not. A thing such as logic did not exist down here. The golden-eyed breed are pure evil, ungracious and malevolent, unknowing of such a concept. Without Neil Farris here, they would become sick and lame with injury and disease. Enter the new doctor. They kidnap me, hold me and my family hostage until I cure each and every goddamned one. Make them strong.

Savior. Yes, that's what they call me. Now I understood why. I was here to save their race from extinction. And soon, from what I could fathom, they'd be done with me. As they were at the time with Neil Farris.

"*Maltor!*" Fenal screamed. The breed repeated his demand, the roar of it deafening.

"No," I said feebly, knowing very well I was simply prolonging their game by not cooperating.

A demon appeared from just behind Fenal, groveling toward me on its knees, a great tormented grin pulling its lips wide.

In one dirty, twisted claw it held Jessica's teddy bear, its one button eye still dangling from withered threads.

Dear God . . . They had violated my asylum, the one place where I found my only peace of mind. The place of my purest and most precious possession, the *only* place still sacred in my life. My daughter's room.

My God, how did they get in?

The demon dug its claws into the teddy bear and shredded it with one swift motion. Soft white stuffing fell out, so alien here in this befouled place.

"Maltor," it said.

I had no choice, their threat was clear. Kill Phillip, or they would kill my daughter.

I set my eyes upon Phillip. He was crying, tears pouring down his bruised face, through the blood, the dirt, the pain.

I closed my eyes, raised the club, and swung.

With barely the strength to stagger up the stairs, I looked up, pondering the grisly sight that I feared would greet me: my precious beauty torn limb from limb, her innocence splattered on the walls.

My heart tottered as I took each step, my muscles screaming in pain. I reached the landing, turned, and entered Jessica's room. My nerves flared the moment I saw her.

Turning in bed, Jessica faced me. She rubbed her eyes, her golden locks partially covering her face.

"Hi, Daddy." Her voice sweet, tender, innocent.

I smiled and sat next to her on the soft mattress.

She sat up. Her hair fell away from her face, revealing a smear of blood on her forehead.

Shivering, I held her close, knowing I had to come up with a solution, some way to leave Ashborough. My body and mind could not go on any longer. I had to find a way, I had to protect my family from the Isolates.

But was that realistic? The barriers had proved worthless. Attempts by others to leave had only led to death for their efforts. And now, with the breed healthier, stronger . . .

It was not *whether* they would harm my family, but *when*. Possibility became probability.

Leaving was not the answer. In this playground of good and evil, my only solution was to fight back.

My only hope.

"Daddy?"

"Yes?"

"Where's my teddy?"

I stayed silent, watching the sunrise behind the woods. I hugged Jessica, running my fingers through her hair as I regarded the woods from the window, trying desperately to come up with my next move.

Part Three

For the Infestation of Maggots

Chapter Thirty-three

Every day I wanted to give up. Twice, maybe three times, I actually considered suicide. But that, I told myself, might be a form of murder—certainly they'd take my death as a strike against them, and they would respond by killing my family, making me, in theory, a murderer of my own family. It would take the old adage "What goes around comes around" and contort it into something horridly perverse.

So I gave up on the suicidal thoughts. I'd live each day. I'd see (or hear) Christine leaving to take Jessica to school. I'd see two or three unspeaking patients during the day who never seemed to have anything worth seeing a doctor about (I've come to the assumption that the Isolates were sending them here to keep tabs on me, just as they had with Sam Huxtable; paranoid? me? You'd be too). I'd eat, shit, catch an hour or two of sleep, then slip into my office to wait for their signal. During this time Christine would return home, and every time I'd wonder just where the hell she spent her days, what she did. We still weren't speaking; this seemed to be a mutual concession, leading me to believe even more so that she kept some Isolate-induced secret under tight wraps. This too I gave up trying to uncover. In time, I told myself, it would all come out in the open. And then the shit would hit the fan.

Sooner or later, it would have to happen.

Three weeks after the death of Phillip Deighton, it did happen.

And it was all my doing.

Chapter Thirty-four

I awoke to a strong December gale that'd rattled the windows in my office so hard I mistook it for a misguided flock of birds. Startled, I sat up from the couch and peered around the office, which had taken on the alarming appearance of a madman's junk room: books pulled down from the shelves; dirty plates piled high; papers littering nearly every inch of the wood floor. I'd taken up permanent residence here about two weeks prior, my contact with Jessica and Christine now limited to a random crossing of paths en route to the bathroom or refrigerator. By that point my patients had stopped coming completely. I didn't answer the door anymore. The phone had stopped ringing altogether.

I heard Christine leaving every day, beginning with her footsteps in the kitchen, the cold and limited conversation with Jessica, then the slamming of the front door and the eventual starting of the minivan with its tires that crunched over the gravel driveway as it backed away. My days were spent wondering whether the Isolates in fact had Christine under their control, and what dark tasks they might have had her carrying out; had they threatened Jessica, or even perhaps our unborn child, forcing Christine to maintain utter silence and do what they said?

Eventually, when thoughts of my broken family faded from my mind, I stared into the woods and wondered just when they would call on me again.

I hadn't heard a sound from them since I swung the club and murdered my closest neighbor, Phillip Deighton. Every day I saw his tortured eyes, swollen and bruised and shut tight, anticipating the blow that would shatter his skull. I could still see his body so clearly . . . how it fell in a lifeless heap at my feet, twitching, *creeping,* the blood and the brains spilling from the crushed portion of his skull like porridge, the thick warmth of it soaking through my boots to my feet. Every day I saw this scene played out in my mind like a recurring nightmare, and it felt as though insects were crawling feverishly beneath my skin. Eventually I forced myself to sit silently in my office, and clutched myself tightly to prevent lunacy from taking full control. And then, when the hours passed and nighttime fell, I found it in me to rise from my paralysis and take a seat at my desk, my medical bag close by as I waited for their call.

This morning I felt somewhat *different*, for lack of a better word. I'd fallen asleep at my desk prior to midnight—my usual point of turning in—and awakened at some dark hour. I'd carried myself lifelessly to the couch, where I'd slept the entire night soundly for the first time in months.

The clock read six A.M. Christine had yet to get up. With a strangely enthusiastic burst of energy, I stood up and went into the kitchen, where I drank a glass of milk and ate a peanut-butter sandwich. The good night's sleep had revived my senses, making the food taste much better than usual.

The weather outside was typical for December in New England. Cold, blustery, with a dusting of snow. I retrieved a sweater from the laundry basket on the dryer and pulled it on, realizing that I, all of a sudden, had plans to undertake the one task I hadn't had any energy for in the past. In the closet by the front door, I grabbed my coat, and as I shrugged into it I heard Christine moving around upstairs. Blood surging with anxiety, I slipped out the front door and strode briskly to the minivan.

Before getting in, I peeked up at the windows of the house, forgetting for a moment that they were still barricaded, although the wind had loosened the board in front of the extra bedroom, causing it to dangle like a pendulum from one corner. My mind played games with me in that moment of indecision, and I ignored it as best I could. I realized there was nothing much left to lose by unearthing what really went on in Christine's life during the day. Logic told me, as demented as the *logic* was here in Ashborough, that her days consisted of much more than just dropping off Jessica at school and shopping for groceries. I decided that today, I would find out.

I opened the back hatch to the minivan, closed myself in, then nestled down behind the seat and covered myself with the wool blanket there, not only to conceal my presence, but to also keep warm.

About a half hour later, I heard the front door to the house slam shut.

Christine was coming. She and Jessica walked in silence up the path, each of them taking a seat up front. For a moment I anticipated one of them coming back here to get something, or to investigate the strange odor (I hadn't showered in a week), but instead Christine started the car and backed out of the driveway.

I winced at the aches in my joints as I shifted a bit, the jostle of the car sending flares throughout my body. I was sweating like a horse despite the cold, and I pretty much smelled like one too. I closed my eyes to block all the discomforts, and waited out the ride.

The hum of the engine was constant, Christine apparently keeping the car at a very slow and steady speed. She made a few turns, all hard lefts and rights, but it was difficult to tell exactly how many she made after the first few. We all rode in silence, the only sounds outside of the engine being a few random gales against the rear windshield or a kicked-up pebble striking the car's body.

At last the car slowed, made a sluggish right turn, and pulled onto a long, shaky, unpaved road. For a fleeting moment I assumed that we'd arrived at the school, but having been there once before when registering Jessica, I could not recall an unpaved road or driveway leading to the grounds. No, we weren't at the school. We were someplace else.

But where?

The car made a soft left turn, then stopped. Christine shut off the engine.

Sweat flowed over my body, sticking to my clothes. All was silent except for the naked sway of nearby trees. The car door opened and Christine got out in silence. The door slammed shut and I heard her footsteps circling the front of the car. Through the muffled barrier of the car, I heard her say, "C'mon, honey." Her tone was flat and demanding, as though they'd performed this routine a hundred times before.

Jessica's door opened, then closed. Their footsteps crunched gravel and stopped. The creak of something riding metallic hinges—a gate perhaps—sounded, closing out their footsteps, which quickly faded away into the distance.

I waited. Ten minutes or more passed, and when I assumed that they weren't coming back right away, I leaned up and peeked out through the rear window.

Although it was the middle of the morning, the cloud-filled sky and dense clustering of trees set everything around me in darkness. I could see a thin dirt driveway veining away from the minivan to a back road perhaps a hundred yards away. Thick pine trees on both sides of the driveway insulated it from any traffic that might pass by. I popped open the hatch and crawled outside. The wind was strong, and it almost ripped the door from my hands as I got out of the car; I had to push down on it hard to get it to shut. Pulling my jacket up around my neck, I jogged around the rear of the car and hid behind a large elm that stood next to a wrought-iron fence marking the perimeter of someone's property. The high fence marched in a semicircle around a single tattered dwelling. I looked for a *Beware of Dog* sign, but didn't see one. Still, this was the kind of property that stereotypically housed a foam-jawed pit bull or Doberman, so I remained on close guard.

A minute passed. I kept myself pinned to the tree. I didn't want to be seen, especially by Christine, or a dog, or the owner of the house, which was set back a hundred or so feet from the fence. Then, when I was convinced that all was clear, I quickly rushed along the fence to the gate, nestling my freezing body alongside an old oak whose branches groaned restlessly in the wind. My jacket rippled, chilling my bones, which were already gripped in a cold tide of apprehension.

I peered at the single-story house. Even older than mine, and much smaller, it had a wraparound porch with a railing that lacked more than half its supports. Most of the others were whittled and rotting with age. The shingles hung crookedly, withered and gray, and the shutters were mere skeletons of their former selves. The porch itself was slanted and littered with holes and broken glass.

Christine and Jessica were in there, I told myself, detained against their will and being forced to do horrible things to save themselves, and perhaps me. *I'm gonna get you out of there,* I thought. *Gonna save you both, and then we're gonna get out of here. Forever. Even if it means my life.*

I reached through the iron slats and flipped the latch to the gate, peering up at the fancy cathedral shape running eight feet high. The gate creaked anciently as it moved, not unlike the wind. I slipped through it and shut it behind me, suddenly thankful that I didn't have to tackle the pointed staves running the length of the rusty fence. The last thing I needed now was to end this dangerous parade skewered like a loin of lamb at a Brazilian barbecue.

I hurried forward and pressed up against the trunk of an elm in the middle of the yard, feeling the sweat pouring from my body.

Silence dominated except for the wind and the sway of the trees.

Deciding against the porch, I darted from the tree and circled the house into the backyard. There were more trees there, shutting out even more sunlight. It was unusually dark. And cold. Almost like night.

I took a deep breath, wondering if what I was about to do made any sense. My common sense pointed out to me that very little was tolerated by the "law" here, and that there would be no second chances because the Isolates were probably out there right now, watching me, waiting to see what tricks their good doctor had up his sleeve. So . . . if I didn't do this now, then I'd never find out what Christine was doing here at this strange house. She would never tell me. And the Isolates wouldn't allow me back . . . if they let me live.

Right then and there was my only opportunity to uncover some truth in my life . . . what little was left of it.

I took a moment to survey the surroundings. Not much of a yard, perhaps twenty feet leading into a sea of woodland, which more or less went on forever until someone else's home appeared.

At the periphery of woods was a tombstone.

In the instant I saw the marker, a dead man's words came back to me: *There's a grave in her backyard that's supposed to be that of her mother's. It's right at the edge of the woods, you can see it from the road.*

The cement marker was weathered with age, the top smooth and rounded. It jutted crookedly from the ground, the soil frozen and swollen at the base. Crudely carved on its face was one word:

Zellis

From the woods came a sudden rustling sound. I hid behind the closest tree, pressing my face against the rough bark. A wash of golden light splayed over the tree, and then kept moving, like a spotlight in search of lost ships. My heart expanded in my chest, squeezed painfully against my ribs; I hoped like mad that the demon would miss me. The golden light, bright in the shade, ran across the edge of the woods, then tailed back as though retracing its footsteps. I put my face down and tucked my hands in my pockets in an effort to conceal the white of my skin. It passed over the tree again and kept going before dimming out completely. I waited, continuing to press my body against the tree.

Then without letting myself think about it any further,

I pulled away from the tree and darted toward the house.

Old Lady Zellis's house.

Gasping, I reached the back door. Bits of bark clung to my shirt. A sharp pain made itself known in my knee. I stood quietly for a moment, resting, allowing the ache in my knee to level out before drumming up the nerve to go inside. In this nightmarish moment of inaction I felt a type of loathsome honor . . . here I was, some kind of B-movie hero about to rain down on the parade of the evildoers by bounding in and rescuing the poor fair maiden. It made me feel disconnected from reality, being on this mission to save my family from the evil ancient breed who'd taken an entire New England town hostage.

I wanted to scream, but held it inside, along with the deep inner coldness I knew would stay with me for as long as I kept breathing. I drew my arms around my body, shivered, then again looked at the house.

At the back door.

I reached out and grabbed the doorknob. It was rough with rust.

I turned it.

And then I went inside.

Chapter Thirty-five

I walked into a small vestibule. Stopped. Inhaled deeply. The air tasted bitter, of age and dust. I moved forward into a small kitchen. The room sat in a spiritless light, the windows caked with soil and grime and barely able to accept what little illumination the outside world had to offer. In an alarming moment, I tried to envision my wife and daughter here in this strange, dark environment, but had trouble even remembering what they looked like. I'd spent very little time with them over the past couple of months, and over that time they'd changed on not only an emotional level, but on a physical one as well. Staring at the decrepit features of the kitchen, the rusty basin, the rotting cabinets, the shredded wallpaper, I realized that my family had become complete and total strangers, as foreign to me as this place. I could very well make out their features, Christine's swollen belly and permanent frown, Jessica's blond curls and glassy blue eyes, but attempting to re-call how they looked *before* all this happened seemed impossible, as though their happiness had never ex-isted. And then, when I tried to muster up some images of happiness amongst us in the future, only dark shad-ows arose.

Momentarily keeping thoughts of my family at bay, I set my sights past the doorway in the kitchen, toward what would be the living room—although from this an-gle it didn't appear that much living went on in it. I could see outside beyond the two front windows, to the porch and then to the wrought-iron fence. As before, everything appeared lifeless. If it wasn't for the minivan, I'd've assumed the place to have been long aban-doned.

But Christine and Jessica are here somewhere. The car is parked outside.

Did you actually see them going into the house?

No.

I walked into the living room. It was empty save for some broken pottery and a broom with a splintered handle. A thick layer of dust coated the floor.

In the nearest corner of the room, by a small door-way, were two sets of shoe prints, one of an adult and one of a child.

I walked across the living room, stared down at the footprints, then opened the thin wooden door.

Steps, leading down into a cellar.

Christine? Jessica? Where are you?

I wondered for a moment if I were in control of my

own actions. Somehow, the inability to summon up any happiness in my past led me to believe that I was being psychologically influenced by the Isolates as well. Could this journey be yet another element in their grand scheme? Was I really in control?

I thought of the tombstone out back, only this time envisioned it with *my* name crudely etched into the stone: *CAYLE*. Perhaps in a moment I would be dead, and in need of a marker.

The stairs were set in darkness. But below, somewhere in the basement, candles flickered; a gentle orange glow dancing against the cinder walls leading down. The first wooden step met my feet with a harsh creak, and when I turned my head, I saw that my footprints had vanished in the dust on the living room floor. So had the others.

My God . . .

My heart thumped slow and hard in my chest. I turned back to face the dark stairwell. *(The lesser of two evils?)* I told myself, rightly so, that going down these steps would become a defining moment. That there were people down there in this basement, Christine and Jessica and maybe even Old Lady Zellis. Or an Isolate or two.

I looked back into the living room. My footsteps . . . they were still gone. It wasn't my tired eyes playing games with me. It was the damn Isolates. Somehow they had covered my trail, as if to destroy all evidence of me coming here. In that moment Phillip's voice came back to me from the day we went walking in the woods: *The old lady's eyes started glowing this odd golden color and they had me hypnotized. . . .*

Was it possible that some form of magic existed here in Ashborough? That the Isolates maintained not only a physically intimidating prowess, but a strong hypnotic power as well? If so, was I now under some form of hypnosis, leading me to believe that my footprints had vanished? A trance not unlike the one leading me into the woods to the circle of stones, forcing me to kill Jimmy Page? At that point, anything was possible.

I took the steps one at a time, staring into my soul and seeing that, life or death, I had no choice but to go ahead with this. I told myself that it might be easier to head back outside into the minivan and return home, leave it all behind to run its course. But in doing so, I'd be failing myself, and my family, and then death would most certainly be the only option. So I placed my hands against the cinder walls, reached bottom, and turned into the basement.

Dear God . . . this can't be. . . .

A horror so intense met my gaze . . . so awful and surreal it seemed wholly impossible, like a nightmare. But this was no dream, this was real—as real as the fear pumping through my veins.

They were here. Christine and Jessica. At first sight of them I clapped my hands to my face, fury immediately rising up in me, overturning all those emotions, cold and dark, that had ruled my body and soul for so long.

Then my legs went weak and rubbery on me, stomach twisting madly and shooting acids up into my throat. My anger escalated . . . but so did my fear. I'd never felt such a spectacular combination of emotions, and it tore me even further away from reality, as though I were an astral traveler exploring the heavens while my body lay resting somewhere a million miles away.

I stepped toward them, my feet moving by themselves. An odor hit me and I began to gag. It was awful, and familiar. I gripped the staircase wall, holding on to my balance and breathing heavily.

I took another step forward, shaking so much I thought I would simply collapse. My eyes blurred, making it difficult to focus on the scene before me.

Michael, what you're seeing is absurd. A figment of your spent imagination. You've been through a lot over the past six months, and now it's finally taken its toll on you. Time to check out, my friend. It's been nice knowing you.

There were three people in the basement, Christine, Jessica, and the ancient woman that had come into my office, Old Lady Zellis. They didn't see me, that much was certain. They were surrounded by a circle of candles on the floor, blinded by the shadows. Christine lay fully naked on a concrete slab, spread-eagled. The old witch was hunkered down before her, large callused hands cupping a wriggling mound of a green jellylike substance she'd scooped out of a wooden basin alongside her. Using both hands, she smeared Christine's pregnant belly and vagina with the gelatinous material, using two yellow-clawed fingers to paint odd hieroglyphs upon her skin. Some of the stuff slid away in streaks down Christine's waist, which the old lady eagerly smeared up the sides of her torso to her armpits. This whole time Jessica was sitting on the floor in the furthest corner of the room, seemingly unaware of the wicked event taking place before her, her eyes open, but coated with tears and aimed at some nondescript point in the basement. Her face appeared devilish in the flickering candlelight.

My entire body began to tremble, but I suppressed it. I took another step forward, unsure of what I could possibly do. In that instant, the old lady dipped her hands in the jelly again, only this time, instead of splashing the outside of Christine's body, she clawed a hand into Christine's vagina, up to the wrist. The green matter oozed out at the edges of her orifice as the old lady twisted and turned her arm. Christine seemed not to feel nor care about this, moaning and wincing only slightly as the witch continued thrusting her hand deep inside her. In the corner, Jessica began chanting something alien in a deep-toned voice that wasn't hers, over and over again.

It was at that moment, hearing my little girl speaking in that strange tongue, that the entire scene really hit me . . . really *hit* me, and I began to scream.

My screams clamored piercingly about the basement. I could feel my face contorting—eyes swelling, jaw stretched, skin heated—with noises coming from my throat like sirens, awful screeches that signaled the beginning of insanity, of love lost and then found incomplete and fruitless. Images of the last six months came back to me: Rosy Deighton in her bedroom, the deer in the shed, Lauren Hunter on my walkway, Jimmy

Page's blood on my hands, Old Lady Zellis in my office, Phillip Deighton's exploding skull. But . . . most horrifying of all were the memories of the Isolates themselves, evil demons doing a damn fine job in running my life in their sick, twisted way.

Jessica's moaning stopped.

Old Lady Zellis removed her claw from my wife's vagina.

I'd made my presence known. Now I had to do something about it.

The candles had distorted the appearance and size of the basement, and I could see now that I was closer to the scene than I'd first estimated.

Old Lady Zellis backed away from Christine, slowly, as though trying not to disturb the scene any further. She drifted out of the circle of candles, not toward me but toward the left side of the basement, against the cinder wall near the steps. She stared at me, and the candlelight flickered upon her face, somehow transforming it into something beautiful, princesslike: hair dark and flowing, skin smooth and unblemished, arms waving gracefully in the air. The rags she wore metamorphosed into a silky dress that ran around her neck, across her chest, and down to her ankles; suddenly it appeared to be adorned with golden jewels that glimmered against the dancing flames.

"Michael," she said, her voice soft and musical and seeping out of the gloom like tinkling piano keys.

She was . . . *beautiful.* Suddenly everything I'd feared and suffered seemed extraordinarily distant . . . all I wanted was *her,* her dark beauty, the grace with which she hugged the wall, the way she grinned—so seductively—how she used one single feminine hand to call me to her. This woman before me was the most strangely exotic being I'd ever encountered, stirring thoughts of a breathtaking siren from some untitled silent film.

"Daddy!" I heard the voice filter into my consciousness. In my peripheral vision I saw Jessica struggling to rise from her spot in the far corner; her arms were outstretched toward me.

I turned to look at her. My daughter. "Jessica?"

"Daddy," she cried. "No . . . don't look at her. . . ."

But I did, and she looked back at me, Old Lady Zellis, now a monstrous witch again, grinning at me with hateful eyes that glowed gold and brought pure horror back into me—a horror so cold and icy . . . fouled and fully poisoning my lustful desires of just seconds earlier. Her hands and feet had become claws again, serviceably assisting her in performing a dexterous spiderlike climb up the cinder-block wall. She kept those golden irises pinned on me as she perched herself against the beams in the low ceiling, claws dug deep into the swollen wood. She was more Isolate than human now, a demon showing dark gnarled teeth, hissing at me.

Then, the spell Old Lady Zellis had on Christine and Jessica appeared to weaken. Jessica was now standing with her arms folded tightly across her chest, crying. Her face was corpse-white, wet with tears. Her hair was a tangled mess. Christine looked more surprised than frightened. She sat up from the cement slab, shifting her pregnant belly with two hands. Her breasts, swollen and covered in green sludge, jostled like pendulums as though each might have held a baby too. It seemed as though she was still partially buried in her trance; she scooped up a handful of the green jelly from the floor beneath her crotch and licked it from her palm. Her face went awry and she spit it out as though wholly disgusted. Then she vomited a thick stream of green jelly, splattering the floor beneath the fidgeting witch.

I leaned down to take Christine's hand. She cowered and cried and screamed, like a character in a nightmare, and I wondered if she were actually afraid of *me*. If being saved wasn't what she really wanted. She tried to back away, but Jessica was there, grabbing on to her other arm. We both had her now, pulling with as much strength as we could offer, and virtually dragging her naked pregnant body across the cement floor. A trail of green gunk was left behind like a tire track.

"Christine!" I yelled. "We have to get out of here! Now!"

Jessica had stopped crying and was yelling, "Mommy! Please! Mommy!" and then Christine blurted out a round of hysterics, gazing around the scene and looking tremendously confused. Her trance had definitely lifted, and she was now a naked babe in the woods in search of her mother. Lost and reeling. She screamed, eyes wild and rolling.

"C'mon," I yelled, grabbing her arm. "Let's move!"

Old Lady Zellis began bobbing maniacally from her perch in the ceiling. Her eyes glowed brighter than ever—like those of the Isolates themselves. She let out a hiss that sounded something like a snake in fear of its life. One clawed hand tore away from the cross-beam, taking a thick splinter of wood with it.

"The stairs!" I yelled, pushing Jessica first, and then Christine. Each of us stumbled as we made our way up. When I reached the top step I looked over my shoulder to see if the witch was following us, slicing the air with those claws and hissing that hiss and watching me with those glowing golden eyes. But she wasn't there.

I slammed the door behind us, thinking for a brief moment that it might very well keep the thing away from us. Christine had collapsed on the dusty living room floor, covering herself. There was green jelly everywhere, and suddenly the harsh odor of it rang a bell in my head.

The green tea. Rosy Deighton's recipe.

There were so many assumptions that could be made, none of which we had any time for. I quickly told myself that it was all part of the Grand Scheme, Ashborough's conspiracy against the Cayle family. Hopefully, we'd all live through this nightmare to further reflect on it all. Hopefully.

I reached down to grab Christine. She cried and tried to get up, but slipped back down as a result of the coating of jelly. She looked up at me, her eyes tearing crazily and pleading for forgiveness. Silently I nodded and said, "Let's go, Christine. We have to get out of here now."

She tried to stand, and that was when the basement door burst open. Old Lady Zellis was there, more monstrous than ever, her face a horribly mutated mess, eyes a brilliant gold color.

And then in an instant I saw the beautiful woman again . . . she was holding her arms out to me and pursing her full red lips and saying, "*Come to me, Michael. I want to make love to you, right here and now.*"

I knew I shouldn't have, and didn't really want to, but suddenly she *owned* me, and in the next instant I was holding my arms out toward her, wanting to taste her red-wine lips, her slippery tongue, feel her soft-white skin and run my hands through her shimmering chestnut hair. A pleasure raced through me, replacing all my fears. I could do nothing but want her and submit to her commands. Her fingers met mine, and I could feel my mouth watering for her as a tiny spark of electricity passed between us. Jesus, she was everything I could have ever wanted at the moment. And she was mine for the taking.

Then something happened. The woman shrieked pure evil, a high-pitched shrill of torturous pain. I backed away, breaking our contact. There was a quick movement beside her, and she immediately transformed back into Old Lady Zellis. She backpedaled into the wall, hissing, her face bent into a vulgar mask of fury, agony, and scorn. She turned sideways, and that was when I saw what'd happened to her . . . what Christine had done to her.

There'd only been some broken pottery and a splintered broom handle in the room when I'd first arrived. And of course the dust. But the broom handle's end had broken into a sharp point. Christine had realized this, and competently lodged the handle deep into the side of the witch's neck. Blood shot out in a spectacular display, spraying the wall. The witch fell to her knees, hands blindly grasping at the broom handle. She'd almost gotten hold of it, but I stepped in and kicked her squarely in the face. She choked. Her voice was weakened by the broom handle in her neck, and came out barely more than a harsh whisper. She hit the floor, blood gushing from her wound. I reached down, yanked the wood handle out, and in a quick calculated thrust, slammed it back down into her throat. A moaning, gargling noise came out of her mouth, her lips twisted in an attempt to scream, golden eyes bulging horridly. Her hands clawed the dust on the floor as if vainly attempting to conjure up one last spell. The nauseating stink of hot blood rose up; it colored the floor in a extraordinary puddle, wide and shimmering and spreading. She wheezed and thumped and hissed one last time, and then her eyes, once glowing gold, faded down into pallid gray marbles, staring lifelessly at the ceiling.

Old Lady Zellis was dead.

Common sense told me that in a very short time, we would be too.

Chapter Thirty-six

We fled through the front door. I didn't want to go the back way. The woods were there, filled with poisonous eyes that would spot the murderers of the old witch; we'd never make it out alive. I opted to brave the rotting porch instead, whose holes and soft beams proved easy enough to avoid. We raced across the front yard, and what a sight we must've been. A naked pregnant woman covered in green sludge and dust, with blood on her hands; a grown man leading her away, also with blood on his hands; and then, the most normal one of the crew: a five-year-old girl who from afar may have seemed normal, but who had just emerged from a trance and who was probably traumatized. Luckily, no one was there to see us . . . unless, of course, someone (or something) was hiding amidst the trees leading out to the main road.

We ran in silence to the car, where we all frantically piled in, Christine in the backseat, Jessica beside me in the front.

I felt for the ignition.

The keys . . .

"Shit!" I yelled. "Christine, where are the fucking keys?"

I heard her sob in the backseat. "Jesus Christ . . ."

I glanced around and saw her curled fetally against the seat, shivering uncontrollably. Goose bumps lined her body. The green gunk had somehow made its way from her stomach to her hair. "Where are they?" I demanded.

"In my pocketbook . . ." she said with dismay. Her voice cracked and trembled and she hid her face behind her hands, as if expecting a blow.

"Damn it!" I slammed the steering wheel hard enough to make it vibrate, sending a piercing pain into my fists.

"Daddy . . . please, I want to get out of here." Jessica was looking all around, nervous and desperate.

I had no choice. I had to go back inside.

"Lock the doors after I get out. Whatever you do, don't open them unless I come back."

Jessica nodded weakly.

From the backseat came a despondent voice "What if you don't come back?"

I answered emptily, "Your lives are at stake, not to mention that of my unborn child's. I'll be back, and then we'll get out of here for good. I promise."

I'd lied before. I just lied again.

Honey, those were fireflies you saw in the woods. . . .

303

"It's in the basement," Christine said. "With my clothes, on the floor in the far corner."

I nodded, then got out of the minivan. I glanced around to make sure there were no Isolates nearby, then shut the door. The locks clicked. Jessica looked at me through the windshield, and I smiled as best I could to offer her some reassurance. She did nothing, just looked away.

I stepped around to the back of the car, opened the hatch, reached in and grabbed the wool blanket I'd hidden under earlier, and tossed it over the seat to Christine.

Surprisingly enough, my travel medical kit was still back here. I opened it and removed the only scalpel. It was a small one, with a one-inch blade. Better than nothing, I supposed.

I closed the hatch, then quickly raced to the gate, which I'd left open. The wind picked up for a moment and jarred the pines, making a harsh breathlike noise that went fittingly with the cold dismal setting. I ran across the front lawn, sidestepped the holes in the porch, and went back inside Old Lady Zellis's house.

And there she was. Old Lady Zellis. Her rictus grin, spotted with blood, laughing at me. Her eyes, gray and lifeless, stared up at the ceiling. The broomstick protruded from her throat like a stake in a vampire's heart. Blood had puddled out from the wound in a semicircle across five feet of flooring. The room possessed a hot organic stench. I'd smelled this scent before while performing emergency-room work during my internship at Columbia. It was a unique smell, one you never forgot.

To avoid the blood, I stepped over her body (cringing as I did so; my mind imagined her feigning death, launching a hand up and grabbing my ankle) and staggered back down into the basement, hands against the cinder walls, leaving ghostly bloodstains behind on the cement. I wondered just what the hell Old Lady Zellis was all about. Without question she had some Isolate blood in her, as evident by the glow in her eyes and her sharp yellow claws. But still . . . she maintained human qualities. Was she the result of mixed parents? A mixed-breed of human and Isolate? Somehow I couldn't see a human willfully entangling with one of those things. So then, how?

Perhaps the dead person in the grave out back can explain that to you?

Phillip's words seeped back to me yet again: *There's a grave in her backyard that's supposed to be that of her mother's. It's right at the edge of the woods, you can even see it from the road.*

The candles were still burning in the basement. Wax pooled at their bottoms like lilypads. I looked into the far corner opposite the steps and spotted Christine's clothes and purse. I ran over, hurriedly snatched them up, and tucked everything under my arm, all the while holding the scalpel out. Then, quietly, I went back up the steps into the living room.

When I reached the top step, I stopped.

My body went numb.

There were footprints in Old Lady Zellis's blood.

Isolate footprints.

There was only one set, but it was enough to scare

the hell out of me. They passed through the blood alongside the body, then backtracked out, trailing bloodstains into the kitchen. I imagined one of them having come here to investigate the ruckus only to find the old lady in a less than desirable state. It was probably out back now, alerting its brothers and sisters of the sudden tragedy. Shit . . . they'd be on me in seconds.

I ran like an animal in the scope of a hunter's rifle, out the front door and simply forgetting about the holes in the porch. If there was ever a time I was close to just giving up, this was it. My foot went through a soft spot in the porch like a thumb into a piece of rotten fruit. My leg sank in up to the knee, and I jammed my elbow against the edge to stop from sinking in further. My jeans tore, and I could see a cherry-red gleam of fresh skin from the middle of my shin to a spot just below my knee; a hunk of flayed skin hung at the top of the wound, where it dangled painfully. My breath escaped me and left my lungs burning. I threw down the clothes and purse, then pressed my left hand against what I hoped was a more stable area of the porch. The splinter of wood that'd made a mess of my shin came back at me for a second helping, sending a jolt of pain through me that damn near made me swoon. Then I looked over at the minivan. Jessica and Christine were pressed against the windows, watching me the intense way children watch an animal at the zoo. God . . . I didn't want this to be the last time I saw them. I had to get myself out and move fast, find some inner strength and go for it. Jesus, I'd done pretty well up until this point—there was no sense giving up now.

Was there?

I stretched forward and grabbed the lip of the top step. Using this as leverage, I pulled myself out of the hole, then quickly grabbed the purse, electing to leave Christine's clothes behind. I tumbled down the three steps of the porch, and fell to my knees on the concrete walkway.

Something came at me from the house. In my peripheral vision I saw the lanky figure leap over the porch and sail at me through the air. I dived sideways, but the thing managed to get a claw on my waist, taking me to the ground. Still holding the scalpel—and what a miracle that was—I stabbed at it. The Isolate lunged at me, teeth gnashing as it tried to bite me, but the blade was there first, leaving a gaping gash on its cheek. I could see its face, the head whipping around as it struggled to find some part of me to bite down on. I continued to thrust the scalpel, catching it wherever I could, on the shoulders, chest, and neck. Hot blood sprayed out everywhere; I could feel it on my skin, through my shirt. Its arms and legs flailed crazily, loathsome claws scratching me, seeking purchase, but succeeding only in tattering my clothes. The thing yelped and in a moment of pain, withdrew just enough for me to bring the scalpel home into one of its glowing golden eyes.

Howling, the Isolate reared back, batting at the scalpel that took away the color in its eye. Thick yellow pudding blobbed out from the socket and oozed down its cheek. *It looks like tapioca,* I thought crazily. It fell down on its back, fists pounding the snowy grass in agony, the scalpel sticking straight out of its eye socket like . . . like the broomstick in the old lady's throat.

I got up clumsily, like a palsied child. I squinted obliquely toward the car; the world started spinning around me. I heard Jessica's voice calling, "Daddy! Hurry!"

Instinctively, I started lunging toward the car. I'd only taken a few steps when Jessica yelled, "The purse, Daddy, the purse!"

It lay next to the writhing Isolate. I darted over as quickly as my numbing feet could take me, then leaned down and grabbed it. The Isolate staggered up, the scalpel still in its left eye; the other eye glowed like fire and pinned me angrily—there was still some fight left in this bad boy.

Despite the pain and fatigue and damn near willingness to pack it all in, I ran. Fast. Back to the minivan to the driver's side door. I pulled on the handle and it snapped back. The doors were still locked! "Open the fucking door, Jessica!" Inside I saw my daughter scrambling at the controls on the passenger side. With an audible *click*, the doors unlocked. I pulled it open and shoved inside. But the Isolate was there.

Instead of trying to pull me out, the creature pushed me forward into the minivan against Jessica, then leaped inside on top of me. Screams erupted from Jessica and Christine. Limbs flailed wildly from all sources, a barrage of swipes and fists being tossed in all directions. The Isolate's claw slapped my face. Immediately

I could feel blood pouring down from the laceration it made, the cold air biting into my skin like acid. Jessica was hysterical, clawing at the window, attempting to steer clear of the battle taking place right next to her. Christine had sat up and was tentatively hurling fists into the front seat; her aim was good, but she neither hurt nor distracted the creature. It had me on my side and was sitting on top of me, swiping my back and shoulders. Its nails felt like razors as they sliced through my clothes. I knew that if I didn't do something soon, I'd be no better off than Old Lady Zellis. But my strength was fading fast, and I could do nothing at this point but allow my weakening body to be ravaged by the creature.

Suddenly there came a squeal of pure agony. The weight on my back lifted and when I tilted my head up, I saw a thick wash of blood on the windshield. In this brief moment of respite, the pain of my attack rang out, suddenly and excruciatingly. I kicked my legs frantically and felt them connect with the Isolate. It screamed, but didn't fight back. There was a series of coughs. Finally I flipped over and scrambled as much as I could into Jessica's seat, arms outstretched, prepared to throw fists. Jessica was pressed flat against the back of the seat, sweating and trembling.

The Isolate was dead, or approaching its fate fast. The scalpel now protruded from its other eye, a matching tapioca trail painting its other cheek. Its body twitched as though charged with electricity.

"I did it, Daddy . . ." Jessica said. "I . . . I . . ." She was shaking uncontrollably, then broke out in hysterics.

"Michael," Christine said, "is it . . . is it dead?"

I prodded it with my foot. The creature slipped off the steering wheel and fell against the door. The scalpel that Jessica had so bravely pulled from one eye and inserted into the other pressed against the window and sank deeper into its head so only the tip of the handle was exposed.

Then, something came to my attention. I tried to swallow the lump in my throat, with not much success; my stomach wouldn't take it—it was too filled with fear.

"Who shut the car door?" I whispered.

No answer.

I reached over and triggered the locks. "The keys," I said. "Where are they?" I shifted my body against the dead Isolate. Jessica leaned down, grabbed Christine's purse.

"Is it dead, Michael? Is it?" Christine repeated.

Gingerly, I placed a hand against its wrist. Déjà vu. I'd done this a dozen times before in their den. "Yeah, it's dead," I confirmed.

In the alarming silence, I added, "Whatever you do, don't open the doors." I shifted the Isolate's body over my lap, between the two front seats. Christine screamed as the befouled head lolled in her direction.

"Quiet, Christine!" I whispered forcefully, looking out the windows for a sign of them. *Someone closed the door.* . . . "Take the body and put it next to you in the backseat. And again . . . don't open the doors."

Christine said, "I can't look at it . . . it's dripping all over. Can't we throw it out the window?"

I pushed the body into the backseat. Christine slid to

the opposite side, curling the blanket around her body as though it might protect her from the dead creature. "They're out there, watching us," I said. "They know what we did. And now they're waiting."

"Waiting for what?"

"For the right time to kill us."

Chapter Thirty-seven

All was quiet. Too quiet. A bat fluttered overhead, making a noise almost like a snicker. Probably because it knew just how many of those motherfuckers were out there right now, watching us from the woods.

Jessica handed me the keys she'd retrieved from Christine's purse. I slid them into the ignition and started the car. As if in answer, the woods ignited with golden eyes. About two dozen sets, maybe more. Slowly, I took the minivan over the dirt driveway.

With the ease of trained gymnasts, the Isolates darted from the woods after the car. One was already nearby (presumably the same one that'd closed the door, shutting us inside with its brother) and leaped atop the hood of the car. It latched its claws onto the windshield wipers, pressed its horrible face against the glass, and howled at us.

I slammed on the gas. A cloud of dust rose from the back tires, filling the yard. The minivan shot down the long thin driveway. Jessica screamed, "They're coming Daddy! They're coming!" Her voice was jarred because of the bumpy path.

The minivan reached the end of the driveway, and I just took my chances that no other cars would be traveling along the tree-shrouded road. I won this crapshoot. We spun out into the road, wheels skidding on the thin layer of snow. The Isolate on the hood lost its grip on the wipers and sailed off toward the side of the road like a loose piece of luggage. The force of the turn also sent the dead Isolate in the backseat on top of Christine. She screamed, flailed at it, pushed it away with disgust, then continued kicking it once it was back on the other side of the seat, as though that would keep it away for good.

In the rearview mirror, I could see about a dozen Isolates racing from the driveway out into the road, zigzagging like hungry rats in search of food. But the car had built up too much speed for them, and once they seemed to realize that it was completely out of their reach, they all at once raced back into the snowy cloak of the woods.

At this point my intentions were to flee Ashborough. Or at least make some sort of an attempt. All I had to do was drive as fast as I could right the fuck out of town, right? I came to the state road and pondered which way to go, right or left. I couldn't drive east because then I'd have to go right through the village, and there'd be townsfolk and cops there and other scheming obstacles with their Isolate-given edicts and maybe even bats and torches in their hands. And they might as well be wearing T-shirts that say, *Welcome to Ashborough! You'll never get out alive!* So I decided to travel west along the state road, which would take us right past our home, and then into Ellenville.

"We're getting out of here," I said.

"They won't let us," Christine said. "You and I both know that, Michael."

"Fuck 'em," I said, with not an ounce of rationale to back me up.

"If we'd been able to get out of here, then we would've done it a long time ago. So would've all the other people living here. Nothing's changed. They're still not gonna let us go. In fact, they're probably going to kill us now, after what we just did to the woman. You said so yourself."

In an effort to create hope, I changed my tune. "They won't kill us . . . we won't give them the chance." I continued driving along the state road, pushing forty despite the curves. My knuckles were white against the steering wheel. "I mean, how could they possibly get to us now? We're in the fucking car, so let's be serious here!"

Damn it to hell . . . I wasn't making any sense, and I knew it too. They'd managed to trash the car on Christine while it was moving. So why couldn't they do it again? Well . . . they probably could. But the problem was that I had this odd concept called freedom in my head and I was ready, willing, and able to do anything to acquire it.

Jessica started sobbing. "I want to leave here, please, Daddy! Please Daddy!"

"See that, Chris? Your daughter wants to leave, and that's just what we're gonna do. Leave."

"We should go home," Christine said despondently. "It's what they want us to do."

I swallowed a lump in my throat, then said, "You're out of your fucking mind if you expect me to go back to that house. I'm not going there, and I'm not gonna let you or Jessica go back there either."

"We killed the fucking woman!" she screamed, silencing the car. The immediate tension inside felt like humidity on a hot summer day, heavy and oppressive. She added, "Isn't it bad enough that we're simply talking again? We should just go back to the house and lock ourselves in."

I looked into the rearview mirror. Christine's expression was very peculiar. It was as if she'd seen Medusa and had turned to stone. And then her eyes narrowed, as if to confirm her revelation: that all along we'd feared speaking to one another because it would've resulted in severe injury or death. That the Isolates had *owned* us all along.

Now . . . with all that had happened today? I had no choice but to agree with her. We'd killed a woman who might have been their spiritual leader, and now they were going to kill us.

For months they'd been threatening us with death. Those threats were now going to be carried out. The way I looked at it, it didn't make much of a difference what we decided to do. It made much more sense to, at the very least, attempt an escape.

Ignoring Christine's wishes, I floored the accelerator. The minivan took off down the road. It wasn't a bull when it came to pick-up, but it kept us moving, pushing fifty and climbing faster.

Christine screamed for me to stop. But all I could think about was how they could possibly halt us now. Would they really start hurling themselves under the wheels?

Our house was a quarter mile ahead. We passed Phillip Deighton's house on the right, and I quickly wondered how long it'd be before the local real-estate agent ushered in the next young unsuspecting couple with a deal too good to be true.

"Look out, Daddy!" Jessica screamed.

I'd looked away for the briefest moment to peek at Phillip Deighton's house. When I set my sights back to the road, stunned terror hit me like a knockout punch. I slammed down on the brakes. The minivan skidded and three-sixtied, much too late to avoid the ash tree lying end-to-end in the road about twenty feet ahead. We slammed right into it, jolted, went up on two tires, and nearly flipped over. Two loud explosions sounded, that of tires blowing. The tree splintered into a million pieces and rained down all over us. The minivan lurched back down, then tilted forward as the front tires fell away from the axle. The stench of gas immediately invaded my nostrils.

A moment of stunned silence passed between us. I

could hear everyone breathing heavily. Jessica then started crying, and so did Christine. I wanted to cry also, but held back. Someone needed to be strong, and it wasn't going to be my wife or my five-year-old daughter. I looked into the rearview mirror and saw blood on Christine's face, uncertain if it was hers or the dead Isolate's.

"Is everyone okay?" I'd slammed the top of my head nice and hard against the roof of the car. The pain was just now making itself known. Thankfully, despite the fact that none of us had seat belts on, we all seemed to have come out of it okay.

"I smell gas, Michael."

I got out of the minivan. There were pieces of the tree everywhere, many chunks lodged into the grille. One thick shard jutted from the bumper like a stake. The front axle of the car had shattered, causing the two front tires to lay flat on the road. Gas bled out onto the blacktop. Our car had no life left in it . . . just like the witch.

Jessica had gotten out and was standing on the side of the road.

Near the woods.

"Jessica! Get away from the woods!" I had sudden visions of an Isolate leaping out from its camouflage, grabbing her, and pulling her away.

"The car might explode," she said, racing out into the center of the road, far ahead of the car.

Right she was too. I quickly opened the backseat door and eased Christine out. She had the blanket wrapped around her like a shawl, belly and breasts protruding, blood and mud now spotting the dried layer of green slime on her skin. She started laughing, a high, chortling sound that was probably the onset of hysteria.

I pulled her away from the car and we all walked as quickly as possible down the center of the road. When Christine's giggling died down, I said despondently, "I guess we have no choice now but to go back home."

"It's what they want us to do," she exclaimed, suddenly and rather spookily composed.

"You mentioned that earlier. . . ."

Christine answered, "If they'd wanted us dead, then they would have done it already." Shivering, she wiped her nose with the end of the blanket, then promptly changed her tune. "I just don't understand it, though . . . I mean, why don't they just kill us?" She started looking around in a paranoid fashion, over her shoulders and into the woods. Clearly the likelihood of hysteria still loomed. Jessica huddled close to me, something she hadn't done in months.

Then I answered, "They're not killing us because . . . because they need me. That's why."

There was a moment's hesitation, then Christine said, "Michael . . ."

"Yes?"

"We need to talk."

"I . . ." Instantly, my past fears came back to me. I couldn't speak . . . I was afraid to talk to her—it was as though the sudden reminder had retriggered the negative-memory engram in my subconscious. Now *I* was looking over my shoulder, thinking that they were watching us now, listening to us. . . .

"I don't care about their threats anymore," Christine revealed, not so much out of bravery as much as denial. "If they'd wanted us dead, then they would have done it already. Right?" It appeared as if she was trying to convince herself.

"Unless they're waiting for the right moment."

"If that's the case, then we better get home and formulate some sort of plan. Pool our experiences. Maybe we can learn something about them. Maybe they have a weakness, something we can exploit. Something that can help us escape. It doesn't appear as if we have any other choice."

Holy shit . . .

I stopped walking, started thinking. Christine's words, suddenly logical, stirred an amazing revelation in me. *A weakness. Something that can help us escape.* Christine and Jessica stopped and turned to look at me. I stood silently in the center of the road for about thirty seconds, rubbing my face, thinking . . . thinking . . . thinking that there might actually be a way to get out of this after all. Jesus, all I needed was . . .

"Michael? What's wrong?"

I looked back at them. "Farris . . . he was on to something."

"Who? What are you talking about?"

"I don't want to talk about it now. They're probably in the woods, listening to us." Heart pounding, blood racing, I ran back to the minivan, opened the rear passenger door, and scooped out the dead Isolate. It felt like a heavy bag of potatoes, thick and misshapen. It almost slipped through my arms, but I clutched it

319

tighter. Then I walked back to my family, looking over my shoulder the entire time.

"What the hell are you doing, Michael?"

"Let's go home. Then we'll talk."

Chapter Thirty-eight

The walk back home went as quickly and uneventfully as we could've hoped for; most of the short journey was spent in silence, sniffing the cold damp air and peering at the lifeless patches of woodland peeking out from beneath the thin layer of snow. A mere thirty minutes after the minivan had slammed into the ash tree, we found ourselves safely behind the locked doors of 17 Harlan Road, seated around the kitchen table and drinking cold water, with the body of a dead Isolate in our freezer. Christine still had the blanket wrapped around her like a shroud, I still had my injuries, and Jessica looked much dirtier under the fresh light than she did an hour before at the witch's house. After some food, we decided it best to wash up and attempt to clear our bodies and minds of the events of the morning. Two of us stood guard with kitchen knives in the upstairs hallway while the third one showered, and in thirty minutes we were all clean and seated back at the kitchen table, ready to discuss the past, present, and future of the Cayle family.

The living room clock tolled twelve noon. I found it hard to believe that everything that morning had taken place in less than three hours, from the moment I hid in the car to that very minute. It felt like a week had passed by.

"Does Jessica need to hear all this?" I asked Christine.

Jessica remained silent in her seat, eyes wounded with dark circles and tears. Christine said, "Jess, honey, you can stay and listen, and if there's something you think Daddy and I should know, then tell us, okay?"

She nodded weakly, sipping her water, seeming not to care one way or the other. *Yep, that's post-traumatic stress disorder settling itself into her brain, nice and comfortable.*

I went first. I took a deep breath, then told them everything. From the encounter with Rosy Deighton in her bedroom on the first day we moved in (I'd told Christine about this before, but felt the need to begin with that again, for Jessica's sake, I suppose), to the confrontation with the deer in the shed. I detailed the incidents with Lauren Hunter, my dream with Page, and all the circumstances surrounding Phillip Deighton, of how he'd tried to set me up, of his description of Rosy's death, and how he'd ultimately died at my hand. I spoke of my meeting with Old Lady Zellis and Sam Huxtable and how my conversation with him was the catalyst for my wondering if the rest of my family might be involved in what I dubbed as the Grand Scheme. I detailed all my experiences within the den of the Isolates, how I'd been named their "Savior," and described in as much detail as I could everything I'd been forced to endure. When I told Christine about how I slipped into the car, determined to find out exactly what she was up to, I looked at the clock and saw that an hour had passed since I'd begun the whole extraordinary tale.

"As it turned out, I was right. You were as much a prisoner as I was."

Christine frowned, then said, "The only difference is that I really didn't know I was being manipulated. Up until the moment you came into the basement, I was undeniably convinced that I'd been visiting the doctor all along. It just appeared that way to me, everything, the house we were in . . . to me it looked just like a doctor's office. Never once had I seen past the delusion."

"I fell under her spell too once she discovered me in her house," I said. "She appeared to be a beautiful siren. I was captivated. I couldn't move, speak, nothing. It was as though I'd died and gone to heaven and my angel was there to usher me in through the pearly gates. If you hadn't stabbed her with the broomstick, I probably wouldn't be sitting here with you right now."

"You never felt any sort of entrancement with the creatures?" Christine asked.

"No . . . well, except maybe in the dream."

"So . . . is it possible that only the witch possessed this kind of ability?"

I nodded. Then a sudden realization crept up on me, and I asked, "How often did you go there?"

"To the witch's house?"

I nodded again.

Tears filled her eyes. "Every day since Jessica started school."

The truth made me wince. "God, Christine, didn't you bring Jessica to school at all?"

Christine gazed at Jessica remorsefully, then nodded and said, "Every day up until last month. But the doctor—well, the witch, I mean—she insisted that I bring her to our sessions. I felt I had no choice. It was as though something terrible would happen if I didn't."

"That was definitely another part of her spell. Which makes me believe that the Isolates also used some form of mind control against me. I'd been utterly convinced that any conversation I initiated with you or Jessica would result in your deaths. That's why I maintained such a strong silence over the last few months." Frustrated, I ran a hand through my hair. "Jesus, for all we know, there's a great deal more than just blatant threat keeping this town at bay."

"The people I saw carrying the dead body into the house. They looked like zombies. They didn't appear to be acting on their own accord."

I paused in thought, trying to imagine the eerie scene playing out as Christine described it that afternoon. I looked at Jessica. She was focused hypnotically on the grain of the kitchen table, perhaps closing herself out to the unpleasant conversation taking place. I asked her, "Did the old lady do anything to you, honey?"

"No."

"Nothing?"

"No," she said, then added, "The whole time I thought I was in a waiting room. I never saw anything."

"Did the old lady ever threaten you?"

"No," she answered.

I turned back to Christine. "What the hell did the witch want with Jessica?" Of course there was no answer to this question, at least none that we could come up with. At this point, Christine didn't even know what she herself had been doing there.

Christine said, "I don't remember much of anything, but I can recall some conversations I had with who I presumed at the time was the doctor. I remember her telling me that she was a longtime local, and that her mother used to live in the house with her but was now buried in the backyard. For some reason, this piece of information sticks in my mind."

"Because it's true, I saw the grave."

"So then what the hell was she? A human? Or one of those things from the woods?"

"Some kind of half-breed, I guess. Half-Isolate, half-human. With some extraordinary prescient abilities above and beyond those of the Isolates themselves."

"Did you see anything, Michael?" Christine asked, her voice thinning out. "In the basement. Did you see her doing anything to me?"

For a moment I actually considered divulging everything I saw, but quickly decided against it. Some things were better left untold, like when you cheat on your girlfriend. Telling your wife that she had a witch-claw in her vagina would be one too.

You sure about that, Michael? The witch had to have been doing something at that moment. It might be best if you told her. It's her body after all. And your baby.

Dear sweet Jesus, she was doing something to the baby, wasn't she?

"No, all I saw was the old lady bathing you in that stuff."

"The leaves."

"Leaves?"

She shrugged her shoulders. "She made jelly out of these weird leaves. I remember her grinding them in the barrel with a wooden pestle."

"When I went down into the basement, I'd smelled a pungent odor . . . it'd struck me as being very familiar. Then I realized what it was. The tea. Those weird leaves, you grew them in the garden and brewed them to make that tea you were drinking, right?"

Tears filled her eyes. She placed her head against my chest, suppressing her sobs. "How could I have been so stupid?"

"You didn't know. You didn't know."

"I trusted Rosy."

"And I trusted Phillip. But at the time there was no way we could've known what was going on." I rubbed a gentle hand against her back and peered over her shoulder at the kitchen counter, to the few things we'd removed from the freezer when we first got home.

I then looked over at the freezer, and realized with dread that the dead Isolate crammed inside would be our only hope for escape.

Chapter Thirty-nine

The frigid afternoon moved forward with a dusting of snow. One of the three wooden boards had fallen (or had been torn) from the upstairs window, and was now lying on the grass ten feet away near Christine's dying herb garden.

I sifted through the trash on my office floor, realizing that that might very well be the last day I'd ever set foot in there, which was just fine with me. A million thoughts raced through my head, and if all went as planned, we'd be out of there in a day or two. I hoped.

I'd explained my discovery to Christine, along with my intentions. She appeared enthusiastic, yet skeptical. I told her that I saw no other alternative, that we could either attempt to finish what Neil Farris had started, or wait for the Isolates to come after us, which, in my estimation, would be tonight. She nodded, realizing that there'd be no other option but to fight the evil breed known as the Isolates.

I told Christine and Jessica to prepare for an immediate departure, and they both went upstairs to pack up some things, only necessities I told them, such as clothes and food. The minivan was totally undriveable, so my campaign against the Isolates would have to be one-hundred-percent successful if we were to walk part of the way out of Ashborough. I remained convinced that along the way we could probably take someone's car without much resistance.

The dead Isolate I took from the backseat of the minivan was still sufficiently wedged inside the freezer—I'd had to break its thigh bones to get it in, but I'd had no choice since we chose not to weather the horrid stench of the thing, which in turn would send up a giant red flag to its relatives.

I opened the freezer. The creature's skin had adhered to the icy walls and made a tearing sound as I pulled it out. It left patches of dirt and blood against the snowy interior, like abstract paint smears.

With a shiver, I hauled the body into my office and laid it out on the patient's examining bench. Perhaps four feet in length, the monster rested messily, its legs and arms twisted into near-impossible angles, dangling from the table's edge like those of a strewn marionette. Its face had a furry coating of ice on it, like a beard. It could've passed as one of Santa's elves gone to hell and back.

I spread the body out (like a patient, I suppose), the bones making hard white snapping sounds as I wrenched the limbs back into form. Smears of slimy deposits and muck saturated the pure white paper sheathing the table.

The clock in my office tolled four. Darkness crept in like a murderer's hand. Soon, I knew they would be coming for the body. Which meant I had only one chance to get it right. And not much time to do it.

I could hear my wife and daughter pacing about upstairs as they prepared to flee this godforsaken town. I wondered for a moment if the Isolates were out there right now, perching against the barricaded windows and watching us: trying to figure out our intentions. I could only pray that they didn't find out right away.

As I went about mentally preparing my plan, curiosity got the best of me and I took a moment to study the body more closely. Its face was horrible, like that of a child's stricken with progeria: skin pruned, teeth overgrown and terribly misshapen. Wispy strands of hair lay straggled atop its warped head like cobwebs. Its rib cage was sunken, the stomach cavity rippled with sinewy muscle, limbs long and gangly and broomstick-thin. So different than us—yet so genetically similar.

So genetically similar . . .

In an abstract moment I considered the fact—a single tidbit of information culled from my years at Columbia—that only one single gene differentiates man from the apes. And yet, gazing at this creature, I could see that apes differed from humans much more than the Isolates did. Was it possible that these golden-eyed demons were in fact some unique race of homo sapiens?

But what of the glowing eyes? I could only assume them to be the result of adaptation to their subterranean environment. And the feet? Five-toed, yes, but more reptilian than mammalian, something unexplainable by evolutionary theory. Dozens of questions existed, but it seemed they would have to remain unanswered for now.

Or would they?

Despite my obedience to their commands, in the back of my mind I'd always wondered how I might actually go about putting an end to their existence. Setting fire to their lair had been one option. But would there be enough oxygen to keep the flames burning in their subterranean den? Plus, would fire even burn in the dampness? Yes, I might end up killing off a number of them by smoking out the entrance, but as Sam Huxtable had pointed out, there were many other entrances and exits to the great den—ones I had no knowledge of.

Other options seemed even more implausible: flooding them out, sniping at them one by one; it was futile to even consider these. The Isolates' numbers were too extensive, and there seemed no means of alerting outside forces to their presence. As soon as I tried, the Isolates would come after me, capture and torture me. And then they would murder my family and take pleasure in making me watch.

So when Christine mentioned in the road earlier today that they might actually have a weakness, it became immediately obvious to me that they must indeed have some limitations, and that Neil Farris had known about them, and *that* was why he was running. Because the Isolates had caught on to his plan. And they took him down before he could do anything about it.

I saw my only option—I needed to finish what Neil Farris started.

I snapped on a pair of surgical gloves, then went into my office and unlocked the small icebox hugging the corner of the room between the bookshelf and the armoire. This was where Neil Farris had kept samples of his patients' blood. Upon first discovery of the icebox, I'd wondered why in God's name he had done this, putting aside the fact that harboring samples tainted with bubonic plague was a federal violation; the government would toss your ass in jail for thirty years if they found you doing this.

Inside the icebox were seventeen plastic tubes in total, containing four different strains of viruses. Bubonic plague, malaria, HIV+, and hantavirus. I was most interested in the last one: hantavirus.

For the first time in six months, I smiled.

I picked out the *hantavirus* tube and took it back to the examining room, placing it in a clamp on the steel supply table opposite the examining bench. I then retrieved a syringe from the cabinet above my head, armed it with a needle, and confronted the dead beast.

The needle slid into its jugular with ease, and I pulled back on the syringe, filling it with the Isolate's blood, which had only begun to coagulate. I then placed a drop of the blood on a glass specimen slide and hooked it under a microscope.

I looked through the eyepiece. And saw it immediately. Fluttering on the slide. A germ, propelling itself through the blood by means of hairlike flagellum.

This is too easy. . . .

This was Microbiology 101. The presence of the germ in the blood at once confirmed the most profound mystery of all: that these creatures were *human,* grossly infected humans. This germ I was looking at had somehow over the years wreaked havoc on their genetic system and mutated these *people* to a degree previously unheard of. Their warped features, their withered skin and stooped posture, even their maniacal aggressiveness were all results of this little bugger in the microscope, this horribly transfigured germ.

It was an amazing discovery. Perhaps tens of thousands of years ago the spread of this germ had brought disease and eventual death to a large population of humans—a plague of insurmountable proportions. Miraculously, the survivors of the plague had built a resistance to the germ—but not without any consequences. The result of their exposure was pure genetic mutation, a disfigurement of growth, appearance, and demeanor. Over time, through the retardation of genes in conjunction with environmental adaptation, the humans slowly evolved into Isolates and thrived to become the alienated race of creatures living in the woods today.

Genetically altered human beings. *Naturally* genetically altered, like the genus of six-legged frogs found only in one small lake in the northwest United States,

333

or the two-headed snakes indigenous to a mere twenty square miles of Amazonian forest.

So . . . if the Isolates were indeed susceptible to germs, as evident by the bacillus in their blood, then they could catch a virus too, just like other humans do. And with the right virus, they could be killed. Quickly. *Viciously.*

Neil Farris knew this. And now, so do I.

Reflecting again on my past education, I recalled that when biological conditions become unfavorable, certain categories of viral germs become capable of creating bodies called spores. These bodies detach themselves and eventually become free spores, highly resistant to physical and chemical change. Later, when conditions become more favorable for survival, the spores regerminate and reproduce the original qualities of the virus. It is at this point the virus becomes communicable. This is how we end up catching colds, or the flu. Through sporulation.

Deep in their den, where physical contact is high and the damp environment is supporting, sporulation would work masterfully.

A patient came in to me a few years back. He complained of diarrhea, vomiting, fever, congestion, cough. It had all snowballed upon him one day after being bitten by a rat while cleaning out his barn during a weekend getaway in the Hamptons. I'd taken his blood, tested it.

His blood had tested positive for Hantaan virus.

Two days later my patient died from acute respiratory

distress syndrome and hemorrhagic fever—the brutal side effects of the virus.

Hantaan virus is highly communicable, with a near one-hundred-percent death rate if not treated in time.

All I needed to do was infect one of them. Just one.

Chapter Forty

Night fell. Most of the preliminary work had been completed. I waited, peeking though the once-barricaded window in my office, awaiting their emergence from the woods. The body lay on a chair beside me, legs and arms dangling. It had fully defrosted now and was reeking up a storm. The skin had turned a muddy shade of gray. Its eyes were shut and I could see a thin layer of hair on the lids. I raised my right hand, armed with a syringe filled with hantaan-infected blood, and for the hundredth time in the last hour, stared at the syrupy brick-red contents inside.

I waited. Checked the Isolate's body to make certain it was still really there and that this wasn't just another vivid dream: one perhaps mentally induced by the Isolates to trick me into thinking I actually had a chance against them. Despite the amount of time that'd passed since my dream (or sleepwalk, if you must), it still had me in its iron grip.

The clock tolled ten. It was at the tenth chime that I realized I hadn't heard Christine or Jessica moving around in the house for at least an hour now.

I shuddered.

A twinkling flash of golden light flitted in my peripheral vision.

The time has come. . . .

I looked out the window. They appeared like magic, golden eyes, a half dozen or more floating in from the damp gloom of the woods. My heart pounded in my chest so hard that white ghostly images appeared in my sight, and when I looked outside again I saw their dark bodies stepping slowly forward, dry snow clinging to their limbs like patches of cotton. I leaped up, choked back a lump in my throat, and quickly jammed the needle into the dead demon's stomach, injecting half the contents.

I bent down and cradled the body as I would a baby, with care and caution; this horrid corpse was my only weapon against the evil breed and I didn't want anything to happen to it. Carrying the creature, I scooted from the office into the waiting room, then out the side door onto the walkway. A wind picked up and sent the stench of the creature into my nose, making me gag. A full moon splayed dreamy beams across my path; a ground mist encircled my feet. The ground was cold and hard beneath my feet, the frigid air like needles against my face.

This is what hell must be like: cold, forbidding, deadly.

337

The dead Isolate lay limply in my arms, like a virgin sacrifice. When the nausea passed, I turned the corner into the backyard. The Isolates spotted me and immediately bounded forward, some on two legs, most on all fours. They appeared to move as though part of a simulation, like computer-generated beings in some dark game. In a flash, they surrounded me, perhaps eight or nine beasts, teeth bared, sneering, poking at me with their vicious claws. I felt like a pony caught in the center of a pack of jackals.

I handed over the body. It was what they came for, what they wanted. Two of them yanked it from my arms, pawing at it like kittens wrestling over a piece of yarn. The rest of them followed suit, practically dancing in their agitation.

All except one. I grabbed it by its long gangly hair and yanked it back.

Without hesitation I plunged the needle into its jugular and injected it with Hantaan-tainted blood. It howled and its body stiffened, arms reaching for the plunger but unable to grasp it. The wind rose as if to echo the severe act, shrieking through the trees and causing me to look around uneasily. There might be more Isolates nearby, poised to deliver vengeance for the death of Old Lady Zellis. It staggered away as I let it go, the needle still dangling from its neck, its injury unnoticed by its overeager brothers who'd begun to feast on the body of the corpse.

Again, I smiled. And prayed. And then, quickly returned to the sanctuary of my home, wondering as I went inside why they didn't simply kill me for ending the life of the old lady. Perhaps they were grateful for the meal.

Chapter Forty-one

I walked into the living room, grimacing at the sudden stab of pain in my stomach; somewhere along the line, I'd twisted an abdominal muscle and it felt as though I'd been knifed. Christine and Jessica were sitting on the couch like patients in a waiting room, hunched with apprehension, hands folded across their laps. Christine stood in questioning silence, gripping her belly along the way, eyes wide and hopeful for a positive reaction. Jessica remained seated behind her, struggling to remain awake, trying not to miss anything crucial. We stood in silence for a short time, staring at each other and wondering how the hell it had all come down to this. Suddenly the fear I should've felt outside with the Isolates hit me like a barrage of bullets, and I began to teeter back and forth on both feet, trying to keep from succumbing to dizziness.

Your family, Michael. Be strong. Don't give in now!

It didn't really matter, I thought, and before I could say anything to Christine, I collapsed to the floor.

I came to, immediately worried about Christine and Jessica. Christine's face came into view, a cool washcloth in her hand swathing my brow. I tried to perch up on my elbows, but fatigue had me in full grasp, and I slumped back to the floor in exhaustion.

"Don't move," Christine said. "Not yet."

She continued to comfort me with the washcloth. Minutes passed before I could find the strength to ask, "How long was I out for?"

"Only a few minutes."

"Are you all right?"

"Yes," she answered, nodding slightly.

"Jessica?"

"She's fine on the couch."

Despite her reassurances, I felt a vague sense of worry. I kept asking myself, what if it doesn't work? Then what? Are we all dead, like Neil Farris? Perhaps not. After all, they let the Widow Farris go. I wondered if that might've been part of the arrangement, if Farris had been forced to sacrifice himself for the sake of his family. Or was it perhaps just another part of the Grand Scheme? Maybe the widow Farris had taken up a position of border sentry, watching the coming and goings (mostly comings) of those on the outskirts of Ashborough. Like those Sam Huxtable had talked about.

I questioned whether I'd be man enough to surrender my life for the guaranteed safety of my family, but soon realized that only one road led out of Ashborough, and it would be traveled with my family in tow. I clenched my teeth with frustration and worry and wondered how this would all play out. Either life or death, I figured. There didn't seem to be any middle ground. I took a deep breath, held it, and blew it out long and slow, trying to calm down.

Somewhere along the line, I passed out again.

In my swoon, I recalled a dream. A nightmare. Old Lady Zellis had returned from the dead, spoiling all my intentions, everything I'd accomplished up until this point. She escorted me back to the circle of stones, and stood there beside me as the cannibal Isolates gorged themselves on a smiling Lou Scully, who lay naked and spread-eagled on the big center stone. Lou Scully . . . in the past he'd acted as a friend, helping me to find this place . . . this place that was supposed to have been my haven, but turned out to be my curse. At the time he'd seemed to be a godsend . . . now, as far as I could tell, he'd very much been an acting participant in the Grand Scheme, either intentionally, or as a pawn wholly ignorant of his actions. It didn't really matter. He'd led us here. So I gazed around the surreal scene, pulling my sights away from the man whom I suddenly detested.

And from out of nowhere Phillip and Rosy Deighton appeared. They began helping themselves to Lou's flesh, clawing it away in strips and stuffing it gleefully into their gaping mouths just as the Isolates did. Blood poured down their chins, and it was at this moment I realized that Rosy was the woman she used to be before she'd gotten her disfiguring injuries, her jaw complete, her skin unblemished.

To my right I heard a barking noise. I turned away from the feeding and saw Lauren Hunter, just as she'd been in her previously untouched state: neatly clothed, tanned, her hair and makeup perfectly tended to. She sat cross-legged in the soil alongside one of the vertical stones, smiling and clapping her hands in rhythm and periodically breaking the cadence with a series of doglike barks. The tone of the barks sounded eerily familar, and when a deer suddenly appeared alongside her, I realized that she'd been emulating the horrid bleats of the dying deer in my shed.

I looked down at Old Lady Zellis, who used a crooked finger to point toward the left. When I looked in that direction, I saw Sam Huxtable. He was riding atop the back of another deer and guiding it across the open area to the center stone. When he got there, he jumped down and reached deep into Lou's open stomach (who, crazily, was still smiling at me, eyebrows leaping up and down as if to crudely say, "Nice set of titties on that bitch, eh Michael?") and removed a liver or a kidney, caught it before it slipped through his fingers, and slurped it down his throat in a jerking reflexive motion, as though he were taking a mouthful of pills.

All the players were here, smiling gleefully as the feast went on and on.

And then suddenly, rising behind the tallest white stone to a height of the trees behind it was an unnameable creature, with dark hairy skin and glowing golden eyes that spotlighted the six twisting horns and long braided hair atop its head. All those in attendance stopped what they were doing, turned their attention from me, and peered up at this great black beast whose long yellow claws gripped the top of the tallest stone before it.

And then, in the blink of an eye, Christine was here, walking—no, floating—into the scene from behind me. I leaned out to grab her, but she moved out of my reach, unaware of me or ignoring my presence. I tried to scream, but only a harsh whisper emerged from my sore throat. I tried to move, but my feet were glued to the ground, and when I looked down I saw that I was buried into the soil up to my ankles, Isolate claws emerging from the earth, gripping my calves. The crowd parted, pulling Lou Scully's body with them, leaving the center stone bare save for the thick wash of blood coating its surface.

Christine shed her clothing and sat down on the center stone. Her eyes were empty and glazed, staring up at the great creature who stepped out from behind the stone. Its entire body rippled like water, as though insects crawled just beneath the surface of its skin. Clumps of mud and wet leaves fell from its hairy skin in rotten clumps. It emitted a powerful odor, like that of the leaves in Old Lady Zellis's basement—like Rosy Deighton's tea. It leaned down on its knees, one claw breaking its fall. The other gripped what appeared to be its penis, a black mottled spade erect and secreting yellow fluid. Its eyes glowed a miraculous gold.

Christine looked at me. Her eyes glowed gold too, and she smiled. And then she spread her legs.

And then, with a deafening roar, the creature mounted her.

I screamed myself awake.

I sat up in bed, soaked with sweat and shivering. Christine ran to my side, sat on the edge of the bed, and leaned forward to wipe my brow with a damp washcloth. I closed my eyes as I ran my hands across the mattress of my bed. My bed. The one I hadn't slept in for months; the sheets felt good beneath my skin, and for a maddening moment I wondered if they'd been cleaned recently.

The odor of something oddly familiar, something . . . *organic* rose in the air. *Wood burning outside? Rotting leaves in the gutter?*

The leaves . . . the tea.

"Michael . . . are you all right?"

"Jesus . . . I had a dream. A nightmare. I . . . can't explain it . . . it was terrible."

Christine kept wiping my brow. "Shhh, relax . . . don't worry about it now. You're not feeling well."

I turned my head to the side, mind spinning sluggishly, as though drugged. Yellow light came in through the window, and I wondered how long I'd been sleeping.

"What time is it?" I asked.

Christine pulled the washcloth from my forehead. "Late morning," she replied. I caught another whiff of the odor. Like chamomile, only slightly fermented. The tension in the room was calm, yet oppressive. It drew down on me like my memories. And those seemed strangely ancient, as if they'd been recorded in sepia-toned stills.

"You're sick, Michael," she added. "You've been running a high fever for nearly three days now. But it looks as though it might be breaking. You're down to ninety-nine degrees. I'm no doctor, but as the doctor's wife, I'd say the prognosis is pretty good."

Three days?

In a rush of panic, I wrestled up in bed, fighting the fatigue, the dizziness, the aches. "Jesus . . . I . . . why . . ." I was at a loss for words. How could I have been sleeping for the last three days? It didn't make sense. Had I been that exhausted that my body just decided to give up and put me out of commission for all that time? Possible. But the plausibility of something else also came into play, and that gave me a fright, along with a defiant measure of resolve to battle the circumstances. The battle had not been won. Not yet anyway. Finally, I was able to blurt out, "What's been going on? Last thing I remember was . . ."

. . . was that dream. Where the old lady came back and brought you to the circle of stones. Where all your friends played sick roles in some ritualistic game. Where the great golden-eyed demon showed itself to you, then raped your wife . . .

I ran a trembling hand through my hair; my palm came away coated with sweat. Christine stood up quickly, went in the bathroom, and ran water in the sink. She returned with a wet washcloth in her hand, grinned weakly, then stopped, grimaced, and grasped her stomach.

346

"You okay?" I asked. The question seemed to rise from my lips by itself. My mind was utterly distracted with the dream, and the notion that I'd been immobile for three days.

"Baby's kicking," she answered in a strange, flat voice.

"We have to get you out of here," I said, my body seeming to move on its own volition out of the bed. "How long did you say I was out for?"

"Three days."

Three days. It really didn't seem possible. "Are you sure?"

She nodded.

"Jesus, how come I don't remember anything? Did I eat?" I put on a pair of jeans and a sweatshirt and tried to ignore the panging soreness in my muscles.

"You slept a lot," she answered. "Most of the time your fever ran high. You took your aspirin and drank your tea like a good patient and went back down."

Drank your tea.

I went into the bathroom, splashed cold water on my face. The sink had a few spottings of green liquid in it that quickly washed away beneath the flow from the faucet. *Green tea, Michael?* I looked into the mirror for a quick moment and saw a man who'd aged twenty years in the last eight months.

I was going to ask Christine if she was still drinking that tea, or feeding it to me, when she appeared suddenly in the doorway and said, "You never told me what you did." Her face was hard and serious. So were her words . . . they weighed on me like an accusation

347

of murder—not the desperate hope for success I'd expected.

I decided not to say anything. She grimaced again, holding her belly (which seemed to have grown to full term), then backpedaled to the edge of the bed, which she rested against needfully.

"I need to go out there, Christine," I said, referring to the woods. "I need to know if it worked."

Christine sighed, chewed a bottom lip, then asked with more force than needed, "If what worked?"

Odd that she would ask that, since I'd discussed everything with her beforehand. And her tone, it was even odder, as though I'd shocked her by actually following through with my plan. I'd explained to her that our only alternative had been to defeat the Isolates—or at the very least weaken them so we could get out of Ashborough. Now, judging by her manner, it seemed that she'd forgotten these details. I looked at her, unable to cloak my confusion. "The tainted blood," I said, quietly defensive. "The hantavirus. It should've knocked them all out by now."

"Is that what you did?" Her sudden accusatory tone made me think that I hadn't told her what I'd planned to do, and now she was mad at me for not knowing about it. Although I was certain I'd discussed my intentions with her, I couldn't remember actually doing it, and *that* scared me. All I could recall was that sometime after I grabbed that Isolate and poisoned it, I came back into the house and spoke with Christine in the living room, then passed out and experienced the scariest, most surreal nightmare ever.

Automatically, I said, "Yes, that's what I did. I poisoned them. Now go get your bags. There's a good chance we'll be leaving today."

"Good luck," she said, her voice dry and mechanical. She smiled at me. It was clearly forced.

"Thanks."

It was only after I stepped out of the bedroom that I thought of Jessica, and my heart sank into my stomach. I stopped and turned around, looked back. All was deadly quiet beyond the bathroom door. The hallway reverberated with the tension of the moment, and all of a sudden I felt alone in the world. "Christine?"

"Yes?" she called from the bedroom.

"Where's Jessica?"

"In her room."

I spun away, stepped down the hall, and peeked into Jessica's bedroom. The blinds were shuttered, closing out most of the light. Her dolls were lined up on the dresser, a few missing (in addition to the teddy bear), presumably packed away in the duffle bag on the floor beside the bed. She lay in bed, a silent coma beneath the sheets. I walked over to her, ran a finger across her brow, then gently kissed her on the cheek. "Don't worry," I whispered. "I'll get you out of here."

I left her room and went downstairs, into the kitchen. I drank some water, but had no appetite, so decided against eating anything. If everything went as intended, I'd soon behold a scene not suitable for a full stomach. A sense of coldness set upon me. It froze me, perhaps warning me that finishing the task wasn't a very good idea. But . . . beneath the cold premonition grew a

349

flame of eagerness. It protected me against the chill and gave me the incentive to press on, as though a driving force had swooped down from the rafters to guide me in the right direction.

There was no way I could stop now.

I put my boots on and went outside.

Chapter Forty-two

Despite the frigid air, it was the sunniest day of the year. I had no idea what day of the week it was. Last I checked, which had been an indeterminate amount of days ago, it had been December, somewhere around the middle of the month. Jesus, for all I knew it might've been Christmas Day. Or New Year's.

As I entered the woods, I looked down to see if my feet were actually touching the ground. In the dream where I'd killed Page, I'd had the feeling of my feet floating inches above the forest floor. It'd seemed as if the woods had reached out to me, had ushered me along as though I'd been transcendentally connected with them. Now, I could see that my feet were firmly rooted to the forest soil . . . yet my body experienced a level of exhilaration like that in the dream.

I took the path of least resistance: the same one Phillip guided me along when he brought me up here that fateful day. The environment seemed newly familiar to me, all the details coming back to me as if I'd begun reading a book for the second time. The sights were the same, the trees, the hills, the bushes, the filmy snow gently crunching under my footsteps, twigs and needles flattening beneath my weight. Far along, the ground dipped and softened, the gentle crunch turning to *squoosh* as muddy water filled the recesses of the land. The bushes began to thin, and the trees gave way to a clearing where a low fog hung listlessly in the damp air.

Here comes the circle of stones. It's up ahead, a bit to the left. A mere hop, skip, and jump. Take yourself into it with the same bit of confidence that brought you here in the first place. Let the woods guide you, protect you . . . keep the faith. The hard part is over, Michael. Accepting what is becomes the end-all conclusion to the entire saga.

That is, if the Grand Scheme allows it . . .

The fog thickened and rose up to my waist as I made my way forward. All along I'd accepted the abilities of the Isolates as being mortal, commanded solely through strength and an instinctual determination to survive the elements. But the breed also possessed a shrewd intelligence enabling them to dominate the weaker race around them, the human residents of Ashborough, yours truly included.

On the surface it seemed as if Isolates were indeed infected humans.

Or were they?

The fog began to swirl around me as I considered the

possibility of them being much more than infected human beings. There was a sentient presence within this fog, in the woods, I could feel it, I *saw* it. And it became clear to me that it had *everything* to do with the existence and vitality of the Isolates. The germ had to have come from somewhere, *something*. I needed to look no further than my dream, and the great golden-eyed demon that rose up from the depths of the woods and raped my wife. This horned beast . . . it had shown itself as a way of telling me that it had cultivated the germ and transfused it into a select body of humans who in turn became its offspring. *If the germ had been nothing more than just a germ, then it would have spread beyond the confines of Ashborough*. The germ had been sufficiently quarantined within the limits of the town and the surrounding woodland (yet another brilliant survival technique on the part of the Isolates—or should I say on the part of the great demon who created it?).

Common sense dictated that the Isolates were more than just primitive creatures. They were commanded by a much higher force, the glow of their eyes a complex power above and beyond the simplistic chemical reaction I presumed them to be. Once I began to think along these lines, then their mental abilities became all too obvious as well—their capacity to drive the enemy through subjective means was unmistakable. They controlled this town, *owned* it, and not through brute force alone. They controlled everyone's minds as well. In my case, they made me believe that speaking to my wife would mean certain death to her. They made Christine believe she had been visiting an OB/GYN all along.

God, for all I knew, Christine wasn't really pregnant at all. Their real power lay in illusion, not by means of threat or strength (although their aggressiveness was without question formidable, and not to be easily dealt with). There was no telling what was real, and what wasn't.

The fog rose up even further, encapsulating me. It seemed unexplainably alive, swirling and pulsing around me like a toss-up of underwater silt. I felt terribly small and insignificant in its grasp, blind and being led into an inescapable trap. Vainly, I tried to convince myself that the hantavirus germ had worked, that there was nothing to be afraid of.

Nothing to be afraid of? You think the virus worked on that demon?

That was just a dream . . . wasn't it?

There were never more unanswered questions than now.

The trees spread and the fog parted to reveal the circle of stones. I stepped into its center, looking around. Silence dominated at first, but then there was a bit of laughter: low, rasping, mocking. It paralyzed me, nearly stopped my heart, my breath. The fog spread and formed a perfect circle around me, as if to create a broad showcase of light for me to perform under. I stood there for a moment, then took a step forward toward the center stone. The laugh emerged again, louder this time and from a different direction. It seemed to derive from everywhere: before me, behind me, above and below. It *filled* the environment.

The fog then began to move upward. It gathered into

a dense form that rose fifteen feet high and five feet wide, amassing into a compact, recognizable shape: that of the great demon from my dream. In the center of the roiling fog that formed its head, two golden lights burned. A hole broke for its mouth, and the laugh blared forth once again. The fog glowed even brighter, the demon now taking on a more definitive shape. Its skin began to darken. Muscles formed in its arms and legs as they writhed about, seeking mobility. Golden veins pulsed throughout its body, igniting its head so that the six horns and braided hair came into sharp view. A thick black tongue jutted from its mouth, dripping venom that sizzled as it hit the ground. The creature was almost complete now, as it was in my dream, and I could actually see yellow claws emerging from its hands as it reached down to grab its horribly misshapened erection. Tempered puffs of fog shot from its penis in hot steam-engine bursts.

And then it raised its nearly formed head to the sky and bellowed a sound like nothing I'd ever heard before. It silenced the woodland insects and generated a cold turbulent gale that whipped the branches of every tree. The ground resonated beneath my feet.

I peered up at the thing, terrified, awaiting my death. It peered down at me with its glowing golden eyes, then drew its mouth down, the forming lips swelling like balloons and revealing green-black stumps for teeth along a reddened jaw. The wind picked up even stronger, and nearby I could hear branches snapping angrily.

Then, as quickly as it appeared, the fog that had crafted the beast dissipated. I could feel the shifting wind, the fog breaking up and forming a tornado that whipped itself into a frenzy. Snow and leaves exited the area amidst the circle of stones in a windswept rush. A passage into the lair of the Isolates whipped open from the forest floor, and in a drill-like motion, the fog that had been the great creature sank down into it and disappeared.

A surge of adrenaline beat back my fatigue, allowing me to stagger forward toward the entrance. Although the fog-beast was gone, the wind it produced remained as strong as ever, and it whipped at me fiercely, sending soil and wet snow into my face. Once at the entrance, I looked around at the stones that remained undisturbed in their intimidating stance. Their circuitous path made me dizzy, and I swayed and pitched my head forward, gasping for air. I kneeled before the hole, and peered deep into its inviting darkness.

I went in, stepping downward neither quickly nor slowly, following the tunnel, down, down, down, through the blackness. I traveled forward, unable to see, realizing that if I mistakingly ventured off into one of the branching corridors, I might get lost. So I did my damnedest to stay on the path, regulating my breaths with smooth, even inhalations, keeping the pace slow and steady, with my hands out before me to help guide the way. Mud and water sloshed beneath my feet. Roots from the low ceiling pinched my hair. At one point I slipped and fell in the cold mud, but quickly stood up and kept on walking.

I walked in the blackness for nearly fifteen minutes, thinking that I'd never make it there, that I'd perhaps taken a wrong turn and was now on my way to some remote exit in a farmer's field. But soon a faint light flickered into view. I moved toward it, now able to make out the dirt walls around me. I hadn't taken a wrong turn. The hub was just ahead. I continued forward, turned a corner, and beheld the wide-open entrance to the main dwelling place of the Isolates, thirty feet ahead.

Slowly, I walked forward.

Even here, cold silence continued to rule. There was no bustle of activity, only the flickering scatter of diminished wall-torches.

I moved closer to the entrance.

Then, suddenly, I heard them. Moans rife with pain and suffering. I stopped to listen, and stayed there for a few minutes before I could brave the courage to move on. When I finally entered the lair of the Isolates, I beheld them. They were all here. The Isolates.

They were gathered in a seemingly unending collection of withered bodies, knotted together in a great mass of ruin. Many of them were dead, many were still dying and squirming. But not a single golden eye was aglow.

I smiled victoriously as I walked through them, contemplating the results of my labor: a mass execution, the genocide of an entire race of beings now collected in a vast playground perfectly suited for the infestation of maggots. I never felt more in powerful in my life. I won. *I fucking beat them*.

I turned away, my whole body a solid ache of torment. Sweat blanketed me, adding to the discomfort.

Mosquitoes poked my skin. I paced back through the carnage, making sure not to trip over any of the bodies in my path.

Suddenly, in a quickened thrust, something grabbed my ankle. The claws punctured my skin and I yelped out in pain. I looked down. A sick Isolate had me in its grasp, blood and mucus pouring from its nose, foam from its mouth. And then suddenly I recognized this one from the jagged scar racing across its face. Fenal. The glow in his eyes grew sharply bright, then faded down to gray right before my eyes. And then, it died. The hand released its grip. I kicked it away disgustedly. *He wanted you to help him, Michael.*

I turned around one last time to admire my work.

In the distance, in one of the multitude of burrows, I saw a single pair of eyes ignite, their glow intense, pinning me. In their illumination I saw a single bony hand raise up and point an accusatory finger at me.

And as I considered the unexpected possibility that one or more of the beasts might be immune, a single howl like the one I'd heard in the woods ripped the silence to tatters, condemning me back to the hell I had momentarily escaped.

Chapter Forty-three

I waited at the edge of the woods, staring up at my house. The wind had muscled away two more boards from the upstairs windows. The darkness within peered down at me watchfully, daring me to move on.

It had taken me a long time to return home, my body riddled with stiffness and monumental aches. My muscles felt atrophied, my breathing labored, and I wondered if this was what it felt like being on the receiving side of a heart attack. Once I'd escaped the underground den, which had taken the better part of an hour, I'd taken a few moments to rest before journeying back home. Now, darkness was approaching, and the setting sun cast an elongated shadow of myself across the side of the house that seemed to mock me as I finally made my way across the lawn. I wondered if I had the fortitude to actually leave here, and laughed madly at the possibility that after all this time I wouldn't be able to flee because my legs had no strength left in them to take me.

I went into the house via the side door. It was cool and dark and damp inside. I staggered down the hall into the kitchen. My muddy footfalls echoed spookily on the tiles, reminding me of the noise a sickened stomach makes.

"Christine?"

The eerie silence swallowed up my voice like water into a sponge. The wind rattled the boards over the living room windows. Alongside the front door were two duffle bags, presumably the supplies Christine and Jessica packed for the journey out of Ashborough. The sight of them gave me a ray of hope, and I found the strength in me to continue.

"Christine?" I called upstairs.

No answer.

Again I was scared. My heart pounded ferociously. Where were they? What were they doing? Sleeping perhaps, I thought with doubt. I took the steps one at a time, the pessimistic silence making the skin on my back and arms ripple with gooseflesh. The walk was short and terrifying, and I felt like a man walking the plank into shark-infested waters.

I reached the landing and immediately saw a spot-trail of blood leading down the hall past the closed door of the master bedroom. I stared at it for a long time, feeling fear and madness weighing down on me, and I imagined myself as a small house caught in the beginnings of an unstoppable mud slide, wondering how much pressure I could tolerate before caving in.

Soon I stood before the master bedroom. The blood on the floor was thicker here, and it was smeared around as if someone had stepped in it. I grabbed the doorknob with a sweaty palm and put an ear against the door.

From beyond, I heard a gentle cry. A whimper.

I turned the knob and pushed the door open.

I saw Jessica first. My little girl was sitting silently in a chair against the right wall of the bedroom alongside the boarded window frame. She was staring blankly toward the bed, head cocked, eyes cold and hypnotic, and it became immediately apparent that her intense inaction was the handiwork of the Isolates—she looked no different now than she had in the basement of Old Lady Zellis.

Hey, Michael!

The call was propelled from the smidgen of sanity my conscious held on to. It told me that there was much more to take in and that I ought to try and tame the fires of madness in my head because there weren't any calm waters ahead to put them out.

I let the door swing all the way open, and was greeted by the sight of my wife, the woman whom I walked down the aisle with and traded vows with, for richer and for poorer, in sickness and in health. She was lying naked on the bed, head tilted uncomfortably against the headboard, legs spread apart amidst a massive wash of blood. Her arms fidgeted at her sides, fists gripping the stained sheets in bunches. Her belly was no longer swollen with child. Somewhere here was our baby. *Our baby.*

I walked toward her. I saw blood on the footboard of the bed, on the floor, on the walls. It was *everywhere*.

And suddenly, I screamed.

It came from me ungoverned, reverberating around the room and through the halls of 17 Harlan Road, the house that had now become haunted with living ghosts. I realized at this moment that nothing could stop the evil brewing here. It would simply go on and on forever despite any roadblocks; there was nothing more certain than that except for my undying screams. Insanity . . . yeah, it had finally taken over, I could feel it finally. It had come out with all its guns blazing, and all I could think about was the great golden-eyed demon-beast in the woods whose presence brought out the very best in its progeny, and the most abominable conduct in its enemies: the simple folk of Ashborough who had come here seeking charmed lives and died with the blood-soaked consequences.

Christine had heard me scream, of course. I looked at her, dazed. Our eyes locked, mine filled with tears, hers with blood. Christine was gone now. Not dead per se, but gone in mind, in soul, and the thing that had replaced her couldn't have been happier at the moment to let me know all about it. This possessed thing that had become my wife pulled its split lips back into a wicked grin and licked the blood on its teeth, then arched its hips up from the mattress and pressed down on its belly. What had once been Christine's placenta came bursting out from her vagina, ruptured and purple and pumping blood and birth matter in a horrible, flat-ulent spew. I cried for Jessica, who remained in a cat-atonic state. Then I turned and vomited, the gristly odor of blood and feces taking full control of my stomach. Gagging, I turned back to face the scene, and that was when the bathroom door opened.

Here came my newborn child. *Walking.* Half-human, half-Isolate, it staggered out with a full coat of sticky-wet body hair, its face untouched by Isolate genes excepting the hideous glow of its golden eyes. It ca-reened toward me, this thing only eighteen inches high, reptilian feet leaving congealed prints on the hardwood floor. It held up both its hands, not for me to accept it, but to strike. Blood and amniotic fluid dripped from its yellow claws. I staggered back, but the thing latched onto my leg, swaying and clawing and then biting into my shin with its powerful little teeth. I kicked at it, swat-ted at it. My screams and the wails of the demon-child erupted from the room, and that was when Jessica sud-denly sprang into action. This brought a brief flickering light to the end of my long dark tunnel, but it was quickly extinguished when I realized that my daughter was still caught in the throes of her catatonia and had no intentions of assisting me. Instead, she came at me, arms outstretched, hissing like an angry cat. She lanced into my legs, tripping me up as I frantically attempted to shake the baby-beast away. I fell back on my ass, and felt the wind bullet out from my lungs in a sharp unintentional exhale. The baby-beast fell away and ca-reened against the bathroom door, then immediately righted itself and scowled as it looked back at me, its gaze glowing and resentful. I scrambled to the wall, staring dumbfounded up at the three bodies in the room with me.

The new and not necessarily improved Cayle family.

Christine crawled forward on the bed like a serpent. She was doused in blood, her face twisting and writhing, mouth panting and full of foam. Jessica staggered up, adjusted her cotton nightie, which had bunched up around her chest, then leaped up on the bed, joining her mother. She giggled in her little-girl voice and licked the blood from her fingers, as did the baby beast, which also climbed onto the bed to be with its family.

"Jessica . . ." I managed. "No, honey . . ."

She giggled and playfully tossed herself down on the blood-soaked bed.

Christine looked back at Jessica and ran a gentle hand through her blond locks. When she pulled away, a stark bloody streak marred the previously untainted curls.

"Christine . . . what in God's name are you doing? You're hypnotized! Shake it off! *Shake it off!*" I sat there, stupefied, surveying the evil scene before me, convinced for these futile moments that all I had to do was convince them that it was all some form of mind control at play here, and that once they realized this—as they had in Old Lady Zellis's basement—we could get the fuck out of here while the Isolates were still out of commission.

But there would be no Cayle family exodus—that much made itself very clear in the following seconds;

in my mind heinous images played out, images of the great horned beast in the woods who'd sent me a message in my swoon, telling me that the fight was unwinnable, and that no matter what I did to knock his children down, he'd be there stronger than ever to pick them up again.

I pictured the thing with its spectacular erection, mounting my wife.

And then, I thought back to a brief moment in time five months ago when Christine and I were talking in the kitchen, when she revealed the pregnancy and said, *Damn it Michael, you wore a condom.* I realized now that the great beast had already been upon her at that time, and that the grinning, walking, scowling Isolate baby on the bed with my family had no genes of mine in it, but those of its father in the woods. It would grow up a mix breed like Old Lady Zellis, and perhaps assume her position as Ashborough's spiritual leader.

I tried to stand, and at that moment became terribly aware that it wasn't just hypnosis or some form of mind control that'd had my family stricken. It was much, much more than that.

I looked at Christine and Jessica, bloodied and on the bed, now gleefully cradling the newborn beast in their hands. I collapsed back down to the floor.

They both looked up and smiled at me.

Their eyes were glowing gold.

I could do nothing but stay there defeated, staring at the utter evil before me. There was absolutely nothing I could do. Nothing except give in. I crumpled to the floor and pulled myself into a ball, trying to make myself as small as possible. I cried hysterically, hoping I'd disappear from this world forever and ever.

Quite soon, I did.

Epilogue

"When I awoke, many hours later, Christine, Jessica, and the baby-beast were gone. I never looked for them. I knew they weren't in the house . . . gut feeling, I suppose. Perhaps I didn't care. I went downstairs. The bags were still by the front door. I'd considered taking one and walking out the front door to see how far I'd get before they pulled a Neil Farris on me. Trying to leave meant certain death, I knew that already, and to be frank, I didn't really care at the moment if I died, I just didn't want to give them the benefit of making it happen. So I washed up and went back to sleep for many hours.

"When I awoke, I went into my office, grabbed the things I needed, along with whatever food was left in the house, and locked myself down here in the basement, where I remain to this day, perhaps two weeks after my family disappeared.

"It has been my intention to chronicle the events taking place here at 17 Harlan Road. I feel that with these tapes, I have done that. I do hope that the recordings on these tapes find the ears of an impartial listener, although I doubt that once you find your way into Ashborough, you will find your way out.

"My work, for now, is done, dear listener. I have only one decision left to make. If I am nowhere to be found, then I have decided to look for Christine and Jessica and I have perhaps fallen victim to the great demon's plague, although he might not allow me to escape, since I'd murdered so many of his progeny. I assume that he wants me to suffer for as long as possible, and by leaving me alone, he is doing just that. Either that, or I have indeed escaped the bonds of Ashborough, although that's highly improbable.

"My only other alternative is to take my own life, which I have planned for should it become necessary. On the table in front of me sits a needle. In it, hantavirus-tainted blood. If you find my body alongside these tapes, then you know the decision I have made and I wish you more successful results in your quest to escape the guard of the Isolates.

"At this point, I bid you farewell, dear listener. Thank you for your time and your ears. For that, I am truly grateful.

"Good night."

*　　*　　*

Dark basement.

   Heavy breathing.

   The grainy shuffle of feet on a cement floor. Edgy fingers tapping a table's rough surface. The reek of things moist and damp.

   Somewhere upstairs a clock chimes. A useless breeze sweeps a single candle's flame.

   A hand moves to a small tape recorder, sitting on the tabletop.

   One hesitant finger seeks out the stop button. Presses it.

   Ten seconds of deep, labored breaths. Then a hand moves to grab the needle. . . .

GRAHAM
MASTERTON
THE DOORKEEPERS

Julia Winward has been missing in England for nearly a year. When her mutilated body is finally found floating in the Thames, her brother, Josh, is determined to find out what happened to his sister and exactly who—or what—killed her.

But nothing Josh discovers makes any sense. Julia had been working for a company that went out of business sixty years ago, and living at an address that hasn't existed since World War II. The only one who might help Josh is a strange woman with psychic abilities. But the doors she can open with her mind are far better left closed. For behind these doors lie secrets too horrible to imagine.

STRANGER

SIMON CLARK

The small town of Sullivan has barricaded itself against the outside world. It is one of the last enclaves of civilization and the residents are determined that their town remain free from the strange and terrifying plague that is sweeping the land—a plague that transforms ordinary people into murderous, bloodthirsty madmen. But the transformation is only the beginning. With the shocking realization that mankind is evolving into something different, something horrifying, the struggle for survival becomes a battle to save humanity.

Dorchester Publishing Co., Inc.
P.O. Box 6640 _____ 5076-5
Wayne, PA 19087-8640 $6.99 US/$8.99 CAN

Please add $2.50 for shipping and handling for the first book and $.75 for each additional book. NY and PA residents, add appropriate sales tax. No cash, stamps, or CODs. Canadian orders require $2.00 for shipping and handling and must be paid in U.S. dollars. Prices and availability subject to change. **Payment must accompany all orders.**

Name: _____

Address: _____

City: _____ State: _____ Zip: _____

E-mail: _____

I have enclosed $_____ in payment for the checked book(s).

CHECK OUT OUR WEBSITE! <u>www.dorchesterpub.com</u>
_____ Please send me a free catalog.

Vampyrrhic
Simon Clark

Leppington is a small town, quiet and unassuming. Yet beneath its streets terrifying creatures stir. Driven by an ancient need, united in their burning hunger, they share an unending craving. They are vampires. They lurk in the dark, in tunnels and sewers . . . but they come out to feed. For untold years they have remained hidden, seen only by their unfortunate victims. Now the truth of their vile existence is about to be revealed—but will anyone believe it? Or is it already too late?

SIMON CLARK
DARKER

Richard Young is looking forward to a quiet week with his wife and their little daughter. Firing up the barbecue should be the most stressful task he'll face. He has no idea of the hell that awaits him, the nightmare that will begin with an insistent pounding at his door.

The stranger begging to be let in is being hunted. Not by a man or an animal, but by something that cannot be seen or heard, yet which has the power to crush and destroy anything in its path. It is a relentless, pounding force that has existed for centuries and has now been unleashed to terrify, to ravage . . . to kill.

ATTENTION
BOOK LOVERS!

Can't get enough
of your favorite **HORROR**?

Call **1-800-481-9191** to:

— order books —
— receive a **FREE** catalog —
— join our book clubs to **SAVE 20%!** —

Open Mon.-Fri. 10 AM-9 PM EST

Visit
www.dorchesterpub.com
for special offers and inside
information on the authors you love.

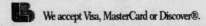